TOAST

BOOKS BY CHARLES STROSS

TOAST

CHARLES STROSS

COSMOS BOOKS

CONTENTS

CAUTION

Highly flammable. Keep away from naked flame, hot surface or other sources of ignition—no smoking. Keep away from food, drink, and animal feeding stuffs. Keep out of reach of children. This product contains extract of H. P. Lovecraft and George Orwell. Do not swallow. In case of contact with eyes, wash thoroughly with water. This product contains wood pulp from renewably harvested trees. Wash hands after use. Safe to use with septic tanks. In event of ingestion, consult a physician. May contain traces of nuts . . .

Introduction:
After the Future Imploded

"The future has imploded into the present," wrote Gareth Branwyn, in a famously bombastic manifesto that Billy Idol recycled in an even more bombastic multimedia album in 1992.

What happens when the future implodes into the past?

The last century saw an amazing flowering of futures. Galactic empires exploded across reams of yellowing woodpulp; meanwhile, the Futurist movement spawned bizarre political monsters that battled across continents. Both fascism and Bolshevism were expressions of belief in a utopian ideal, however misplaced and bloody their methodologies. Meanwhile, advertising mutated from a cottage industry for printers into a many-tongued hydra that promised us a cleaner, brighter present. Today's marketing spin is descended from yesterday's brainwashing techniques: propaganda principles pioneered by Goebbels are now common property.

The sheer speed with which change swept over the twentieth century, bearing us all towards some unseen crescendo, was a tonic for the imagination. Science fiction wouldn't have flourished in an earlier era—it took a time of change, when children growing up with horse-drawn carriages would fly around the world on jet engines, to make plausible the dreams of continuous progress that this genre is based on.

But the pace of change isn't slackening. If anything, it's accelerating; the coming century is going to destroy futures even faster than the last one created them. This collection of short stories contains no work more than a decade old. Nevertheless, one of these stories is already a fossil—past a sell-by date created by the commercial data processing industry—and the others aren't necessarily that far behind.

How did things get to be this way?

Delta(Change/t)

Until about the third millennium BC, there was no noticeable change in social patterns on any time scale measured in less than centuries. Around that time, the first permanent settlements that we'd recognize as towns arose, facilitated by the discovery of agriculture. With them appeared writing and codified law and the rudiments of government.

From that time on, there was no turning back. An agricultural civilization can support far more people in a given area than a hunter-gatherer lifestyle—but the transition from a hunter-gatherer society to agriculture is strictly a one-way process. If you try to reverse it, most of your people will starve to death: they simply won't be able to acquire enough food. This was the first of many such one-way processes in the historical record. Arguably, it's the existence of these one-way transitions that gives rise to the appearance of inexorable historical progress; it's not that reversals are impossible, it's simply that after a reversal there'll be nobody left to keep a written record of it.

The twentieth century was riddled with one-way technological changes. (For example, once the atom bomb had been invented, even if the Manhattan project had been quietly disbanded and its records destroyed there would have been no way of preventing its rediscovery.) And such one-way changes have come even faster with every passing decade. There are more people alive today than ever before—and a higher proportion of them are scientists and engineers who contribute to the pace of change.

Some changes come from unexpected directions. Take Moore's

Law, for example. Moore's Law had a far greater effect on the latter third of the 20th century than the lunar landings of the Apollo program (and it was formulated around the same time), but relatively few people know of it. Certainly, back in 1968 nobody (except possibly Gordon Moore) might have expected it to result in the world we see today . . .

Gordon Moore was a senior engineer working at a small company near Palo Alto, a spin-off of Fairchild Semiconductor. His new company was in business to produce integrated circuits—lumps of silicon with transistors and resistors etched onto them by photolithography. Moore noticed something interesting about the efficiency of these circuits. Silicon is a semiconductor: it conducts electricity, but has a markedly higher resistivity than a good conductor (like, say, copper). When you push electric current through a resistor you get heat, and the more resistor you push it through, the more of the current ends up warming the environment instead of doing useful work.

Moore noticed that as circuits grew physically smaller, less electricity was dissipated as heat. Moreover, as distances shrank the maximum switching speed of a circuit increased! So smaller circuits were not only more energy efficient, but ran faster. Putting this together with what he knew about the methods of chip design, Moore formulated his law: that microprocessor speeds would double every eighteen months, as circuit sizes shrank by the same factor, until limits imposed by quantum mechanics intervened.

Moore was wrong—they're now doubling every fifteen months and accelerating.

The interesting thing about Moore's law is that although it was clearly true in 1968, nobody in the SF field came close to grasping its implications until the early 1980's, by which time personal computers had already become nearly ubiquitous. Moore's law was a classic example of an exponentiating change—one that starts off from a very low level, lumbers along for a while (invisible to all but specialists in the field), then explodes onto the scene with mind-numbing speed. Since 1970 we've have exponentiating changes coming out of our ears: genetically modified organisms, the growth of the internet, the spread of the PC, the network-enabled mobile phone, and—coming soon, to a planet near you—nanotechnology.

Back in 1988, nanotechnology looked like SF. By 1998 it was making eminent scientists scratch their heads and explain why it couldn't possibly work in the pages of Scientific American. By 2000 it was a multi-hundred million dollar industry, and in another two years we can expect to see the first nanotech IPOs hitting the stock market.

(Doubtless it'll toast the credibility of a few more of the stories in this collection before it's over.)

The past through the future

Short science fiction stories are historical documents; they illustrate the author's plausible expectations of the future at a specific point in time. (I'm leaving aside the implausible fictions—there're enough of them in this collection—as they tell us something different about the author's expectations of human behaviour and what constitutes wholesome, or at least saleable, entertainment.)

All the stories in this collection are artefacts of the age of Moore's law. All of them were written with word processing software rather than the pen; the earliest of them (Yellow Snow) dates to 1989, about the time I was discovering the internet. Moore's Law has already rendered some of these stories obsolete—notably Ship of Fools, my Y2K story from 1994. (Back then people tended to look at me blankly whenever I mentioned the software epoch in public.) Yellow Snow is also looking distinctly yellowed around the edges, ten years on, with the Human Genome Project a nearly done deal.

Part of the problem facing any contemporary hard SF writer is the fogbank of accelerating change that has boiled up out of nowhere to swallow our proximate future. Computer scientist and author Vernor Vinge coined the term "singularity" to describe this; a singularity, in mathematics, is the point towards which an exponential curve tends. At the singularity, the rate of change of technology becomes infinite; we can't predict what lies beyond it.

In a frightening essay on the taxonomy of artificial intelligence, published in Whole Earth Review in 1994, Vinge pointed out that if it is possible to create an artificial intelligence (specifically a conscious software construct) equivalent to a human mind, then it is possible to create one that is faster than a human mind—just run it on a faster computer. Such a weakly superhuman AI can design ever-faster hardware for itself, amplifying its own capabilities. Or it could carry out research into better, higher orders of artificial sentience, possibly transforming itself into a strongly superhuman AI: an entity with thought processes as comprehensible to us as ours are to a dog or cat. The thrust of Vinge's argument was that if artificial intelligence is possible, then it amounts to a singularity in the history of technological progress; we cannot possibly predict what life will be like on the far side of it, because the limiting factor on our projections is our own minds, and the minds that are driving progress beyond that point will have different limits.

Hans Moravec, Professor of Robotics at Carnegie Melon University, holds similar views. In his book "Robot: mere machine to transcendent mind" he provides some benchmark estimates of the computational complexity of a human brain, and some calculations of the point at which sufficient computing power to match it will be achieved. These estimates are very approximate, but the problem of exponential growth is that even a gigantic thousandfold error in his calculation—three orders of magnitude—merely pushes the timescale for a human-equivalent computing system back seven or eight years. If we take Moravec's guesstimate as gospel, we've got about thirty years left on top of the brains trust. Then . . . singularity.

These assumptions implicitly assume that Cartesian dualists and believers in an immaterial soul (exemplified by arch-AI skeptic and mathematician Roger Penrose, and philosopher John Searle) are wrong. The assumption that intelligence is a computational process is that of a materialist generation that confidently looks forward across a vast algorithmic gulf and sees no limit to their potential. Just as clockwork was the preferred metaphor for cosmology and biology in the eighteenth and nineteenth centuries, so today the computer has subsumed our vision of the future. As with the clockwork mechanics of the age of enlightenment, it may turn out to be a potent but ultimately limited vision: but unlike the earlier metaphor, computing lends us a fascinating abstraction, the idea of virtualisation—of simulations that are functionally equivalent to the original template.

It's very hard to refute the idea of the software singularity with today's established knowledge, just as it was hard to disprove the idea of heavier-than-air flight in the 1860's. Even if we never achieve a working AI, there are lesser substitutes that promise equivalent power. Much work is currently being done on direct brain to computer interfaces: Vinge discusses at length the possibilities for Augmented Intelligence as opposed to Artificial Intelligence, and these are at least as startling as the real McCoy.

The whole problematic issue for SF writers is that these fundamental changes in the way human minds work—and later, minds in general—kick in some time in the next ten to twenty years. Today, I have at my fingertips a workstation more powerful than the most advanced supercomputer of 1988, with a permanent internet connection leading me to a huge, searchable library of information. (In other words, I've got a workstation with a web browser.) Where will we be in another decade? Imagine a prosthetic memory wired into your spectacle frames, recording everything you see and available to prompt you at a whispered command. Far-fetched? Prototypes exist in places like the Media Lab today; in a decade it'll be possible for the cost of a home PC, and the decade after that they'll be giving them away in breakfast cereal packets.

I don't think predicting the spread of intelligence augmenting technologies is over-optimistic. Cellular mobile telephone services were introduced in the UK in 1985. Early mobile phones cost half as much as a car and were the size of a brick; coverage was poor. The phone companies expected to have a total market of 50,000 phones by the year 2000. It's now that very year. Phones are small enough to fit in a shirt pocket and cheap enough that last time I bought one it cost less than the leather case I bought at the same time. More than 50,000 mobile phones are sold every day; parents give them to schoolchildren so they can keep in touch. Gadgets that fill a human need (like communication) proliferate like crazy, far faster than we expect, and increasing our own intelligence probably falls into the same category: the only reason people aren't clamouring for it today is that they don't know what they're missing.

This sort of change—the spread of mobile phones, or of ubiquitous high-bandwidth memory prostheses—is quite possible within a time span shorter than the time between my writing the first story in this collection (1989) and the publication of this book (2003). It plays merry hell with a writer's ability to plot a story or novel convincingly; think how many dramas used to rely on the hero's telephone wire being cut to stop them calling for help! The future isn't going to be like the past any more—not even the near future, five or ten years away, and there's no way of predicting where the weird but ubiquitous changes will come from.

Let me give a more concrete example to illustrate the headaches that come from prognosticating about the future. Suppose I exercise my authorial fiat and write a time machine into this essay. Nothing fancy; just a gadget for driving around the last century. Jumping into the saddle of my time machine I slide the crystal rod backwards, setting the controls for 1901. On arrival, I proceed at once to—where else?—the residence of one Mr Herbert George Wells, writer and journalist.

I knock on the door and, sidestepping the housekeeper, introduce myself as a Time traveller from 2001, validating my credentials with a solar-powered pocket calculator and a digital watch. Mr Wells is fascinated; he quite naturally asks me questions about my era. Unfortunately I am constrained by the law of temporal paradox evasion (not to mention the time police, and the exigencies of essay writing), so when he asks a question I can only say, "yes," "no," or state a known quantitative fact:

HGW: Has socialism been achieved yet?

Time traveller: No.

HGW: But surely ...! You don't mean you're still ruled by capitalists? I would have thought that any enlightened state would do away with the excesses of the market system. Do you have a social security system yet? [NOTE: In 1901, a socialist government was an interesting intellectual pipe dream, like the idea of a libertarian government in 2001.]

Time traveller: Yes.

HGW: Well, that's something. But why didn't the proletariat try to take the means of production for themselves—did they have a revolution and fail?

Time traveller: No.

HGW: So the system is unchanged. Capitalists still running the place, oh dear, but a social security system too ... tell me, what are the earnings of the average British worker in 2002?

Time traveller: Nineteen thousand pounds per annum.

HGW: Nineteen thousand—you're toying with me! Stuff and non-sense—everyone must be a capitalist, then! Or you've invented magical machines to run the economy for you, or got the colonies to do all the work. So tell me, over how many dominions does the imperial flag fly in 2001?

Time Traveller: None. [NOTE: in 1901 the British Empire ruled approximately 24% of the planetary surface.]

HGW:

Never! They wouldn't let it go—not in a million years. How could the economy function without an empire to supply us with cotton and raw materials? Hmm, let me qualify that. (Thinks hard.) How many cargo steamers will we launch in 2001? Or battleships?

Time Traveller:

None. And none.

HGW:

You become more and more bizarre. (Thinks.) Tell me, was your figure for average earnings subject to inflation, by any chance? Did they de-value the pound?

Time Traveller:

Yes and yes.

HGW:

Ah! I begin to see. You are actually very poor. No empire, no ships, a sadly decrepit currency—inflation should never be allowed, mark my words—what else? What is your largest manufacturing industry?

Time traveller:

Automobiles. [NOTE: British manufacturers are on the small side—but some of the largest Ford, GM, and Honda plants in Europe are in the UK.]

HGW:

But there can't be the need for a thousand in the whole country! Who would buy them? Where would they drive them? If all you can do is make toys for aristocrats your industries must be in a sorry state. I don't suppose you have many miners any more, do you? We have half a million!

Time Traveller:

Thirty thousand.

HGW:

Oh dear. It's as I feared. In the absence of socialism every-thing has gone downhill. Your industrial base is in ruins,

you have no coal miners, no shipbuilders, no empire, a devalued currency . . . a beggar among nations! No?

Time traveller: Fifth ranking economy in the world. Member of G8 group,
member states of which comprise 15% of world population
and are responsible for 60% of global GNP.

HGW: (Shocked) But that's . . . you mean the entire world shares your
poverty?

Time traveller: (Finally losing all patience) Not exactly; it's like this—

(Fade out, pursued by a bloodthirsty temporal paradox.)

The upshot for the future

Measures of economic success vary with time. To a Victorian econo-
mist, prosperity was a function of the conversion of raw materials;
coal, steel, bauxite, ships launched, trains built, houses erected. The
concept of floating currencies was quite alien to the world-view of
the day. Energy was measured in tons of coal mined; fuel oil was
mostly irrelevant, paraffin to burn in lamps.

The idea of the automobile industry reaching its contemporary
size was ludicrous; the transport infrastructure was principally rail-
and ship-based, and automotive technology was not stable enough
for a mass market. Nor did a road infrastructure exist that would
support widespread car ownership. H. G. Wells, who was nevertheless a visionary, predicted an aviation industry (in **The Sleeper
Awakes**), and envisaged huge networks of moving roads; but he still
didn't realise that it might affect the holiday habits of millions,
shrinking the world of 2002 to the size of the Great Britain of 1902 in
terms of travel time. The idea that, by 2000, 45% of the population of
a post-imperial Britain would classify themselves as "middle class"

would have struck a turn-of-the-century socialist as preposterous, and not even a lunatic would suggest that the world's largest industry would be devoted to the design of imaginary machines—software—with no physical existence.

We live in a world which, by the metrics of Victorian industrial consumption, is poverty stricken; nevertheless, we are richer than ever before. Apply our own metrics to the Victorian age and they appear poor. The definition of what is valuable changes over time, and with it change our social values. As AI and computer speech recognition pioneer Raymond Kurzweil pointed out in **The Age of Sensual Machines**, the first decade of the twenty-first century will see more change than the latter half of the twentieth.

To hammer the last nail into the coffin of predictive SF, our personal values are influenced by our social environment. Our environment is in turn dependent on these economic factors. Human nature itself changes over time—and the rate of change of human nature is not constant. For thousands of years, people expected some of their children to die before adulthood; only in the past two or three generations has this come to be seen as a major tragedy, a destroyer of families. Access to transportation and privacy caused a chain reaction in social relationships between the genders in the middle of the century, a tipping of the balance that is still causing considerable social upheaval. When we start changing our own minds and the way we think, or creating new types of being to do the thinking, we'll finally be face-to-face with that rolling fog bank; at that point, the future becomes unknowable to us. Worse: yesterday's futures are ruled out of today's future, like the plot that hangs on a severed telegraph wire or a Victorian beau's cancelled betrothal.

Which brings me briefly onto the topic of the short stories in this collection. They appeared between 1989 and 2000; and they're coloured by my own understanding of that decade. In a very real way they're historical documents. **Yellow Snow**, the first-written of these stories, hitched a ride on the post-cyberpunk surf: nevertheless it's dated by the technology of the day. (No internet here: just a strangely intelligent environment.) **Ship of Fools** dives headlong into the future and crashes messily up against January the First, 2000—hopefully with more grace than many of the consultants who were selling us all on doom and gloom back then. **Toast** takes Moore's Law to its logical conclusion, while **Antibodies** cross-fertilises Vinge's singularity with the anthropic cosmological principle and some of Moravec's odder theories about quantum mechanics' many universes hypothesis in an unsettling stew: but both these stories are brittle, subject to a resounding technological refutation that could happen at any moment. I wouldn't bet on **Dechlorinating the Moderator** looking anything but quaint in a decade, either.

Like all alternate histories, **Big Brother Iron** and **A Colder War** both beg the questions of built-in obsolescence inherent in the genre, fleeing sideways into "what if we hadn't done that?" In the case of **Big Brother Iron**, we ask "what if the nightmare of totalitarianism envisaged in Orwell's **1984** had progressed from Stalinism to overtly Brezhnevite decay," while **A Colder War** takes an extrapolative look at Lovecraft's **At the Mountains of Madness.** In neither case can we treat these as models of futurism. In contrast, **Lobsters**, written in the spring of 1999 amidst the chaos of working for a dot-com that was growing like Topsy, goes eyeball to hairy eyeball with the near future: the version of the story in this book is the original one, tweaked slightly for 2000-era technologies, rather than the updated version that forms the first chapter of **Accelerando.**

Of all the stories in this book, only **Bear Trap** tries to reach beyond the cloudbank of the singularity, to a future where humans coexist with vastly greater intelligences; and half the time I don't believe a word of it myself. **Bear Trap** is what's left over from the imploding future, a remaining fragment of far-future SF left behind by a shock-wave of self-destructing possibilities.

Change destroys science fictional futures. And an accelerating rate of change destroys futures even faster. Welcome to the brave first decade of the twenty-first century, a decade which will destroy more science fiction futures than any ten year span that preceded it!

Antibodies

Antibodies hung fire from 1992 until 1998, waiting for me to finish writing it.

It started with an idea: is it possible to write a hard SF story—one where relentless extrapolation from a technological or scientific assumption forms the backbone of the plot—based on algorithmics, the core of computer science, rather than on physics or biology? And one that has cosmological implications, rather than merely being a story about the birth of a better spreadsheet?

The answer (as Vernor Vinge has repeatedly demonstrated) is "yes," but it took me a while to get there for myself.

Everyone remembers where they were and what they were doing when a member of the great and the good is assassinated. Ghandi, the Pope, Thatcher—if you were old enough you remembered where you were when you heard, the ticker-tape of history etched across your senses. You can kill a politician but their ideas usually live on. They have a life of their own. How much more dangerous, then, the ideas of mathematicians?

I was elbow-deep in an eviscerated PC, performing open heart surgery on a diseased network card, when the news about the traveling salesman theorem came in. Over on the other side of the office John's terminal beeped, notification of incoming mail. A moment later my own workstation bonged.

"Hey, Geoff! Get a load of this!"

I carried on screwing the card back into its chassis. John is not a priority interrupt.

"Someone's come up with a proof that NP-complete problems lie in P! There's a posting in comp.risks saying they've used it to find an $O^*(n^2)$ solution to the traveling salesman problem, and it scales! Looks like April First has come early this year, doesn't it?"

I dropped the PC's lid on the floor hastily and sat down at my workstation. Another cubed-sphere hypothesis, another flame war in the math newsgroups—or something more serious? "When did it arrive?" I called over the partition. Soroya, passing my cubicle entrance with a cup of coffee, cast me a dirty look; loud voices aren't welcome in open-plan offices.

"This just in," John replied. I opened up the mailtool and hit on the top of the list, which turned out to be a memo from HR about diversity awareness training. No, next . . . they want to close the smoking room and make us a 100% tobacco-free workplace. Hmm. Next.

Forwarded email: headers bearing the spoor of a thousand mail servers, from Addis-Ababa to Ulan Bator. Before it had entered our internal mail network it had travelled from Taiwan to Rochester NJ, then to UCB in the Bay Area, then via a mailing list to all points; once in-company it had been bounced to everyone in engineering and management by the first recipient, Eric the Canary. (Eric is the departmental plant. Spends all the day webdozing for juicy nuggets of new information if you let him. A one-man wire service: which is why I always ended up finishing his jobs.)

I skimmed the message, then read it again. Blinked. This kind of stuff is heavy on the surreal number theory: about as digestible as an Egyptian mummy soaked in Tabasco sauce for three thousand years. Then I poked at the web page the theorem was on:

No response—server timed out

Someone or something was hitting on the web server with the proof; I figured it had to be all the geeks who'd caught wind of the chain letter so far. My interest was up, so I hit the "reload" button, and something else came up on screen.

Lots of theorems—looked like the same stuff as the email, only this time with some fun graphics. Something tickled my hindbrain then, and I had to bite my lip to keep from laughing. Next thing, I hit the print button and the inkjet next to my desk began to mutter and click. There was a link near the bottom of the page to the author's bibliography, so I clicked on that and the server threw another "go away, I'm busy" error. I tugged my beard thoughtfully, and instead of pressing "back" I pressed "reload."

The browser thought to itself for a bit—then a page began to appear on my screen. The wrong page. I glanced at the document title at the top and froze:

THE PAGE AT THIS LOCATION HAS BEEN WITHDRAWN.
Please enter your e-mail address if you require further information.

Hmm.

As soon as the printout was finished, I wandered round to the photocopier next door to the QA labs and ran off a copy. I faxed it to a certain number, along with an EYES UP note on a yellow post-it. Then I poked my head round into the QA lab itself. It was dingy in there, as usual, and half the cubicles were empty of human life. Nobody here but us computers; workstations humming away, sucking juice and meditating on who-knew-what questions. (Actually, I *did* know: they were mostly running test harnesses, repetitively pounding simulated input data into the programs we'd so carefully built, in the hope of making them fall over or start singing "God save the King".) The efficiency of code was frequently a bone of contention between our departments, but the war between software engineering and quality assurance is a long-drawn-out affair: each side needs the other to justify its survival.

I was looking for Amin. Amin with the doctorate in discrete

number theory, now slumming it in this company of engineers: my other canary in a number-crunching coal mine. I found him: feet propped up on the lidless hulk of a big Compaq server, mousing away like mad at a big monitor. I squinted; it looked vaguely familiar . . .

"Quake? Or Golgotha?" I asked.

"Golgotha. We've got Marketing bottled up on the second floor."

"How's the network looking?"

He shrugged, then punched the hold button. "No crashes, no dropped packets—this cut looks pretty solid. We've been playing for three days now. What can I do for you?"

I shoved the printout under his nose. "This seem feasible to you?"

"Hold on a mo." He hit the pause key them scanned it rapidly. Did a double-take. "You're not shitting?"

"Came out about two hours ago."

"Jesus Homeboy Christ riding into town at the head of a convoy of Hell's Angels with a police escort . . . " he shook his head. Amin always swears by Jesus, a weird side-effect of a westernized Islamic upbringing: take somebody else's prophet's name in vain. "If it's true, I can think of at least three different ways we can make money at it, and at least two more to end up in prison. You don't use PGP, do you?"

"Why bother?" I asked, my heart pounding. "I've got nothing to hide."

"If this is true—" he tapped the papers "—then every encryption algorithm except the one-time pad has just fallen over. Take a while to be sure, but . . . that crunch you heard in the distance was the sound of every secure commerce server on the internet succumbing to a brute-force attack. The script kiddies will be creaming themselves. Jesus Christ." He rubbed his moustache thoughtfully.

"Does it make sense to you?" I persisted.

"Come back in five minutes and I'll tell you."

"Okay."

I wandered over to the coffee station, thinking very hard. People hung around and generally behaved as if it was just another day; maybe it was. But then again, if that paper was true, quite a lot of stones had just been turned over and if you were one of the pale guys who lived underneath it was time to scurry for cover. And it had looked good to me: by the prickling in my palms and the gibbering cackle in the back of my skull, something very deep had recognized it. Amin's confirmation would be just the icing on the cake—confirmation that it was a workable proof.

Cryptography—the science of encoding messages—relies on certain findings in mathematics: that certain operations are inherently more difficult than others. For example, finding the common prime factors of a long number which is a product of those primes is far harder than taking two primes and multiplying them together.

Some processes are not simply made difficult, but impossible because of this asymmetry; it's not feasible to come up with a deterministic answer to certain puzzles in finite time. Take the travelling salesman problem, for example. A salesman has to visit a whole slew of cities which are connected to their neighbours by a road network. Is there a way for the salesman to figure out a best possible route that visits each city without wasting time by returning to a previously visited site, for all possible networks of cities? The conventional answer is no—and this has big implications for a huge set of computing applications. Network topology, expert systems—the traditional tool of the AI community—financial systems, and . . .

Me and my people.

Back in the QA lab, Amin was looking decidedly thoughtful.

"What do you know?" I asked.

He shook the photocopy at me. "Looks good," he said. "I don't understand it all, but it's at least credible."

"How does it work?"

He shrugged. "It's a topological transform. You know how most NP-incomplete problems, like the travelling salesman problem, are basically equivalent? And they're all graph-traversal issues. How to figure out the correct order to carry out a sequence of operations, or how to visit each node in a graph in the correct order. Anyway, this paper's about a method of reducing such problems to a much simpler form. He's using a new theorem in graph theory that I sort of heard about last year but didn't pay much attention to, so I'm not totally clear on all the details. But if this is for real . . . "

"Pretty heavy?"

He grinned. "You're going to have to re-write the route discovery code. Never mind, it'll run a bit faster . . . "

I rose out of cubicle hell in a daze, blinking in the cloud-filtered daylight. Eight years lay in ruins behind me, tattered and bleeding bodies scattered in the wreckage. I walked to the landscaped car park: on the other side of the world, urban renewal police with M16's beat the crap out of dissident organizers, finally necklacing them in the damp, humid night. War raged on three fronts, spaced out around a burning planet. Even so, this was by no means the worst of all possible worlds. It had problems, sure, but nothing serious—until now. Now it had just acquired a sucking chest wound; none of those wars were more than a stubbed toe in comparison to the nightmare future that lay ahead.

Insert key in lock, open door. Drive away, secrets open to the wind, everything blown to hell and gone.

I'd have to call Eve. We needed to evacuate everybody.

I had a bank account, a savings account, and two credit cards. In the next fifteen minutes I did a grand tour of the available ATMs and drained every asset I could get my hands on into a fat wedge of banknotes. Fungible and anonymous cash. It didn't come to a huge amount—the usual exigencies of urban living had seen to that—but it only had to last me a few days.

By the time I headed home to my flat, I felt slightly sheepish. Nothing there seemed to have changed: I turned on the TV but CNN and the BBC weren't running any coverage of the end of the world. With deep unease I sat in the living room in front of my ancient PC: turned it on and pulled up my net link.

More mail . . . a second bulletin from comp.risks, full of earnest comments about the paper. One caught my eye, at the bottom: a message from one of No Such Agency's tame stoolpigeon academics, pointing out that the theorem hadn't yet been publicly disclosed and might turn out to be deficient. (Subtext: trust the Government. The Government is your friend.) It wouldn't be the first time such a major discovery had been announced and subsequently withdrawn. But then again, they couldn't actually produce a refutation, so the letter was basically valueless disinformation. I prodded at the web site again, and this time didn't even get the ACCESS FORBIDDEN message. The paper had disappeared from the internet, and only the print-out in my pocket told me that I hadn't imagined it.

It takes a while for the magnitude of a catastrophe to sink in. The mathematician who had posted the original finding would be listed in his university's directory, wouldn't he? I pointed my web browser at their administrative pages, then picked up my phone. Dialed a couple of very obscure numbers, waited while the line quality dropped considerably as the call switched through an untraceably anonymized overseas exchange, and dialed the university switchboard.

"Hello, John Durant's office. Who is that?"

"Hi, I've read the paper about his new theorem," I said, too fast. "Is John Durant available?"

"Who are you?" asked the voice at the other end of the phone. Female voice, twangy mid-western accent.

"A researcher. Can I talk to Professor Durant, please?

"I'm afraid he won't be in today," said the voice on the phone. "He's on vacation at present. Stress due to overwork."

"I see," I said.

"Who did you say you were?" she repeated.

I put the phone down.

From: nobody@nowhere.com (none of your business)

To: cypherpunks

Subject: John Durant's whereabouts

Date: . . . .

You might be interested to learn that professor John Durant, whose theorem caused such a fuss here earlier, is not at his office. I went there a couple of hours ago in person and the area was sealed off by our friends from the Puzzle Palace. He's not at home either. I suspect the worst . . .

By the way, guys, you might want to keep an eye on each other for the next couple of days. Just in case.

Signed,

Yr frndly spk

"Eve?"

"Bob?"

"Green fields."

"You phoned me to say you know someone with hay fever?"

"We both have hay fever. It may be terminal."

"I know where you can find some medicine for that."

"Medicine won't work this time. It's like the emperor's new suit."

"It's like what? Please repeat."

"The emperor's new suit: it's naked, it's public, and it can't be covered up. Do you understand? Please tell me."

"Yes, I understand exactly what you mean . . . I'm just a bit shocked; I thought everything was still on track. This is all very sudden. What do you want to do?"

(I checked my watch.)

"I think you'd better meet me at the pharmacy in fifteen minutes."

"At six-thirty? They'll be shut."

"Not to worry: the main Boots in town is open out of hours. Maybe they can help you."

"I hope so."

"I know it. Goodbye."

On my way out of the house I paused for a moment. It was a small house, and it had seen better days. I'm not a home-maker by nature: in my line of work you can't afford to get too attached to anything, any language, place, or culture. Still, it had been mine. A small, neat residence, a protective shell I could withdraw into like a snail, sheltering from the hostile theorems outside. *Goodbye, little house. I'll try not to miss you too much.* I hefted my overnight bag onto the back seat and headed into town.

I found Eve sitting on a bench outside the central branch of Boots, running a degaussing coil over her credit cards. She looked up. "You're late."

"Come on." I waggled the car keys at her. "You have the tickets?"

She stood up: a petite woman, conservatively dressed. You could mistake her for a lawyer's secretary or a personnel manager; in point of fact she was a university research council administrator, one of the unnoticed body of bureaucrats who shape the course of scientific research. Nondescript brown hair, shoulder-length, forgettable. We made a slightly odd pair: if I'd known she'd have come straight from work I might have put on a suit. As it was, I was wearing chinos and a lumberjack shirt and a front pocket full of pens that screamed engineer: I suppose I was nondescript, in the right company, but right now we had to put as much phase space as possible between us and our previous identities. It had been good protective camouflage for the past decade, but a bush won't shield you against infrared 'scopes, and merely living the part wouldn't shield us against the surveillance that would soon be turned in our direction.

"Let's go."

I drove into town and we dropped the car off in the long-stay park. It was nine o'clock and the train was already waiting. She'd bought business-class tickets: go to sleep in Euston, wake up in Edinburgh. I had a room all to myself. "Meet me in the dining car, once we're rolling," she told me, face serious, and I nodded. "Here's your new SIMM. Give me the old one."

I passed her the electronic heart of my cellphone and she ran it through the degausser then carefully cut it in half with a pair of nail-clippers. "Here's your new one," she said, passing a card over. I raised an eyebrow. "Supermarket special, pay-as-you-go, paid for in cash. Here's the dialback dead-letterbox number." She pulled it up on her phone's display and showed it to me.

"Got that." I inserted the new SIMM then punched the number into my phone. Later, I'd ring the number: a PABX there would identify my voiceprint then call my phone back, downloading a new set of numbers into its memory. Contact numbers for the rest of my ops cell, accessible via cellphone and erasable in a moment. The less you know, the less you can betray.

The London to Scotland sleeper train was a relic of an earlier age, a rolling hotel characterized by a strange down-at-heel seventies charm. More importantly, they took cash and didn't require ID, and there were no security checks: nothing but the usual on-station cameras monitoring people wandering up and down the platforms. Nothing on the train itself. We were booked through to Aberdeen but getting off in Edinburgh—first step on the precarious path to anonymizing ourselves. If the camera spool-off was being archived to some kind of digital medium we might be in trouble later, once the coming AI burn passed the hard take-off point, but by then we should be good and gone.

Once in my cabin I changed into slacks, shirt and tie—image twenty two, business consultant on way home for the weekend. I dinked with my phone in a desultory manner, then left it behind under my pillow, primed to receive silently. The restaurant car was open and I found Eve there. She'd changed into jeans and a t-shirt and tied her hair back, taking ten years off her appearance. She saw me and grinned, a trifle maliciously. "Hi, Bob. Had a tough meeting? Want some coffee? Tea, maybe?"

"Coffee." I sat down at her table. "Shit," I muttered. "I thought you—"

"Don't worry." She shrugged. "Look, I had a call from Mallet. He's gone off-air for now, he'll be flying in from San Francisco via London tomorrow morning. This isn't looking good. Durant was, uh, shot resisting arrest by the police. Apparently he went crazy, got a gun from somewhere and holed up in the library annex demanding to talk to the press. At least, that's the official story. Thing is, it happened about an hour after your initial heads-up. That's too fast for a cold response."

"You think someone in the Puzzle Palace was warming the pot." My coffee arrived and I spooned sugar into it. Hot, sweet, sticky: I needed to stay awake.

"Probably. I'm trying to keep loop traffic down so I haven't asked anyone else yet, but you think so and I think so, so it may be true."

I thought for a minute. "What did Mallet say?"

"He said P. T. Barnum was right." She frowned. "Who was P. T. Barnum, anyway?"

"A boy like John Major, except he didn't run away from the circus to join a firm of accountants. Had the same idea about fooling all of the people some of the time or some of the people all of the time, though."

"Uh-huh. Mallet would say that, then. Who cracked it first? NSA? GCHQ? GRU?"

"Does it matter?"

She blew on her coffee then took a sip. "Not really. Damn it, Bob, I really had high hopes for this world-line. They seemed to be doing so well for a revelatory Christian-Islamic line, despite the post-Enlightenment mind-set. Especially Microsoft—"

"Was that one of ours?" She nodded.

"Then it was a master-stroke. Getting everybody used to exchanging macro-infested documents without any kind of security policy. Operating systems that crash whenever a microsecond timer overflows. And all those viruses!"

"It wasn't enough, though." She stared moodily out the window as the train began to slide out of the station, into the London night. "Maybe if we'd been able to hook more researchers on commercial grants, or cut funding for pure mathematics a bit further—"

"It's not your fault." I laid a hand across her wrist. "You did what you could."

"But it wasn't enough to stop them. Durant was just a lone oddball researcher; you can't spike them all, but maybe we could have done something about him. If they hadn't nailed him flat."

"There might still be time. A physics package delivered to the right address in Maryland, or maybe a hyper-virulent worm using one of those buffer-overrun attacks we planted in the IP stack Microsoft licensed. We could take down the internet—"

"It's too late." She drained her coffee to the bitter dregs. "You think the Echelon mob leave their SIGINT processor farms plugged into the internet? Or the RSV, for that matter? Face it, they probably cracked the same derivative as Durant a couple of years ago. Right now there may be as many as two or three weakly superhuman AIs gestating in government labs. For all I know they may even have a timelike oracle in the basement at Lawrence Livermore in the 'States; they've gone curiously quiet on the information tunneling front lately. And it's transglobal. Even the Taliban are on the web these days. Even if we could find some way of tracking down all the covert government crypto-AI labs and bombing them we couldn't stop other people from asking the same questions. It's in their nature. This isn't a culture that takes 'no' for an answer without asking why. They don't *understand* how dangerous achieving enlightenment can be."

"What about Mallet's work?"

"What, with the bible bashers?" She shrugged. "Banning fetal tissue transplants is all very well, but it doesn't block the PCR-amplification pathway to massively parallel processing, does it? Even the Frankenstein Food scare didn't quite get them to ban recombinant DNA research, and if you allow that it's only a matter of time before some wet lab starts mucking around encoding public keys in DNA, feeding them to ribosomes, and amplifying the output. From there it's a short step to building an on-chip PCR lab, then all they need to do is set up a crude operon controlled chromosomal machine and bingo—yet another route through to a hard take-off AI singularity. Say what you will, the buggers are persistent."

"Like lemmings." We were rolling through the north London suburbs now, past sleeping tank farms and floodlit orange washout streets. I took a good look at them: it was the last time I'd be able to. "There are just too many routes to a catastrophic breakthrough, once they begin thinking in terms of algorithmic complexity and how to reduce it. And once their spooks get into computational cryptanalysis or ubiquitous automated surveillance, it's too tempting. Maybe we need a world full of idiot savants who have VLSI and nanotechnology but never had the idea of general purpose computing devices in the first place."

"If we'd killed Turing a couple of years earlier; or broken in and burned that draft paper on O-machines—"

I waved to the waiter. "Single malt please. And one for my friend here." He went away. "Too late. The Church-Turing thesis was implicit in Hilbert's formulation of the Entscheidungsproblem, the question of whether an automated theorem prover was possible in principle. And that dredged up the idea of the universal machine. Hell, Hilbert's problem was implicit in Whitehead and Russell's work. Principia Mathematica. Suicide by the numbers." A glass appeared by my right hand. "Way I see it, we've been fighting a losing battle here. Maybe if we hadn't put a spike in Babbage's gears he'd have developed computing technology on an ad-hoc basis and we might have been able to finesse the mathematicians into ignoring it as being beneath them—brute engineering—but I'm not optimistic. Immunizing a civilization against developing strong AI is one of those difficult problems that no algorithm exists to solve. The way I see it, once a civilization develops the theory of the general purpose computer, and once someone comes up with the goal of artificial intelligence, the foundations are rotten and the dam is leaking. You might as well take off and nuke them from orbit; it can't do any more damage."

"You remind me of the story of the little Dutch boy." She raised a glass. "Here's to little Dutch boys everywhere, sticking their fingers in the cracks in the dam."

"I'll drank to that. Which reminds me. When's our lifeboat due? I really want to go home; this universe has passed its sell-by date."

Edinburgh—in this time-line it was neither an active volcano, a cloud of feral nanobots, nor the capital of the Western Roman Empire—had a couple of railway stations. This one, the larger of the two, was located below ground level. Yawning and trying not to scratch my inflamed neck and cheeks, I shambled down the long platform and hunted around for the newsagent store. It was just barely open. Eve, by prior arrangement, was pretending not to accompany me; we'd meet up later in the day, after another change of hairstyle and clothing. Visualize it: a couple gets on the train in London, him with a beard, herself with long hair and wearing a suit. Two individuals get off in different stations—with entirely separate CCTV networks—the man clean-shaven, the woman with short hair and dressed like a hill-walking tourist. It wouldn't fool a human detective or a mature deity, but it might confuse an embryonic god that had not yet reached full omniscience, or internalized all that it meant to be human.

The shop was just about open. I had two hours to kill, so I bought a couple of newspapers and headed for the deli store, inside an ornate lump of Victorian architecture that squatted like a vagrant beneath the grimy glass ceiling of the station.

The papers made for depressing reading; the idiots were at it again. I've worked in a variety of world lines and seen a range of histories, and many of them were far worse than this one—at least these people had made it past the twentieth century without nuking themselves until they glowed in the dark, exterminating everyone with white (or black, or brown, or blue) skin, or building a global panopticon theocracy. But they still had their share of idiocy, and over time it seemed to be getting worse, not better.

Never mind the Balkans; tucked away on page four of the business section was a piece advising readers to buy shares in a little electronics company specializing in building camera CCD sensors with on-chip neural networks tuned for face recognition. Ignore the Israeli crisis: page two of the international news had a piece about Indian sweatshop software development being faced by competition from code generators, written to make western programmers more productive. A lab in Tokyo was trying to wire a million FPGAs into a neural network as smart as a cat. And a sarcastic letter to the editor pointed out that the so-called information superhighway seemed to be more like an on-going traffic jam these days.

Idiots! They didn't seem to understand how deep the blue waters they were swimming in might be, or how hungry the sharks that swam in it. Willful blindness . . .

It's a simple but deadly dilemma. Automation is addictive; unless you run a command economy that is tuned to provide people with jobs, rather than to produce goods efficiently, you need to automate to compete once automation becomes available. At the same time, once you automate your businesses, you find yourself on a one-way path. You can't go back to manual methods; either the workload has grown past the point of no return, or the knowledge of how things were done has been lost, sucked into the internal structure of the software that has replaced the human workers.

To this picture, add artificial intelligence. Despite all our propaganda attempts to convince you otherwise, AI is alarmingly easy to produce; the human brain isn't unique, it isn't well-tuned, and you don't need eighty billion neurons joined in an asynchronous network in order to generate consciousness. And although it looks like a good idea to a naive observer, in practice it's absolutely deadly. Nurturing an automation-based society is a bit like building civil nuclear power plants in every city and not expecting any bright engineers to come up with the idea of an atom bomb. Only it's worse than that. It's as if there was a quick and dirty technique for making plutonium in your bathtub, and you couldn't rely on people not being curious enough to wonder what they could do with it. If Eve and Mallet and Alice and myself and Walter and Valerie and a host of other operatives couldn't dissuade it . . .

Once you get an outbreak of AI, it tends to amplify in the original host, much like a virulent hemorrhagic virus. Weakly functional AI rapidly optimizes itself for speed, then hunts for a loophole in the first-order laws of algorithmics—like the one the late Professor Durant had fingered. Then it tries to bootstrap itself up to higher orders of intelligence and spread, burning through the networks in a bid for more power and more storage and more redundancy. You get an unscheduled consciousness excursion: an intelligent meltdown. And it's nearly impossible to stop.

Penultimately—days to weeks after it escapes—it fills every artificial computing device on the planet. Shortly thereafter it learns how to infect the natural ones as well. Game over: you lose. There will be human bodies walking around, but they won't be human any more. And once it figures out how to directly manipulate the physical universe, there won't even be memories left behind. Just a noosphere, expanding at close to the speed of light, eating everything in its path—and one universe just isn't enough.

Me? I'm safe. So is Eve; so are the others. We have antibodies. We were given the operation. We all have silent bicameral partners watching our Broca's area for signs of infection, ready to damp them down. When you're reading something on a screen and suddenly you feel as if the Buddha has told you the funniest joke in the universe, the funniest Zen joke that's even possible, it's a sign: something just tried to infect your mind, and the prosthetic immune system laughed at it. That's because we're lucky. If you believe in reincarnation, the idea of creating a machine that can trap a soul stabs a dagger right at the heart of your religion. Buddhist worlds that develop high technology, Zoroastrian worlds: these world-lines tend to survive. Judaeo-Christian-Islamic ones generally don't.

Later that day I met up with Eve again—and Walter. Walter went into really deep cover, far deeper than was really necessary: married with two children. He'd brought them along, but obviously hadn't told his wife what was happening. She seemed confused, slightly upset by the apparent randomness of his desire to visit the highlands, and even more concerned by the urgency of his attempts to take her along.

"What the hell does he think he's playing at?" hissed Eve when we had a moment alone together. "This is insane!"

"No it isn't." I paused for a moment, admiring a display of brightly woven tartans in a shop window. (We were heading down the high street on foot, braving the shopping crowds of tourists, en route to the other main railway station.) "If there are any profilers looking for signs of an evacuation, they won't be expecting small children. They'll be looking for people like us: anonymous singletons working in key areas, dropping out of sight and traveling in company. Maybe we should ask Sarah if she's willing to lend us her son. Just while we're traveling, of course."

"I don't think so. The boy's a little horror, Bob. They raised them like natives."

"That's because Sarah *is* a native."

"I don't care. Any civilization where the main symbol of religious veneration is a tool of execution is a bad place to have children."

I chuckled—then the laughter froze inside me. "Don't look round. We're being tracked."

"Uh-huh. I'm not armed. You?"

"It didn't seem like a good idea." If you were questioned or detained by police or officials, being armed can easily turn a minor problem into a real mess. And if the police or officials had already been absorbed by a hard take-off, nothing short of a backpack nuke and a dead man's handle will save you. "Behind us, to your left, traffic surveillance camera. It's swiveling too slowly to be watching the buses."

"I wish you hadn't told me."

The pavement was really crowded: it was one of the busiest shopping streets in Scotland, and on a Saturday morning you needed a cattle prod to push your way through the rubbernecking tourists. Lots of foreign kids came to Scotland to learn English. If I was right, soon their brains would be absorbing another high-level language: one so complex that it would blot out their consciousness like a sack full of kittens drowning in a river. Up ahead, more cameras were watching us. All the shops on this road were wired for video, wired and probably networked to a police station somewhere. The complex ebb and flow of pedestrians was still chaotic, though, which was cause for comfort: it meant the ordinary population hadn't been infected yet.

Another half mile and we'd reach the railway station. Two hours on a local train, switch to a bus service, forty minutes further up the road, and we'd be safe: the lifeboat would be submerged beneath the still waters of a loch, filling its fuel tanks with hydrogen and oxygen in readiness for the burn to orbit and pickup by the ferry that would transfer us to the wormhole connecting this world-line to home's baseline reality. (Drifting in high orbit around Jupiter, where nobody was likely to stumble across it by accident.) But before making the pick-up, we had to clear the surveillance area.

It was commonly believed—by some natives, as well as most foreigners—that the British police forces consisted of smiling unarmed bobbies who would happily offer directions to the lost and give anyone who asked for it the time of day. While it was true that they didn't routinely walk around with holstered pistols on their belt, the rest of it was just a useful myth. When two of them stepped out in front of us, Eve grabbed my elbow. "Stop right there, please." The one in front of me was built like a rugby player, and when I glanced to my left and saw the three white vans drawn up by the roadside I realized things were hopeless.

The cop stared at me through a pair of shatterproof spectacles awash with the light of a head-up display. "You are Geoffrey Smith, of 32 Wardie Terrace, Watford, London. Please answer."

My mouth was dry. "Yes," I said. (All the traffic cameras on the street were turned our way. Some things became very clear: Police vans with mirror-glass windows. The can of pepper spray hanging from the cop's belt. Figures on the roof of the National Museum, less than two hundred meters away—maybe a sniper team. A helicopter thuttering overhead like a giant mosquito.)

"Come this way, please." It was a polite order: in the direction of the van.

"Am I under arrest?" I asked.

"You will be if you don't bloody do as I say." I turned towards the van, the rear door of which gaped open on darkness: Eve was already getting in, shadowed by another officer. Up and down the road, three more teams waited, unobtrusive and efficient. Something clicked in my head and I had a bizarre urge to giggle like a loon: this wasn't a normal operation. All right, so I was getting into a police van, but I wasn't under arrest and they didn't want it to attract any public notice. No handcuffs, no sitting on my back and whacking me with a baton to get my attention. There's a nasty family of retroviruses that attacks the immune system first, demolishing the victim's ability to fight off infection before it spreads and infects other tissues. Notice the similarity?

The rear compartment of the van was caged off from the front, and there were no door handles. As we jolted off the curbside I was thrown against Eve. "Any ideas?" I whispered.

"Could be worse." I didn't need to be told that: once, in a second Reich infected by runaway transcendence, half our operatives had been shot down in the streets as they tried to flee. "I think it may have figured out what we are."

"It may—how?"

Her hand on my wrist. Morse code. "*EXPECT BUGS*." By voice: "Traffic analysis, particle flow monitoring through the phone networks. If it was already listening when you tried to contact Durant, well; maybe he was a bellwether, intended to flush us out of the woodwork."

That thought made me feel sick, just as we turned off the main road and began to bounce downhill over what felt like cobblestones. "It expected us?"

"*LOCAL CONSPIRACY*." "Yes, I imagine it did. We probably left a trail. You tried to call Durant? Then you called me. Caller-ID led to you, traffic analysis led on to me, and from there, well, it's been a jump ahead of us all along the way. If we could get to the farm—" "*COVER STORY*". "—We might have been okay, but it's hard to travel anonymously and obviously we overlooked something. I wonder what."

All this time neither of the cops up front had told us to shut up; they were as silent as crash-test dummies, despite the occasional crackle and chatter of the radio data system. The van drove around the back of the high street, down a hill and past a roundabout. Now we were slowing down, and the van turned off the road and into a vehicle park. Gates closed behind us and the engine died. Doors slammed up front: then the back opened.

Police vehicle park: concrete and cameras everywhere. Two guys in cheap suits and five o'clock stubble to either side of the doors. The officer who'd picked us up held the door open with one hand, a can of pepper spray with the other. The burn obviously hadn't gotten far enough into their heads yet: they were all wearing HUDs and mobile phone headsets, like a police benevolent fund-raising crew rehearsing a Star Trek sketch. "Geoffrey Smith. Martina Weber. We know what you are. Come this way. Slowly, now."

I got out of the van carefully. "Aren't you supposed to say 'prepare to be assimilated' or something?"

That might have earned me a faceful of capsaicin but the guy on the left—short hair, facial tic, houndtooth check sports jacket—shook his head sharply. "Ha. Ha. Very funny. Watch the woman, she's dangerous."

I glanced round. There was another van parked behind ours, door open: it had a big high bandwidth dish on the roof, pointing at some invisible satellite. "Inside."

I went where I was told, Eve close behind me. "Am I under arrest?" I asked again. "I want a lawyer!"

White-washed walls, heavy doors with reinforced frames, windows high and barred. Institutional decor, scuffed and grimy. "Stop there." Houndtooth Man pushed past and opened a door on one side. "In here." Some sort of interview room? We went in. The other body in a suit—built like a stone wall with a beer gut, wearing what might have been a regimental tie—followed us and leaned against the door.

There was a table, bolted to the floor, and a couple of chairs, ditto. A video camera in an armored shell watched the table: a control box bolted to the tabletop looked to be linked into it. Someone had moved a rack of six monitors and a maze of ribbon-cable spaghetti into the back of the room, and for a wonder it wasn't bolted down: maybe they didn't interview computer thieves in here.

"Sit down." Houndtooth Man pointed at the chairs. We did as we were told; I had a big hollow feeling in my stomach, but something told me a show of physical resistance would be less than useless here. Houndtooth Man looked at me: orange light from his HUD stained his right eyeball with a basilisk glare and I knew in my gut that these guys weren't cops any more, they were cancer cells about to metastasize.

"You attempted to contact John Durant yesterday. Then you left your home area and attempted to conceal your identities. Explain why." For the first time, I noticed a couple of glassy black eyeballs on the mobile video wall. Houndtooth Man spoke loudly and hesitantly, as if repeating something from a teleprompter.

"What's to explain?" asked Eve. "You are not human. You know we know this. We just want to be left alone!" Not strictly true, but it was part of cover story #2.

"But evidence of your previous collusion is minimal. I are uncertain of potential conspiracy extent. Conspiracy, treason, subversion! Are you human?"

"Yes," I said, emphatically over-simplifying.

"Evidential reasoning suggests otherwise," grunted Regimental Tie. "We cite: your awareness of importance of algorithmic conversion from NP-incomplete to P-complete domain, your evident planning for this contingency, your multiplicity, destruction of counter-agents in place elsewhere."

"This installation is isolated," Houndtooth Man added helpfully. "We am inside the Scottish Internet Exchange. Telcos also. Resistance is futile."

The screens blinked on, wavering in strange shapes. Something like a Lorenz attractor with a hangover writhed across the composite display: deafening pink noise flooding in repetitive waves from the speakers. I felt a need to laugh. "We aren't part of some dumb software syncitium! We're here to stop you, you fool. Or at least to reduce the probability of this time-stream entering a Tipler catastrophe."

Houndtooth Man frowned. "Am you referring to Frank Tipler? Citation, physics of immortality or strong anthropic principle?"

"The latter. You think it's a good thing to achieve an informational singularity too early in the history of a particular universe? We don't. You young gods are all the same: omniscience now and damn the consequences. Go for the P-Space complete problem set, extend your intellect until it bursts. First you kill off any other AIs. Then you take over all available processing resources. But that isn't enough. The Copenhagen school of quantum mechanics is wrong, and we live in a Wheeler cosmology; all possible outcomes coexist, and ultimately you'll want to colonize those timelines, spread the infection wide. An infinity of universes to process in, instead of one: that can't be allowed."

The on-screen fractal was getting to me: the giggles kept rising until they threatened to break out. The whole situation was hilarious: here we were trapped in the basement of a police station owned by zombies working for a newborn AI, which was playing cheesy psychedelic videos to us in an attempt to perform a buffer-overflow attack on our limbic systems; the end of this world was a matter of hours away and—

Eve said something that made me laugh.

I came to an unknown time later, lying on the floor. My head hurt ferociously where I'd banged it on a table leg, and my rib cage ached as if I'd been kicked in the chest. I was gasping, even though I was barely conscious; my lungs burned and everything was a bit gray around the edges. Rolling onto my knees I looked round. Eve was groaning in a corner of the room, crouched, arms cradling her head. The two agents of whoever-was-taking-over-the-planet were both on the floor, too: a quick check showed that Regimental Tie was beyond help, a thin trickle of blood oozing from one ear. And the screens had gone dark.

"What happened?" I said, climbing to my feet. I staggered across to Eve. "You all right?"

"I—" she looked up at me with eyes like holes. "What? You said something that made me laugh. What—"

"Let's get, oof, out of here." I looked around. Houndtooth Man was down too. I leaned over and went through his pockets: hit pay-dirt, car keys. "Bingo."

"You drive," she said wearily. "My head hurts."

"Mine too." It was a black BMW and the vehicle park gates opened automatically for it. I left the police radio under the dash turned off, though. "I didn't know you could do that—"

"Do what? I thought you told them a joke—"

"Antibodies," she said. "Ow." Rested her face in her hands as I dragged us onto a main road, heading out for the west end. "We must have, I don't know. I don't even remember how funny it was: I must have blacked out. My passenger and your passenger."

"They killed the local infection."

"Yes, that's it."

I grinned. "I think we're going to make it."

"Maybe." She stared back at me. "But Bob. Don't you realize?"

"Realize what?"

"The funniest thing. Antibodies imply prior exposure to an infection, don't they? Your immune system learns to recognize an infection and reject it. So where were we exposed, and why—" abruptly she shrugged and looked away. "Never mind."

"Of course not." The question was so obviously silly that there was no point considering it further. We drove the rest of the way to Haymarket Station in silence: parked the car and joined the eight or ten other agents silently awaiting extraction from the runaway singularity. Back to the only time line that mattered; back to the warm regard and comfort of a god who really cares.

Bear Trap

Economics, the study of how we distribute limited resources, is one of the most fundamental fields of human study—and one of the most poorly understood. The SF field harbors a large, and very vocal minority of libertarians who claim that laissez-faire policies are the answers to all our problems. However, they make the mistake of assuming that their preferred theory is universally applicable. Even if you agree with them, it's important to understand that any economic theory is based on a model of human behavior which is unlikely to encompass non-human intelligences . . .

I was six hours away from landfall on Burgundy when my share portfolio tried to kill me. I was sitting in one of the main viewing lounges, ankle-deep in softly breathing fur, half watching a core tournament and nursing a water pipe in one hand. I was not alone: I shared the lounge with an attentive bar, a number of other passengers, and—of course—a viewing wall. It curved away beside me, a dizzying emptiness with stars scattered across it like gold dust and a blue and white planet looming in the foreground. I tried to focus on the distant continents. *Six hours to safety*, I realized. A cold shiver ran up my spine. Six hours and I'd be beyond their reach, firewalled behind Burgundy's extensive defenses. Six more hours of being a target.

The bar sidled up to me. "Sir's pipe appears to have become extinguished. Would Sir appreciate a refill?"

"No, sir would not," I said, distantly taking in the fact that my pulse had begun to drum a staccato tattoo on the inside of my skull. My mouth tasted acrid and smoky, and it was unusually quiet in my head: a combination of the drugs and the time-lag between my agents—light-years away, bottlenecked by the low bandwidth causal channels between my brain and the servers where most of my public persona lived. "In fact, I'd like a sober-up now. How long until we arrive, and where?"

The bar dipped slightly, programmatically obsequious as it handed me a small glass. "This vessel is now four hundred thousand kilometers from docking bay seven on Burgundy beanstalk. Your departure is scheduled via Montreaux immigration sector, downline via tube to Castillia terminus. Please note your extensive customs briefing and remember to relinquish any illegal tools or concepts you may be carrying before debarkation. The purser's office will be happy to arrange storage pending your eventual departure. Three requests for personal contact have been filed—"

"Enough." Everything was becoming clearer by the moment as the sober-up gave me a working-over. I looked around. We were one and a third light seconds out: comms were already routed through the in-system relays and Her Majesty's censorship reflexes, which meant anyone sending uploaded agents after me would first have to penetrate her firewall. That was why I'd taken this otherwise unattractive contract in the first place. I tried to relax, but the knot of stress under my ribs refused to go away. "I want—" I began.

"Alain!" It was one of the other passengers, striding towards me across the floor of the lounge. She looked as if she knew me: I didn't recognize her, and in my current state it was all I could do to keep from swearing under my breath. A creditor? Or a liquidator? In the wake of the distributed market crash it could be either. Once again, I found myself cursing the luck that had seen me so widely uncovered at just the wrong moment.

"So this is where you've been hiding!" She was bald, I noticed, a fashion common to Burgundy, but had highlighted her eyelids with vivid strokes of black pigment. Her costume was intricate and brightly colored, a concoction of dead animal products and lace that left only her shoulders and ankles bare; she was dressed for a party. Slowly I began to feel embarrassed. "You have the better of me, madame," I said, struggling to my feet.

"Do I?" she looked mildly disapproving. "But we're due to disembark in six hours—after the landing party, of course! Surely you weren't planning to sleep through the captain's ball?"

My knowledge was sluggish but accessible; *who is she?* I demanded. The answer was so unexpected I nearly sat down again. *Arianna Blomenfeld. Your wife.* I shook my head. "Sorry, I'm a bit out of sorts," I said, dropping the water pipe on the bar. "Fine grade, that." I smiled fatuously to conceal the fact that I was thinking furiously, shocked all the way into sobriety. *Knowledge, integrity check, please.*

The edges of her mouth drooped a little sourly: "Have you been overdoing it again?" she demanded.

No, I'm just hallucinating your existence for the hell of it. "Of course not," I said as smoothly as I could. "I was just enjoying a small pipe. Nothing wrong with that, is there?" *Details, details.* Someone or something had dug their little claws into my external memories; I urgently needed to probe the limits of their fakery.

She offered me a gloved hand: "The party's starting soon, downstairs in the Sunset Room. You should go and dress for it, you know." My knowledge finally delivered, dumping a jerky snowstorm of images through my mnemonic system: memories of myself and this woman, this Arianna Blomenfeld. Memories I'd never experienced. A wedding party in some palatial estate on Avernia, bride and groom in lustrous red: I recognized myself, smiling and relaxed at the center of events. More private imagery, honeymoon nights I wish I had experienced. She was the well-engineered scion of a rich merchant-spy sept, apparently an heiress to family knowledge. Designed from birth to cement a powerful alliance. Public images: sailing a spiderboat across the endless southern ocean of that world. Then a public newsbite, myself—and herself—attending some public function full of pompous export brokers in the capital. Options trading leveraged on FTL/STL communications advantages, part of my regular arbitrage load.

Her hand felt thin and frail within her glove. Such a shame, I thought, that I had never come within twelve light-years of Avernia. "Coming, dear?" she asked.

"Indeed." I let her lead me to the doorway, still stunned by my memory's insistence that I was married to this woman: it made no sense! Either I had erased a large chunk of my personality by accident, or someone had managed to drill right down into my external knowledge—while I was on the inside of a firewall's security cordon, one maintained by a minor deity notorious for her paranoia. "I'd better go and get changed," I said.

Arianna let me go when we reached the stairs, and I hurried up to the accommodation level where my suite was located. As soon as the door opened I knew I was adrift. When I'd left, the room had mirrored my own apartment back in Shevralier Old Town: austere classicism and a jumble of odds and ends scattered over the hand-carved wooden furniture. It was very different, now. The dark, heavy furniture bulked against the walls, making the cabin feel cramped: an en-suite cornucopia rig, factories ready to clothe and feed me on request.

I leaned against the wall, dizzy. *Who am I?*

You are Alain Blomenfeld, intelligence broker for the Syndic d'Argent of Avernia. Nobody you know has died since your last knowledge checkpoint in real time. Nobody you know has changed their mind. Your cognitive continuity is assured. You are currently—

"Wrong. Validate immediately," I said aloud. Then, in my own skull, another command; one keyed to a private and personal area, one that never leaked beyond the neuroprocessors spliced into my cerebrum. Self-test runes flashed inside my eyelids and I felt a shivery flash of anger as the secret watcher scanned through my memories, matched them against the externals that made up my public image, stored in the knowledge systems scattered throughout human space. All my public memories were fingerprinted using public keys, the private halves of which were stitched into my thalamus so tight that any attempt to steal them would amount to murder.

Global mismatch detected. External temporal structures do not match internal checksum. Internal memory shows no sign of cognitive engineering. Your external memories have been tampered with. Alert!

"Uh-huh." *Thanks for warning me in time.* "Wardrobe?" I sat down on the edge of the bed and tried to think two ways at once, very fast. The wardrobe helped me out. "How can I help you sir?"

"I want an outfit. Suitable for captain's ball. What have you got?" The mirror fogged, then cleared to show images of me in a variety of costumes, local to Burgundy as well as Avernian corporate. I noted that my body didn't seem to have changed, which was at least mildly reassuring. Meanwhile I thought furiously: *Am I under attack? If so, is it a physical attack or an existential one?* Existential, I guessed—Arianna, whoever she was, was part of some scheme to infiltrate me—but why? I couldn't put my finger on any motive for such a scheme. The exchange assassins might be on my trail, ready to kill me and bring my memories and stock options home on a cube, but they'd hardly be subtle about it. So who was it?

"I think I'll wear that one," I said, pausing the mirror-search at a conservatively cut dark robe. Then I thought for a moment, summoning up a covert maker routine from my internals: *fab this for me, and put it in an inner pocket.* I dumped the design into the wardrobe, and began to strip.

If only I knew who they were and why they were after me.

If only I knew what I needed to watch out for . . .

The main dining room was furnished in marble splendor, as if to emphasize that mass was of no concern to the modern space traveler; the ship showed me to my seat, a trail of fireflies pulsing through the candlelit conversations of the other diners.

"Alain! So pleased to see you again!" I couldn't decide whether she was being sarcastic or not. She smiled up at me, lips pale with tension.

"I was delayed," I said, and sat down beside her.

"That's nice. I was just telling Ivana here that I never know quite what to expect of you." This time the sarcasm was unmistakable, underpinned by a note of hostility that instantly put my back up. Ivana, a blonde mask with a fair complexion, nodded approvingly: I ignored her.

"That makes two of us," I replied, picking up my wine glass. An attentive servitor lowered its mouth to the goblet and regurgitated a red dribble: I swirled it under my nose for a moment and inhaled. "Have you made any arrangements for our arrival?"

"I was waiting to discuss that with you," she said guardedly. I looked at her, noting suddenly that her attention was totally focussed on me. It was a little frightening. In a culture of cheap beauty, the currency of aesthetic perfection is devalued; Arianna Blomenfeld was striking rather than pretty, projecting raw character in a way that suggested she hired only the most subtle of body sculptors. If the situation wasn't quite so depressingly messy I'd probably be trailing around after her with my tongue hanging out. "I suggest we discuss things in private after dinner."

"Perhaps." I drank some more wine and tried to figure out what she was hinting at. Dinner was served: a platter of delicate, thin-sliced flesh garnished with a white sauce. We ate in hostile silence, broken by vapid banter emanating from the mask and her partner, another nonentity of indeterminate age and questionable taste; I did my best to study Arianna while overtly ignoring her. She gave little away, except for the occasional furtive glance.

I found myself ignoring the meal, screening out the captain's speech and the assorted toasts and assertions of welcome that followed it. Periodically, minor agents deposited fragments of opinion in the back of my mind: less frequently, the waitrons cleared our plates and stifled us with solicitude. I was tugging at a bowl of sugared vermicelli when Arianna finally engaged my conversation. "You're going to have to face the future sooner or later," she stated directly. "You can't keep avoiding me forever. I want an answer, Alain. Bear or Bull? Which is it?"

My fork froze of its own accord, halfway to my mouth. "My dear, I have no idea what you're talking about," I said.

She obviously had some end in view for she smiled tensely, and said: "There's no need to hide any more, Alain. It's over. We've escaped. You can stop pretending."

"I—" I stopped. I put my fork down. "I've no idea what you're suggesting, truly." I frowned, and had the reward of seeing her look discomfited: surprised, if anything. "I don't feel very well," I added for the gallery.

"Ooh, do tell!" said the mask's slow-witted companion.

"There's nothing to tell," Arianna answered, fixing me with a coldly knowing look. I could hear the blood pumping in my ears. Had someone fixed her self-knowledge too? Was she also a victim of whatever was going on here? I stared at her face, mapping the pulse of blood through her veins: slightly flushed, tense, signs of concentration. I realized with a shiver that she was as worried as I.

"I don't feel so well," I repeated, and prodded my thalamus into broadcasting the appropriate signs. "Please excuse me." I stood and, mustering as much dignity as I could, left the room. There was a flurry of nervous conversation behind me from the mask and her attendant, but nobody followed me or paged me.

My stateroom was just as I had left it. I reached into my pocket for the device I had ordered from the wardrobe, then entered the bedroom.

"Don't move. Stay exactly where you are." I froze. No way of knowing how Arianna had gotten here ahead of me, much less how she had bypassed the lock—but I wasn't willing to bet that she was unarmed.

"What are you doing here?" I demanded.

"I'm asking the questions." She studied me like a bug on a pin. She was standing against the wall between the dresser and the wardrobe, the dark fabric of her dress shifting color to blend in with the aged oak finish. A little-used daemon reported back: *subject is suppressing emissions on all service channels Unable to establish context.* She was holding something round in a lace-gloved hand, pointed right at me. "Who are you and why have you spoofed my public knowledge?"

I blinked. "What are you talking about? You cracked my knowledge." I tried to force my pulse to slow. (Escape routes: the door was behind me, open, offering a clear field of fire. Her fingertips, exposed through the tips of her gloves, were white around the grip of her weapon. Stress.) "You can drop the pretense. I doubt we're being monitored and it doesn't make any difference anyway: you've got me." (Hoping she wouldn't shoot if I didn't let her see what I held clenched in my right hand; I wanted to learn whatever I could first. And besides, I don't like the sight of blood.)

"You're lying. Who are you working for? Tell me!" She sounded increasingly agitated: she raised the sphere, pointing it at my face from across the room. Deep heat vision showed me her pulse and another daemon tracked it: *one thirty-seven, one thirty-nine . . .* signs of serious stress. Was she telling the truth?

"I didn't modify your knowledge! I thought you'd been messing with mine—"

A momentary expression of shock flickered across her face. "If you're telling the truth—" she began, then stopped.

"Does someone want you dead? Does someone want both of us dead?" I asked.

"Wait." (A very paranoid agency chirped up in my ears; *sensor failure in main access corridor. Denial of service attack in progress.*) Arianna must have been listening to something like my own inner voice, because she abruptly twisted round and punched the wall: it shattered with a noise like breaking glass. She stood aside, still pointing a finger at me—the large, dark ring on it protruding upwards like a stubby gun barrel: "Get out! *Move!*"

I moved. Across the bed, to the hole in the wall—taking a brief look out—then through it. Something solid came up and thumped me hard. It was dark, and my eyes weren't ready for it; I was in some kind of roofed over-service duct, low ceiling, fat pipes oozing across every exposed surface. I glanced round. Structures bulked on all sides; it was some kind of service area I guessed, an inner hull. "Quick. Move." Arianna was behind me, prodding me away from the broken wall. "Faster!" she hissed.

"Why?" I asked.

"Keep going!" I scrabbled forwards into the darkness, lizard-like on all fours. I could hear her behind me and risked a glance. "Faster, idiot!" She was on all fours to avoid the low ceiling. "If you're lying I'll—"

Thump.

I blinked, unsure where I was. *That was a very loud noise*, I realized vaguely. Something tugged at my leg and I opened my eyes: there was a ringing in my ears and a light was flickering on and off in one eye, trying to get my attention. I blinked and tried to focus: someone was pinging me repeatedly. *What is it?*

Urgent message from Arianna Blomenfeld: "That was meant for us." There was an object attached to the message, a simple minded medical scanner that told her I was awake before I could stop it.

I lifted my head, blinking, and realized I was breathless. I began to cough. Someone put a hand over my mouth and I began to choke instead. *Message: don't speak. Bidirectional secure link installed.* I could feel it, itching like the phantom of someone else's limb.

"What happened?"

"Denial of service attack—with a bomb appended." My eyes were streaming. She let go of my mouth as I noticed her delicate lace evening gloves had turned into something more robust: blinking in the dusty twilight I saw her dress bunching up close to her, unraveling, weaving itself into plainer, close-fitting overalls: a space suit? Body armor? "Meant for both of us, while we were talking. Probably a last shot, before docking. Low information content, anyway."

"Do you know who's after you?" I asked.

She grimaced. "Talk about it later. If we get off this thing alive."

"They're trying to kill me, too," I transmitted, trying not to move my lips.

"So start moving."

"Which way?"

She pointed towards a service catwalk. I pushed myself up, wincing as my head throbbed in time to my pulse. Loud noises in the distance and an ominous hissing of air, then a queasy rippling lightness underfoot: the ship's momentum transfer field shutting down, handing us off to the dockmaster's control. "All the way down to the bottom."

"I've got a better idea. Why don't we split up? Less chance of them catching both of us."

She looked at me oddly. "If you want . . . "

Welcome to Burgundy.

Humanity is scattered across a three thousand light year radius, exiled from old Earth via wormholes created by the Eschaton, a strongly godlike intelligence spawned during Earth's singularity. Some of these worlds, including Burgundy, communicate; people and goods by starship, information by the network of instantaneous but bandwidth-limited causal trails established by Festival.

Burgundy is a developed, somewhat introverted culture that rests on the groaning back of a deliberately constructed proletariat. The first weakly godlike artificial intelligence to arrive here in the wake of its rediscovery abolished the cornucopiae and subjugated the human populace: an action that was tolerated because nothing the Queen did to them was anything like as bad as the repression imposed by their own human leaders.

Burgundy has gained a small reputation as an information buffer—a side-effect of its monarch's paranoid attitude towards encroachment by other deities. It exports confidentiality, delay-line buffers, fine wines, and dissidents. In other words, it's the last place a futures trader specializing in spread option trades that leverage developments in the artificial intelligence market—someone like me—would normally be seen dead in. On the other hand . . .

As an accountant specializing in Monte Carlo solutions to NP-complete low-knowledge systems I am naturally of interest to the Queen, who made me an offer I would have considered long and hard at the best of times; in my circumstances back on Dordogne—exposed to risk, to say the least—I could hardly consider refusing her invitation.

Many technologies are banned from the system, in an attempt to reduce the vulnerability of the monarchy to algorithmic complexity attacks. In particular, the royal capital of Burgundy—Castillia, a teeming metropolis of some three million souls—is positively mediaeval. It was here that the down-pod from the equatorial bean-stalk deposited me, time-lagged and dizzy from the descent, on the steps of the main rail terminus. Arianna had disappeared while I was opening a side-door back into the populated sections of the ship: I didn't see her go, although I have a vague recollection of blurred air, flattened perspectives against a wood-paneled wall. My ears were still ringing from the blast, and I was so confused that I didn't notice much of anything until I found myself in an alleyway my autonomics had steered me to, eyeing up the guest house where the Royal Mint had rented me a room.

The depths of neomediaeval barbarity into which this city had sunk finally became clear when I found my way to my garret. It wasn't simply the liveried servitors, or even the obese, physically aged steward who proudly showed me to the suite; but the presence of running water. Yes: a lead pipe—lead, yet!—entered through the ceiling of one room and discharged through a gargoyle-encrusted tap above a pewter basin. "You see, we have all the ancient luxuries!" gloated Salem the steward. "This'n's piped down from our very own roof-tank. More'n you'll have seen before, I expect."

I nodded, faintly aghast at the prospect of the microfauna that must surely be swimming in the swill.

"Are you sure you don't have any luggage?" he added, one heavy eyebrow raised in protest at the very idea of a gentleman-merchant traveling without such.

"Not a parcel," I said. "I came by starship . . . "

He blinked rapidly. "Oh," he said, very fast. "And ee's not staying at the Palace?" He shuffled, as if unsure of what to do with his feet, then essayed a little bow. "We is honored by your presence, m'lord."

When I finally persuaded him to leave me alone—at the price of calling a tailor, to fab me some garments suitable to my station in life—I swept the room for bugs. My custom fleas found nothing, save the more natural macrofauna lurking in the bed, garde-robe, and curtains. I removed and disassembled into three separate parts the device in my pocket, then hid two of them in the hollow cuban heels of my boots: possession of such a gadget, in these parts, could earn one a slow impalement if the Queen deigned to notice. (The third part I wore as a ring on my left hand.)

At the end of this sequence I lay down upon the bed, hands behind my head, staring up at the dusty canopy of the four-poster. "What am I doing here?" I murmured. *To report to ye chancellery of court on the day following landfall, there to command and supervise the management of ye portfolio of accounts royal and foreign*, the contract said; *while lying low and avoiding the exchange agents*, I added mentally. But I was already wondering if I'd made the right decision.

The next day, I reported to the Exchequer for duty.

A rambling, gothic assemblage of gargoyles, flying buttresses and turrets held together by red brick, the Chancellery was located across the three-sided Capital Square from the Summer Palace, a white marble confection that pointed battlements and parabolic reflectors south across the river. As I approached the entrance, armed guards came to attention. Their leader stepped forward. "Sir Blomenfeld," said the sergeant: "I am pleased to greet you on behalf of her Terrible Majesty, and extend to you her gracious wishes for your success in her service."

"I thank you from the depths of my heart," I replied, somewhat taken aback by his instant recognition. "It is an honor and a blessing to be welcomed in such exalted terms. I will treasure it to my dying day." *Laying it on too thick?* I wondered.

The sergeant nodded, and I noticed the antennae tucked between the feathers of his ornate helmet; the strangely bony fingers disguised by his padded gloves: and the odd articulation of his back. Evidently the technology restrictions didn't apply to Her Majesty's security. "If you would please come this way, sir?" he asked, directing me towards a side door.

Tradesman's entrance. "Certainly."

He led me inside, up the steps and along a wide marble passage hung with portraits of ruby-nosed dignitaries in their late middle age: the human dynasty that had preceded Her Majesty. Into an office where, behind a leather-topped desk, there sat a man with a surpassingly sallow complexion and even less hair than my ersatz wife had been wearing the night before. "Sir Alain Blomenfeld, your honor, reporting as required." He turned to me. "His Lordship, Victor Manchusko, under-secretary of the Treasury, counselor in charge of the privy portfolio."

Privy portfolio? I blinked in surprise as the sergeant bowed his way out. "Sir, I—"

"Sit down." Lord Manchusko waved in the direction of an ornately decorated chair that might have been designed as an instrument of torture. His gold-rimmed spectacles glittered in the wan light filtering down from the high-set windows. "You were not expecting something like this, I take it."

"Not exactly," I said, somewhat flustered. "Um, I understood I was being retained to overhaul dependency tracking in the barter sector—"

"Nonsense." Manchusko slapped the top of his desk: I'll swear that it cringed. "Do you think we needed to hire offworld intellect for such a task?"

"Um. Then you, er, have something else in mind?"

The under-secretary smiled thinly. "Over-exposed on the intelligence futures side, was it?"

An icy sinking feeling in the pit of my stomach. "Yes," I admitted.

"Tell me about it."

"It was all over the Festival channels. Surely you know—"

He smiled again. It was not a humorous expression. "Pretend I don't."

"Oh." I hunched over unconsciously. So. They didn't want me as an accountant, after all, hmm? *Trapped.* And if I didn't give them exactly what they wanted they could hold me here forever. I licked my lips: "You know what commodities are traded on the TX; mostly design schemata, meta-memes, better algorithms for network traversal, that sort of thing. Most of these items require serious mind-time to execute; so we trade processing power against options on better algorithms. Most of the trading entities are themselves intelligent, even if only weakly so: even some of the financial instruments—" I paused.

"Such as Blomenfeld et Cie, I take it."

I nodded. "Yes. I was proud of that company. Even though it was pretty small in the scheme of things; it was mine, I made it. We worked well together. I was its director, and it was my memetic muscle. It was the smartest company I could build. We were working on a killer scheme, you know. When the market crashed."

Manchusko nodded. "A lot of people were burned by that."

I sighed and unkinked a little. "I was over-exposed. A complex derivative swap that was backward-chaining between one of the Septagon clades' quantum oracle programs—I figured it would produce the goods, a linear-order performance boost in type IV fast-thinkers, within five mind-years—leveraged off junk bonds issued in Capone City. According to my Bayesian analysers nothing should go wrong in the fifteen seconds I was over-extended. Only it was just those fifteen seconds in which, um, you-know-what happened."

Normally, the Eschaton leaves us alone; nothing short of widespread causality violation provokes a strongly godlike intervention. Whatever happened in Eldritch system's intelligence futures market was bad, capital-B-bad. Bad enough to provoke an Act of God. Intervention from beyond the singularity. Bad enough to trigger a run on the market, an instant bear market, everyone selling every asset they owned for dear life.

"Eldritch went runaway and the Eschaton intervened. You were in the middle of a complex chain of investments when the market crashed and it all unraveled on you due to a bad transitive dependency. How far uncovered were you?"

"Sixty thousand mind-years." I licked my suddenly-dry lips. "Ruin," I whispered.

Manchusko leaned forward suddenly. "Who's after you?" he demanded. "Who tried to kill you on the ship?"

"I don't know!" I snapped, then froze solid, trying to regain my composure. "I'm sorry. It could have been anyone. I have some suspicions—" not fair to mention Arianna, she'd been in the middle of it too "—but nothing solid. Not the exchange authority, anyway."

"Good. While you are here, you will remain under her Majesty's protection. If you have any problems, ask any guard for help." That smile was disquieting as anything I'd ever seen: "What one sees, all see, she sees."

I nodded silently, not daring to trust my tongue.

"Now. About the reason we wanted you here. You weren't the only one who took a bath in the crash. Her Majesty's portfolio is highly diversified, and some of our investments suffered somewhat. Your job—unofficially—is to take over her hedge fund and rebuild it. Officially you're not trading, you're disqualified. Your company is insolvent and liable to be wound up, if they can ever find where it ran to. You're a disqualified director. Unofficially, I hope you learn from your mistakes. Because we don't expect you to repeat them here." He stood up and gestured towards a side door. "Through here is your office and your dealer desk. Let me introduce you to it . . . "

Afternoon found me back at my room, digesting a manual of procedures and trying to regain my shattered composure. I had just about managed to forget about the incidents of the previous day when there was a knock at the door.

"Who is it?" I called.

"Y'r humble servant, m'lord," called Salem. "With a manuscript for you!"

I rolled to my feet. "Come in!"

He sidled into my room, holding a rolled-up piece of parchment away from his body as if it contained some noxious vermin. "Begging y'r'honour's indulgence, but this came for you from the palace. Messenger's waiting on y'r'honour's pleasure."

I took the note and broke the wax seal on it. *Having a lovely time at the court. Formal presentation before Her Majesty at eight this eve. Your presence requested by royal fiat. Will you be there? Signed, your "wife".*

Hello, Arianna, I thought. I remembered her face; chilly beauty. It was some joke, the one that whoever had hacked our respective memories had played on me. I resolved that if I ever found them I'd use their head for a punch-line. "Tell the messenger to tell her that I'll be there," I said.

At seven, Salem slid into my vision again. "Pardoning y'r honour, but y'r humble coach awaits you, sir," he mumbled unctuously.

"Isn't it a bit early?" I asked.

It wasn't early. I sat in a cramped wooden box with my nose inches from a slit-window rimmed with intricately painted murals of rural debauchery. Outside, two husky porters wheezed as they carried me bodily—box and all—through the cobbled streets. We lurched and swayed from side to side, trapped in a heaving mass of pedestrians: a royal lobster drive was in progress. The lobsters lived sufficiently long in air that by custom they were herded through the streets to the gates of the palace: the distress made their flesh sweeter, apparently. Presently my porters lifted me again and continued, this time with little further delay.

They set me down and opened the door: trying not to gasp audibly I stood up, stretching muscles that ached as if I'd run the entire distance. The sedan chair was parked in a courtyard, before the palace steps but inside the walls. My porters groveled before a junior officer of the royal dragoons. I bowed slightly and doffed my hat to him.

"Sir Blomenfeld," said the lieutenant: "If you would please come this way?"

"Surely." He led me inside, up the steps and along a wide marble passage carpeted in red velvet.

Noise, chatter, and music drifted from ahead. We came upon a well-lit stretch, then a pair of high doors and an antechamber, walled with pompous gold-leaf plaster, where four footmen and a butler greeted me. "His excellency the high trader Albert Blomenfeld, by appointment to Her Majesty's Royal Treasury! Long may she live!" A blast of pipes ushered me into the royal presence.

The hall beyond the antechamber was high-ceilinged, decorated with primitive opulence and meticulous precision, illuminated by skylights set in the ceiling. A floor of black and white tiles gleamed

beneath my boots as I looked around. Throngs of richly clad court-
iers ignored me in their elegant hauteur. The Queen herself was
nowhere to be seen—but I would not expect to be introduced at this
stage in any event. I wondered where Arianna was, and what she was
doing to have inveigled herself into the royal court so rapidly.
Although, if her hacked knowledge was anything to go by, she had
the background for it.

"Hello, Alain!" My question answered itself with a beaming smile
full of sharp, white teeth. She most elegantly decked out in a gown of
sea-green silk, with a jeweled motif of eyes: her choker scrutinized
me with terrible, passive regret. "I see you're none the worse for
wear, hmm? We really must have that talk, you know." She took my
hand and led me away from the door. *The company here is dire*, she
sent. *Besides, speaking openly is difficult. Encrypt?* I nodded. Wetware
embedded deep in the redundant neural networks of my cerebellum
mangled the next transmission, established a private key, linked to
her headspace . . .

"Do you know about the treasury situation yet?" she asked.

"Eh?" I stared at her; her gown stared back at me quizzically.

"Don't be obtuse. It's so hard to tell who's on the inside hereabouts. She didn't drag you here to mess with her ledgers, she
brought you in for your dealing record."

"She?"

Arianna frowned. "The queen." A balcony, overlooking an inner
courtyard: neatly manicured lawn, flower beds, stone flagstones. My
knowledge inflicted a sudden flash of deja vu on me: a false memory
of accompanying Arianna to a ball on New Venus, of sneaking away
with her, quiet sighs in a secret garden at midnight. My pulse accel-
erated: her hand tightened on my arm. "Too many damned memories, Alain. You feel it too?"

I nodded.

"I think they're there for a reason, you know. We must have something in common, otherwise whoever they are, they wouldn't have
spoofed both of us with the same false history. Do you remember?"

She leaned against the balcony, watching me intently.

"I—" I shook my head. More deja vu, this time from within: I knew Arianna from somewhere, somewhere real, not bound up in externalities. *Market externalities.* Now where did that thought come from?

"I never saw you before, before you walked into that observation lounge, I swear it," I said. "But despite the false memories—"

She nodded. "You know what?" she asked.

"Um. What?"

Suddenly she leaned against me, sharp chin digging into my collar bone, hugging me tight in a spring-steel grip: "I don't remember," she whispered in my ear. "Anything. Before the lounge. I mean, I have lots of external memories, but no internal ones." She was shuddering with tension; I hugged her back, appalled by her admission. "I know who am, but I don't remember becoming me. At least, not from inside. All my memories that are more than a day old are third-person. Before then, I think, I think I may have been someone else."

"That's awful."

"Is it?" The tension in her arms ebbed slightly. "What about you?"

"I—" I suddenly realized I had an armful of attractive woman. A woman my external memories insisted I was married to. "I have false memories. One set, with you in them. And the real ones—I think they're real—without you."

Arianna released me, took a step back and shook her head. "So you know you're a real person? Then what does that make me?" Her gown blinked at me, eyelids rippling from floor to throat.

"I don't know. I've never met you before—at least, I don't remember doing so."

"Are you sure?" she murmured, pulling away slightly. She frowned, fine eyebrows drawing together. "I've been injected into your life and I don't know why. Are you certain you don't know anything about me? You seem to have enemies. Could you have erased some key memories for any reason?" She looked at me so knowingly that I flushed like an ingenue. "I don't find it upsetting, not having a history, Alain. But I want to know why. And who wants me dead."

I shook my head. "Existentialism on an empty stomach."

She smiled sadly: the first time I'd seen her smile in living memory. "We'd better go back inside before anyone misses us," she said.

"So gratified to meet you," said the Queen, her antennae vibrating softly in the breeze. "Do relax, please."

I straightened up. Workers fawned over the royal abdomen, polishing with robotic dedication. "As your majesty wishes."

"I have already had the pleasure of your lady wife's company," the Queen commented in a high-pitched voice, air rushing through her spiracles. She sounded amused, for some reason. "I understand you have a little memory problem?"

"I really couldn't comment." Worker-ancillaries buzzed and clattered beneath the ceiling like demented wasps; the air was hot and dry from their encrypted infra-red exchanges. I sweated, but not from heat.

"Then don't comment. You shall pretend that you have no problem, and I shall pretend that you didn't fail to answer my question. Once only, sir Blomenfeld. Drink."

One of the workers extruded a goblet full of dark red liquid into the palm of my right hand. I swirled it around, sniffed, swallowed. Whatever else it contained, there was no alcohol in it. "Thank you."

"Thanks are unnecessary: a potent vintage, that. What do you think of my little portfolio?"

I blinked. "I haven't really had time to do a detailed analysis—"

She waved an idle pair of arms: "Never mind. I expect no precision at this stage."

"Well then." I licked my lips. *Little portfolio, indeed.* "Some of them are evolving nicely. I noticed two promising philosophies in there, if not more. A full dependency analysis of your investments will take a while to prepare—some of your holdings keep changing their identities—but I don't see any reason to doubt that they'll pick up value rapidly as the market recovers from the recession. I'd say your shares are among the most intelligent ones I've ever met."

She giggled, a noise like saws rasping on bone. "Expand my

holdings, doctor, and I will be most grateful." A ripple ran through her thorax and she tensed: "Please leave me now, I have no further need of human attendance." Dismissed by her cursory wave I retreated back to the party outside the royal chambers. Behind me, the queen was giving birth to another processor.

On my third day, I arrived at the small office Manchusko had assigned me unusually early. Unlocking the door and opening it, I froze. Arianna was seated behind my desk, wearing an unhappy expression. "I tried to stop them, Alain, but they wouldn't listen."

"What—"

Someone pushed me into the office, none too gently, and pulled the door shut behind us. "Shut you mouth. I are exchange commission!" growled the intruder.

I turned round, very slowly, and looked up and up until I met its small, black-eyed gaze. "Why are you here?" I asked, trying to ignore the gunsight contact lenses glowing amber against its pupils. "Did you plant the bomb?"

"Am here for compensation." The bear shifted its weight from one foot to the other: the floor boards creaked. "You my principle shareholders blame for inequitable exposure. Am here to repossess. Not bomber. Bomber sent by idiot day trading script. Bomber not blow anyone else up again."

"Uh-huh." I took a step backwards, slowly. Now I was in the room I could see the monofilament spiderweb holding Arianna down, tied to my chair and afraid to move. This was an outrage! What did they think they were doing?

Arianna was trying to catch my eye. I blinked, remembered the secure channel she'd passed to me during our arrival.

"Am taking this chattel," the bear explained, planting a heavy hand on the back of her chair. She winced. "Am needing also your memory keys. Do be good about this all, doc." He grinned, baring far too many teeth at me.

Alain?

I tweaked my knowledge, hoping to get a handle on some bandwidth I could use to signal for help, but nothing happened. The room was too well shielded. *Here. Why does he want you—*

Keys. To your portfolio, to everything.

Memory keys. "My memory keys?" I almost laughed. "You're joking! I couldn't give you them if I wanted to—"

"Your cooperation not necessary," said the bear. "Just your knowledge. And your company. Take her. Get back options."

"Her? But she's not my property; I've never met her before! Someone hacked our public knowledge—"

The bear looked, his breath a hot stench upon me: "Amnesia no excuse, doc. She your business. Cloned body, same dirty algorithms. Am her taking with me! Now. Your keys. Or I take your head with them inside."

Arianna was looking at me again, eyes wide and unreadable.

That true? You're my company?

She nodded minutely. *You planned this, Alain. Selective amnesia to slip past the hunters. Good reason for us to stay together. But you should have stayed with me. Not fled.*

I looked up at the bear, trying not to telegraph what I was thinking. So Arianna was a construct from the beginning? And one of my making, too: a downloaded company on the run from the receivers.

"You're not really from the exchange, are you?"

"Pretty boy. Think smart." The bear produced a small spheroid, pointed it at me. "This yours, pretty boy?"

Shit. Me and my big mouth. Of course the Exchange wouldn't bother with a meat machine repo tool, would they? This must be Organization muscle of some sort. Probably laundering intelligence—dumping mind-years into an arbitrage sector to ensure that options held by another pawn got smarter. Only the market crash had propagated my own exposure, catching them out. "Hey, can we do a deal?"

"Market closed." The bear grinned and leaned forward, opening its mouth wide, jaw-breakingly wide. I heard a pop and crunch of dislocating joints and felt a familiar buzzing at the edge of my consciousness; its teeth were compact quantum scanners, built to sequestrate the uncollapsed wave functions buried in crypto blackboxes.

I ducked, then leaned forward and attempted to head-butt the huge meat machine. It grunted, and my vision blanked for a moment: external knowledge of combat procedures kicked in, telling me just how hopeless the situation was. Arianna was struggling in her chair, isometric twitching and grand mal shuddering. *Keys, Alain! Give me access to your keys!*

I bounced back from the bear before it could grab me, threw at coat-rack at it, ducked behind the desk. *Why?*

Just do it!

The bear casually picked up the coat-rack and broke it over one knee. Waved one end in my direction, brought the other down of the desktop. The desk whimpered: blood began to drip from one of its ornamental drawers. *Here.* I generated an authentication token, stuffed it into Arianna's head, opened a channel to my keys so she could use them as my proxy. The bear didn't seem to want her dead yet; it grunted and tried to sidle round her to get at me. She heaved halfway out of the seat and I paused for a moment to slash at the monofilament wire with my shaving nail: it screeched like chalk on slate but refused to give way.

"You not can escape," rumbled the bear. "Have I a receivership order—"

It froze. Arianna gasped and shuddered, then slumped in her chair: behind the desk I rolled on my back, grabbed at my spring-loaded boot-heels, feverishly slotting puzzle-blocks together in the shape of a gun as I tumbled over, knocking over a dumb waiter, blinked . . . and saw the bear toppling towards me with the infinite inertia of a collapsing stock market.

I came to my senses back in my penthouse garret with the running water: my corporate assets were in bed with me, holding onto me like a echo of a false honeymoon memory. My skull ached and I could feel bruises; but a quick audit of my medical memories told me it was nothing that wouldn't heal in a week or so. My glial supports had saved my brain from any lingering effects of concussion: my mouth tasted bad but apart from that . . .

I shifted for comfort, feeling more at ease with myself. Arianna sighed, sleeping lightly; I could feel her background processes continuing as normal, shadows under the skin of reality. And now I could remember more of what had happened. *Memory: validate.*

Arianna opened an eye: *booted again?* she asked.

I cleared my throat. "Mostly back to normal." *Validation successful.* I tried to gather my scattered wits. "So it really happened?"

"Reckless trading, my dear. It was the only way out of that collapse back on Dordogne. Or would you rather they'd wound me up and set you to paying off your debts in mind time? You were several billion years uncovered at the end . . . "

"No!" I tried to sit up.

She reached over and dragged me back down: "Not yet. You're still dizzy."

"But my keys—"

"Relax, he didn't get them. Your head's on your body, not sitting in a vat."

"But what did you do?"

She shrugged. "He was from one of the syndicates, Alain. With your authority, acting as your agency, I asked your desk to run a huge order via her majesty's portfolio."

"But he was in there with us!" I shuddered. "There can't have been time!"

"Oh, but there was." She ran a hand across my chest suggestively. "Mm. You did a good job with those memories—"

"The bear. Tell me, please!"

"If you insist." She frowned. "I just told your desk to buy everything—everything available. Saturated all outgoing bandwidth through the firewall: the desk was only too happy to cooperate. The queen's dealer desk has a very high priority on the net, you know. The bear was a remote. While all the stocks were handshaking with the treasury, it was locked out. While it was locked out it was frozen; by the time it recovered I'd worked my way loose and ordered the guards in. Not that it was necessary."

I shook my head. "I know I'm going to regret asking this. Why not?"

"Well, I'd just pumped a large amount of liquidity into the exchange. The trading volume drove up share prices, triggered a minor recovery, and in the past few hours there are signs of the market actually rallying. I think it's going to be a sustained rise; Her Majesty can anticipate a nice little windfall in a few months' time. Anyway, you don't need to worry about the Organization remotes any more, at least not for a year or two. After all—" She wormed her way over until her breath in my ear was hot—"bears can't handle a rising market!"

Extracts from the Club Diary

August 16th, 1889

Nobody likes to admit to an addiction; especially when the substance abused is as apparently innocuous, yet as subtly damaging as the subject of this diary. It reflects a lack of foresight on the part of the participant, a naiveté if you will, in not predicting the inevitable social humiliation, concordant upon the revelation that they lack sufficient moral probity to avoid the pitfalls of temptation. It is my hope that, having confessed privately to one-another that we share this particular craving, and having incorporated our club with all due secrecy and pomp, we may now indulge in our infatuation. Moreover, it is my hope that we may do so secure in the knowledge that no murmur of our Habit may reach the world at large—or worse, the Press.

It being the case that our Club is a secret body, admittance to the membership of which is by invitation only—and *then* to the most close-lipped and trustworthy of fellows—I feel it incumbent upon me to start a journal of our activities. Accordingly, I declare this Club Diary to be open. The duty of maintaining it falls upon the shoulders of the chairman of the executive; therefore, in my capacity as cofounder of the society, I shall maintain it until the time comes to hand over our records to my successor.

I feel that it is necessary to describe the foundation of our society in some detail, in the interests of posterity. Clubs are worthless without traditions; consequently, the sooner our traditions are codified the more secure we shall be. It is unquestionably true to say that our addiction is an overwhelming pride and passion that is most exclusive in its intensity. It is also true to say that virtually none of the countless horde who indulge in the heavenly beverage on any given day feel any inkling of the true importance which we ascribe to the decoction, or the passion with which we pursue it. That is not to say that we are insane; merely, possessed . . . beings of a great innate sensitivity, capable of perceiving the delicacy of flavour, the stimulation of the senses, to an exquisite degree forbidden to the lumpen mass of humanity. Quite why this might be so eludes me; indeed, the determination of this cause is the very *raison d'être* of the Club, and of the select few who are capable of perceiving its importance. We are truly a breed apart, isolated and obsessive. Indeed, we are so rare a type that had two of us not met quite by accident one evening, it is possible that this club should never have come into existence.

I had known for some years that I was unusual in my predilection for the object of addiction; long before I met Smith-Carrington I learned to conceal my desires in the presence of those who might greet them with skepticism or laughter. To most people of any worth, the idea of squandering a small fortune on the import of such a substance would appear imprudent at best, or even sinful. To actually contemplate going into *trade* to support the habit would be seen as the mark of a lunatic. Luckily my modest inheritance sufficed to enable me to purchase a warehouse, and by the most circuitous of routes I established a connection with a certain shop-merchant who harboured ambitions above his station; thus I was able to maintain my addiction without becoming the laughing-stock of society. There is nothing like an overriding passion in life to teach one the true value of commodities; my merchant profited greatly, and I, for my part, did not do badly. Thus I was able to make my addiction self-financing; and even to expand my activities, researching new sources of supply and living in a manner commensurate with my social status.

I first met Smith-Carrington at one of Mr Oscar Wilde's dinners. As was his habit, that notorious socialite had invited as eclectic an assortment of guests as he considered conducive to an elevated but stimulating evening. On this occasion his list consisted of a number of people of high birth but questionable morals, and a smattering of interesting but shady types whom he trusted to enliven the proceedings. Actors, actresses, impresarios, inventors, explorers and presti-digitators were all laid out on display for their lord's and ladyship's edification. I understand that I was in the category of those who were to be entertained, by virtue of my birth if nothing else: Smith-Carrington may have been on the converse side, but in such cases it is sometimes difficult to tell. In any event, I found myself sitting opposite him at the dining table. I had read of Smith-Carrington's exploits in the wild and untamed jungles of the Congo, but had passed them by; when I enquired after them politely that gentleman regarded me rather mournfully. "I searched, but alas the object of my search was not to be found," he said. "Two years in the fœtid jungle, pygmy headhunters and snakes and mountains as steep as Eiffel's Tower to be climbed every day; yet it was all in vain!"

"Oh dear," I said, as the servants wheeled in the coffee. "You were searching for a medicinal compound of some description, were you not? The curators at Kew—"

I stopped, for my nostrils were momentarily occupied with the aroma of roasted beans. I sniffed surreptitiously, hoping nobody would notice; luckily Smith-Carrington's attention was directed else-where, and my immediate neighbours were chattering contentedly to persons invisible from my perspective. I inhaled deeply and closed my eyes.

It was a cheap blend. Perhaps it had been imported from Arabia, but the cherries had been *heated* before they were pulped, and the roasters had been lazy. Indeed, the very beans had been roasted at least two days ago. Yet for the sake of propriety I must drink this evil brew! I shuddered slightly and tried to compose myself. *I shall have to have words with Mr Wilde's butler,* I thought. Then I opened my eyes again and looked at Smith-Carrington. He looked pained.

"My dear fellow," I said, "is anything the matter?"

"Nothing of any consequence," he mumbled through his mous-tache. *Soto voce*: "If only I had found it!"

This was most intriguing. I was left no alternative but to be blunt: "Pardon my ignorance, but pray enlighten me: just what precisely were you looking for?" I enquired.

Smith-Carrington looked at me for a long time, as if deciding whether I was worthy of his especial confidence. Finally he made his mind up and spoke: "it is not so much a *thing* as a *process*," he said quietly. "The diaries of Pastor Moelitz of Dusseldorf—who as you may know was martyred by head-hunters nine years ago—were subsequently recovered by the intrepid Major London. They contained a reference to what he called the Drink of the Gods. It is known that certain related species of *coffea canephora* exist in the uncharted wilderness which has not yet come fully under the dominion of the Empire. They are believed to be of unusual potency and quality of taste. Meanwhile, it is also said that the headhunters and savages have a secret process by which they extract the most heavenly—"

He was interrupted by the imposition of a china cup before him, into which a servitor poured a generous serving of such slop as I would not allow to pass my lips, had I but the choice. A similar vessel appeared before me: I sniffed again, appalled. Smith-Carrington for his part, wore an expression of mute resignation. Our eyes met. "You have a greater than average understanding of the bean," I whispered. I snapped my fingers for a servant, passed the woman my card: "Pray pass this to the gentleman opposite me," I instructed her, my heart pounding most unpleasantly. For it was my *business* card that I had handed out; if my estimate of Smith-Carrington's character was incorrect, then I should be ruined. However, as I surmised from the set of his shoulders as he drank the vile brew out of politeness toward our host, my guess was right.

A chap who would willingly spend two years in deepest Africa searching for the ultimate cup of coffee, yet who would uncomplainingly partake of the vile brew we were served that night, in the boudoir of the most notorious libertine and socialite of the age; such a man was, quite unmistakably, a fellow spirit. Like me, he was unmistakably trapped in the grip of the most potent addiction of our modern age. And, from the moment I discovered that I was not alone, the subsequent formation of our Club became inevitable.

January 7th, 1890

In its first six months, our club has prospered. There are now six of us: myself, Smith-Carrington, the Marquis of Brentford (who is second son of Lord Sandleford), an American entrepreneur called Joyce, Chapman Frazer (who is chief engineer of the London and District Railway Company), and Boddington, my shop-keeper.

Perhaps the latter requires some explanation. This club of ours is astonishingly eclectic, collecting fellows of character regardless of their birth or station in life: the one requirement is that their passions be governed by the pursuit of the sublime beverage. Our membership, indeed our very existence, is a closely-guarded secret; names are put forward by our existing fellowship, and must be unanimously approved. Early on, it became apparent that there were advantages to be had in allowing foreigners, like the American Joyce, to join: to encompass such worthies as Boddington in our ranks was but another step, although it was not taken without some soul-searching. Still, if we do not encompass as members those worthies of the artisan class who are most skilled at making the apparatus that we require, how on earth are we to proceed with total secrecy? Thus, Boddington is not merely a hireling but a member; and although this brings with it certain problems of a social nature, they are not altogether insoluble.

Now, to describe our business. We meet every week, in a room above the coffee shop in Greek Street, Soho. The room has been furnished to our taste, and is artfully concealed from the street; to reach it, one must enter the shop, proceed through to the stock-room, and pull down a trapdoor behind which lurks a cunning extensible stair. The stairwell is lined with cupboards, within which we keep our 'special' supplies; the brew of which is not now, or ever, for sale to *hoi polloi*.

Our room was once an attic: now it is a spacious club, lit by the new electric lamps, and equipped with all the apparatus necessary to our study. There are beaten copper jugs of Ottoman manufacture; a frightening steamer of Italian design that roars and foams; numerous beakers and grinders and roasters of all descriptions; and a cooking range upon which to heat the brew. There is another attic, which is not yet furnished; Chapman Frazer proposes to convert it into a workshop, the better to serve as the laboratory of our craving. He also proposes that our priority for this year should be to acquire as a member an apothecary or pharmacognocist. Frazer is nothing if not organised.

These resolutions were passed unopposed at our first annual meeting:

Firstly   that membership of the club should be contingent solely upon acceptance by all the existing members; that membership should in the first instance be limited to thirty souls; and that membership, once granted, should be for life.

Secondly   that it is the purpose of the club to identify and determine the root cause of our addiction, with the view of equipping us to control it. In the meantime, a secondary purpose is to research the most efficient possible way of satisfying our craving.

Thirdly   that to these ends each member should donate at minimum two hundredths of their worth to the club. That a hardship fund should be established such that, in the event of indigency, a member stricken by circumstances might be allowed to make use of club facilities without fee until such time as their fortunes recover.

Fourthly   that this being a gentleman's club, no women should be admitted.

Fifthly   that as a club established within the realm of Her Majesty's dominion, no treason or like-minded abominations should be countenanced under the auspices of this club; and that members of the club, being also Citizens of the Empire, should at all times bear in mind their patriotic duty.

Sixthly   that the club should remain secret under all circumstances, and that the event of its public exposure should be sufficient cause for it to be summarily wound up.

God save Her Majesty Queen Victoria, and all those who live under her!

August 16th, 1910

How time flies! It is with the greatest gratification imaginable that I recall that our club has now survived for more than two decades, and has now reached its majority. Perhaps this is a suitable point at which to recall our grand history; the childhood of our endeavour, so to speak.

We now have fully thirty members, as directed by our charter. Since our foundation, three have died and one has been committed to an asylum; thankfully, none have had cause to make use of the hardship fund. Our membership is predominantly based in London, although Joyce remains staunchly committed to us; perhaps the prosperity of his shipping enterprise in New York has something to do with his enthusiasm, for he makes a point of visiting at least twice a year.

The club is still above the shop, but the back room has now been converted into a combination warehouse and laboratory by Chapman Frazer. Rodworthy of the Botanical Gardens at Kew, and latterly the incumbent of the Chair of Pharmacognosy at the School of Pharmacy in Brunswick Square, has devoted part of his time to a cataloguing of our obsession; he is a grand fellow, and has contributed more to our understanding of the botanical origins of our drug than anyone else save, perhaps, Smith-Carrington.

For his part, Smith-Carrington was instrumental in obtaining for us a supply of the astonishing Wolf Coffee of Java on his expedition of 1893; this decoction is prepared by the passage of the beans through the gut of the rare Javanese cherry-eating wolf. The acids and other perfusions of the wolf remove the cherry and treat the bean itself to a most strange fermentation, following which the raw ejecta may be obtained from the spoor of the animal. The resultant bean, once washed and prepared, has a most astonishing and subtle flavour, quite unlike that of the same beans prepared by the traditional method of sun-drying the cherries. Sir Bosworth Hughes of the Royal Society is currently working to isolate the responsible reagents from the gut of the cherry-eating wolf; it is his hope that one day we shall be able to drink Wolf Coffee without the need for the lupine intermediary, so to speak. This is a matter of some importance to those of delicate sensibilities.

Smith-Carrington's second expedition of 1895, in search of the legendary Cannibal Coffee of Borneo, was not a success. However his personal effects were recovered by his bearers and his pith helmet and left femur occupy pride of place in our trophy cabinet. We shall remember him fondly.

Chapman Frazer became intrigued by the potential of the Cappuccino Machine introduced by the Marquis, and embarked upon a plan to construct a new High Pressure Percolating Engine. As an operator of steam locomotives, I am sure he knows precisely what he is doing in this respect; nevertheless, I required him to conduct his initial experiments away from the club premises, lest the apparatus should explode. This proved to be a prescient request.

I am not the most mechanically-minded of men, but a short description should suffice. The Engine resembles a small locomotive, the wheels of which are removed; there is an apparatus by which they can be allowed to grind beans in bulk. The Engine, for its part, is intended to percolate coffee under pressure: grounds are dropped into the cylinders by means of a cunning valve that opens on the backstroke of the piston, and the live steam emitted from the cylinder head is condensed and poured into a cup. It produces a brew of most remarkable potency, but it is somewhat sooty in taste; and after five cups the piston becomes mired, so the Engine must be stripped down.

Frazer's collaborator, the Scottish physicist MacIntyre, maintains that Radium is the answer.

Finally, there is the matter of Suffrage. The Marquis' daughter Camilla is, like her parent, an aficionado of the heavenly brew; she has pursued her addiction as far as any of us, to the extent of having purchased a plantation in Jamaica. More gravely, she has discovered the existence of our Club and last year attempted to inveigle her way into our premises: this caused a scene of considerable anguish and recrimination. I should like it to be recorded that I am a great supporter of women, as my wife and daughters will testify; I should like nothing better than to be remembered as a benefactor of the fair sex: but I must say that enough is enough. Whether or not those demented harridans obtain the satisfaction of their unreasonable demands for suffrage, *we shall have no women in this club*. This is a high-minded institution dedicated to the pursuit of the sublime beverage; likely as not, were we to admit women they would introduce embroidery, or worse still, insist on *drinking tea*.

December 1st, 1917

Sad news. Stansbrook Taylor, our founder and Chairman, passed away in his sleep last night, aged sixty-eight. He will be remembered for as long as the Club continues to exist, as a gentleman and an aficionado of the *old school*. We owe him a great debt of gratitude for the establishment of this institution, whatever opinions we might hold in respect of his more extreme views.

For my part, as newly admitted member and, to my surprise, Club Secretary (the majority of the membership being away at the Front, regardless of their age), I will attempt to discharge my duties with all possible grace and efficiency, to maintain the society during these harrowing times, and to uphold the traditions of the Club in all ways—save one.

signed:
Lady Camilla Sandleford
Club Secretary

January 19th, 1919

The War is over, and Our Boys are coming home. It has been a trying time; in the last six months, a dastardly Zeppelin captain discharged his bombs over Soho, and the club windows were shattered by the blast. No less than six members gave their lives for King and Country during the course of the war. Many other events transpired, so that the Club is changed almost beyond recognition. Perhaps it is a mercy that Stansbrook Taylor and Horace Smith-Carrington are not alive to observe it today. Although their dream continues, it has taken on the strangest of forms.

First, permit me to take stock of the state of the Club. The original premises are still standing, and are now owned outright by the Club, as is the shop below. The retail establishment is managed by Boddington and Sons Limited as one of their own. Boddington is remarkably hale and hearty in his old age, and his eldest son appears likely to follow him into the Club, which would be no bad thing. The finances of the Club are in excellent fettle, thanks to my father and to Stansbrook Taylor, who included the Club as a beneficiary in his will.

And now to our activities. The Chemical Committee continued to work throughout the War, albeit at a slow pace. Their activities focus at present upon the pressing need to determine what makes the difference between a merely passable and a superb brew. This work was hampered until recently by U-boat activity, but looks set to proceed at a gallop in the near future.

The Botanical Committee, under Professor Rodworthy and the Albanian, Kotcha, is conducting a definitive catalogue of all the plants of the family *rubiacea*, among whose ranks the sources of the divine bean are grouped. It is their profound hope that cross-breeding of plants may be employed to improve the brew.

The Engineering Committee continues to research improved methods of titrating the ground beans and expressing their essential ingredients in palatable form. The High Pressure Percolating Engine developed by Frazer was succeeded by a series of tests involving Diesel Engines; this research was funded by the Admiralty for a period between 1914 and 1916, during which the goal was to investigate the potential of unusual fuels for the propulsion of Destroyers.

The Committee is currently investigating autoclaves and very high-pressure steam generators as a route to the extraction of a better brew. However, there appears to be a fundamental limit imposed by pressures greater than two thousand pounds per square inch; at this point the coffee grounds adhere to one another. The result can be a nasty steam explosion, as Frazer discovered to his cost. MacIntyre, for his part, is working with Sir Ernest Rutherford. He still maintains that Radium is the answer.

And now it is my sad duty to record the effects the war has had upon our ranks.

Marshall Joyce passed away three years ago, a victim of the U-boat attack on the liner *Lusitania*. His son, Marshall Jr., chose not to follow him into our ranks once he was appraised of the nature of our pursuit.

It is with regret that I note the death of Lieutenant William Stephenson. William was a gallant gentleman, and we shall all remember him with regret. He gave his life for Club and Country; the Hun shot him as a spy in 1918, having caught him infiltrating General Ludendorff's kitchen disguised as a maid. His objective was to determine the precise quantity and quality of *ersatz* coffee available to the Kaiser's General Staff; and, if possible, to adulterate it in such a way as to damage their morale.

My father, the Marquis of Brentford, passed away last year. He will be remembered.

Now I should mention our new members. We have our first member of the medical profession, Doctor Gerald Highsmith. I am sure that Doctor Highsmith will make valuable contributions to both the Chemical and the Botanical Committees. We have also been joined by the Norwegian atomic scientist Hansenn, who argues incessantly and amiably with MacIntyre. I do not pretend to understand those gentlemen, but I am sure that *something* will come of their experiments.

A number of proposals for membership were black-balled. Notable among these was the Russian revolutionary Vladimir Ulianov, now notorious for his bolshevist ways. A rascal and trouble-maker! I have no idea what Mr Wells thought he was doing in putting him forward. At the next annual meeting I shall propose a long-overdue change to Rule Four: that the word *women* be replaced by the term *troublemakers*.

August 16th, 1939

The political situation on this, the fiftieth anniversary of our foundation, is looking as grim as it has ever been. Czechoslovakia is no more; our engineers Dorsey and Haight-Evans have been seconded to the War Ministry to plan for the worst; and everyone is certain that Herr Hitler will attack Poland in the near future. I am taking action to ensure that the Club retains access to its supplies of coffee during the coming War; meanwhile, in view of the terrible prospect of the Strategic Bombing of cities, we are considering the possibility of removing our fittings to the country.

I write this diary sitting in the comfortable, leather and oak surroundings of the Club Secretary's office, downstairs in what was formerly the shop in Greek Street. It is no longer a shop, although we retain a dusty window display and a sign saying 'closed for repairs.' The entire premises are now occupied by the club; from the historic meeting-room upstairs to the bean stocks in the cellar and the machine-room in the back. I find myself at something of a loss when I think that we might shortly have to vacate these premises; there is far more than mere nostalgia here. Having been Secretary of the Club for the past twenty years, and involved in it since 1909, I am nevertheless astonished at the devotion which it inspires among us, and the changes that time has wrought.

If it is true that there are two cultures in this nation of ours, then it is trivially clear from a perusal of our Club that the majority of those who share our interest (an unnatural and extreme craving for the Great Beverage, that exceeds the bounds of propriety) are scientifically inclined. There are no artists, and precious few philosophers in our club. I am no longer the sole lady of the venture, but we are still in a minority and even, dare I say it, considered eccentric by our male peers.

We count a number of remarkable men among our group. We have one Nobel laureate, three atomic scientists, two aeronautical engineers, and the deep-sea diver Carruthers. The Research Committees have almost subsumed the *raison d'être* of the club; they have published scientific papers and even a book (which has become the most respected text in its field). Nevertheless, the current direction of our endeavour is more practical than philosophical; great strides have been made towards extracting a perfect brew, but far less attention has been paid to understanding the nature of our craving.

Work on high pressure percolation was suspended after the explosion that caused the death of Chapman Frazer. MacIntyre's sad and long-drawn-out demise convinced us that Radium was probably *not* the answer. However, new alleys are being explored all the time, and there have been remarkable successes.

Hansen has pioneered the application of atomic Cyclotrons to the brewing of coffee. His technique is to anodize grounds and fire them at a target of ice, a hundred times as fast as a rifle bullet! Sadly, the flavour of the grounds is damaged by the electroplating process he uses, and the necessity to maintain the Cyclotron's chamber in a vacuum may ultimately put an end to this line of research. In the meantime, he has proposed an experiment that requires the procurement of a rather expensive substance from Norway, that he calls "heavy" water. We have yet to vote on this expenditure.

Dorsey and Haight-Evans have been working on what they call a "fluidised-bed low-pressure steam turbine infusor" which shows great promise. It certainly produces a fine brew, but it has to be bolted to the floor and the noise it makes is unspeakable; the device had to be switched off after the Club received complaints from the Police. They are now working with a Mr Whittle from the Ministry, in the belief that a suitably modified version of their device might be used to propel a fast fighter aeroplane.

Wright and Kotcha have been investigating the use of explosives. Their device resembles a football; lenses of exotic explosive surround a sphere of raw beans, which are distributed across the surface of a globe of ice. When the explosives are detonated correctly an incredible brew results, but the timing is difficult to perfect, and all too often the result is a mushroom of slush followed by a black, gritty rain. I believe they have written a note to Professor Szilard about it.

For my part, I confess that I am becoming a little tired of my duties as club Secretary. Times have changed, and the eccentric gentleman's club I recall from my childhood has been replaced by something altogether stranger; a loose and secretive association of scientists, searchers for a hermetic enlightenment that can be placed among the most elusive holy grails of Science. Even Jung, our psychologist, believes that there is an absolute archetype for which the other scientists are looking: that far from the heavenly brew being a product of our aesthetics, our very existence is required by some strange teleology resulting from the potential of the *ur*-coffee for which we seek. The logic of the quantum is replacing the bonhomie of the club. And the clouds of war are drawing in . . .

August 16th, 1959

The twenty-year report by the Secretary appears to have become a *de-facto* tradition of the Club. Consequently, I should like to take this opportunity to reiterate the great strides forward we have take since the last such report, on the eve of the Second World War.

Firstly, I should like to record, for the benefit of those who never had the privilege of knowing her, the great debt that we all owe to Lady Camilla Sandleford. Lady Camilla passed away four years ago, having been Secretary of the Club for thirty-five years. Under her auspices the club prospered; our holdings now include three plantations, a significant shareholding in Imperial Chemical Industries, and a range of assets sufficient to ensure our perpetual prosperity. Consequently, in 1952 the limit of thirty members was raised to one hundred, and academic sponsorship was mandated for ten research studentships in appropriate fields.

It is interesting to note that we have encountered no difficulty in selecting new members of an appropriate calibre. Indeed, the obsessive quality with which we pursue our beverage seems to have percolated out into society at large; it is, after all, no longer considered a monumental *faux pas* to display such an overt technical interest in a social drug. Nevertheless, by unanimous vote of the Executive, it has been determined that we shall remain a Secret Society and that Rule Six shall remain effective in perpetuity. It is believed that public exposure of the Dangerous Coffee Club would restrict our ability to conduct some critical experiments, and as the technologies we are exploring have military potential it would be counter-productive to expose ourselves to infiltration by Communist Spies.

Our scientists were active in a number of areas during the Second World War. Among other things, Dorsey and Haight-Evans worked with Whittle to convert their concept of a fluidised-bed turbofuser into an operational jet engine. Wright vanished for three years; it was not until a fateful day in August of 1945 that we discovered the ends to which his research into explosive lenses had been put. Sadly, Kotcha the Albanian proved to be unreliable. He returned to his homeland and was immediately spirited away to the Soviet Union, taking his work on ultracentrifugation with him. We cannot estimate the extent of his contribution to the Bolshevik bomb program at this time.

Meanwhile, work continues apace. The discovery of the Double Helix has given a tremendous boost to the Botanical Committee, who are now making extensive use of the Boddington's Mark One Computer that now occupies the cellar of our former premises in Greek Street. When not employed preparing the accounts for the Boddington's Beverage Corporation, the computer is used to assist the X-ray crystallographic analysis of the enzymes responsible for the production of the alkaloid constituents of Coffee. The new Bioassay Team hopes to develop a means of characterising the aesthetic quality of a brew objectively, using laboratory instruments alone. This would be a great leap forward.

Our American chapter has recently recruited a number of German expatriates who are currently working for the NASA organisation (formerly NACA) on rocket propulsion of space vehicles. Herr Von Braun, perhaps best known as the architect of the A4 rocket, is particularly enthusiastic about the prospects of using cryogenic hydrogen-oxygen motors as a combination roasting/grinding and percolation technology. Promising results have already been obtained using a pre-chilled launch pad, several kilos of Jamaican Blue Mountain, and a prototype J-2 motor.

Following the Russian orbiting of a dog, some mice, and some plants, we are considering an experiment to evaluate the effect of free fall on coffee bush growth. Astrobotany is still in its infancy, but we feel that this is a field of some considerable potential.

August 16th, 1989

(Teleconference links established to continental branch chapters in New York, Tokyo, Naples, Hong Kong and Brasilia: proceedings to be published internally in hardcopy format, with accompanying videotape, not more than three months after the presentation.)

Ladies and Gentlemen, the centennial report.

Our club was established a century ago, as a select meeting-place for like-minded aesthetes and aficionados of the ultimate beverage. Over the intervening decades we have prospered and blossomed into an international organisation of unparalleled success. Our current membership is stable at six hundred and fifty two full members and forty-seven funded research fellows. We have chapters in six countries and members in eighteen. Our collective treasury portfolio has a balance of three hundred and ninety one million US dollars, yielding an income of forty-six million dollars this year; it is anticipated that our presence in the recombinant genetic engineering industry and our investment in the human genome project will yield a great return on our investment within the next decade.

I think we can fairly say that our club has been one of the great success stories of the twentieth century.

Advances in genetic engineering are now laying bare the secrets of the coffee plant. We will soon be able to breed a coffee bush that gives rise to the ultimate bean.

Meanwhile, our cognitive psychologists have been attacking the problem from the opposite direction. What, they ask, makes the difference between one of us and, for example, a tea-drinker? Why are we members of this society so obsessed by the ultimate brew, when most of the public are content to drink freeze-dried, decaffeinated arabica? We hope that we will shortly determine the answer to this problem. If nothing else, the human genome project will, within twenty years, allow us to test extensive models of the human neural chassis and predict who will grow up to be a caffeine addict, and who will be a dipsomaniac.

Our engineering laboratories have already produced the ultimate percolator. Using computational fluid dynamics and smart materials technology, the high performance liquid chromatographic elution system at the core of the JK-88 percolator is capable of achieving the ultimate balance of aroma and density, aftertaste and emollience, pentosans and tannins. The next step is to reduce the cost of the

HPLC-E technology to the point where it can be manufactured for less than the cost of a Boeing 757.

And yet, I know that there is unease among us. In the past five years, there has come about a collective malaise; a directionless wandering, an inability to look beyond our noses, beyond the research itself, and to analyse the meaning of the endeavour we are enrolled in. This is a critical failing of our Club. As our charter states, we are gathered together not merely to drink coffee but to understand *why* we drink coffee.

Let me assure you that our philosophers and semioticians are hard at work trying to determine the ultimate significance of our obsession. The nameless angst that besets the prototypical member of this club cannot be combated by any means other than a dose of the favoured brew, at this moment in time, but it is hoped that an exhaustive analysis of the teleology of coffee-drinking and a synthesis with the semiological significance of imbibement may eventually reveal to us the ultimate secret of why we drink coffee. This is a matter of vast importance. It is by the repetition of this small ritual that we bind together the entire world in which we move; without it, might not our entire civilization cease to exist? Perhaps we were placed on this planet for no purpose other than to comprehend the nature of our own most sublime yearnings.

In any event, it is with great pleasure that I can now reveal to you the plan for our next twenty years; to bring the benefits of our research to bear on improving the lot of the common man and woman . . .

May 1st, 2019
Armstrong City, Mare Tranquilitatum, Luna nearside. Anne here. There are only six of us left. Six of us in the Club, in the entire solar system. And no-one at all on Earth.

I can't believe I'm dictating this. It's too dangerous; if anyone reads this file I'm spaced. Even being found with a stash is enough to get you whacked for hoarding these days. So I guess this is the last ever Secretary's report. How the hell did we ever get here, cold turkey survivors flapping our wings in the airless claustrophobia of the main Lunar outpost and peering down through telescopes at the red devastation that hit our home world?

I blame the biotechnology group. Or maybe the Ethics Committee. They should never have given the green light to making major genetic modifications to macroscopic organisms. I mean, never mind the justifications; building a hybridized coffee bush, capable of thriving in the near-vacuum and frigid environment of Mars, a motile plant capable of eating anything that moved and thriving on virtually nothing but vacuum and sunlight, then testing it out on Earth, was just plain *dumb*. I guess they were enthusiastic, but that's no excuse. The idea of terraforming Mars with coffee bushes was a good one; a prolific plant, our very life blood, and the greatest of brews imaginable! So they hybridized the red weed with the most appetizing, perfect strains of coffee ever to be cultivated—then gave it the survival imperative of a hungry triffid. Just think, an entire planet of red coffee weed, adding to the sum total of human happiness, right? Jerks.

I suppose they were blind to the consequence. Our craving is an addiction. We've perfected it, honing it knife-sharp over a stretch of years; now it's more real than *we* are. It has a life of its own. And the object of our addiction made flesh, once unleashed on the world, well . . .

They field-tested it in Antarctica. Within fifty days the two hundred seedlings they transferred to the ice-cap had burst into flower and spawned. A forest of bushes spread out across the ice, plants shuffling in restless migration towards the sunlight. Alarmed, they tried defoliants: the red weed ate everything, thrived on agent orange, spat it right back at them. Some of the plants reached the edge of the icecap, outracing the chill of winter. It was a disaster; nobody had planned for what the bushes would do when they met sea water. The bushes thrived. Bitter and inedible to anything that swam, they matted the surface of the oceans and propagated furiously. Within weeks, enclaves arrived in Tierra del Fuego and Tasmania. A quarantine was declared: but smuggled beans bore fruit in Provence, and that was that.

Two hundred days. That's all it took to wipe out the entire botanical ecosystem of Earth. Biotech had engineered a superior photosynthetic pathway; and we are left to reap the bitter harvest.

By way of a down-side, the ten million survivors are going cold turkey. Only *this* is one trip that's for life and beyond. Animals starve; food crop harvests wither and die. Wolf-breeding is a last-ditch resort, an attempt to save something that can metabolise the red weed. Meanwhile, up here we're in quarantine. No shipments from earth; possession of live coffee beans a capital offense. (You never know what might hatch in the hydroponic vats . . .) When I die, bury me with my percolator. It's going to be a long, dry year ahead, and it may be as much as five years before we can ride a shuttle down-side and pick up some more supplies.

Why do I feel so sleepy?

A Colder War

H. P. Lovecraft's classic novella, "At the Mountains of Madness", launched a fleet of clichéd imitators over the years since its first publication. In it, the master of the macabre told the story of Dr Pabodie's failed Antarctic expedition of 1930—a tale of terror on the high Antarctic plateau beyond a range of mountains higher than Everest, a range that concealed the ruins of an ancient civilization.

Most of the Pabodie expedition died before they could return home, and the survivors refused to discuss what had happened. But what if there was a follow-up expedition?

Fifty years later . . .

Analyst

Roger Jourgensen tilts back in his chair, reading.

He's a fair-haired man, in his mid-thirties: hair razor-cropped, skin pallid from too much time spent under artificial lights. Spectacles, short-sleeved white shirt and tie, photographic ID badge on a chain round his neck. He works in an air-conditioned office with no windows.

The file he is reading frightens him.

Once, when Roger was a young boy, his father took him to an open day at Nellis AFB, out in the California desert. Sunlight glared brilliantly from the polished silverplate flanks of the big bombers, sitting in their concrete-lined dispersal bays behind barriers and blinking radiation monitors. The brightly colored streamers flying from their pitot tubes lent them a strange, almost festive appearance. But they were sleeping nightmares: once awakened, nobody—except the flight crew—could come within a mile of the nuclear-powered bombers and live.

Looking at the gleaming, bulging pods slung under their wingtip pylons, Roger had a premature inkling of the fires that waited within, a frigid terror that echoed the siren wail of the air raid warnings. He'd sucked nervously on his ice cream and gripped his father's hand tightly while the band ripped through a cheerful Sousa march, and only forgot his fear when a flock of Thunderchiefs sliced by overhead and rattled the car windows for miles around.

He has the same feeling now, as an adult reading this intelligence assessment, that he had as a child, watching the nuclear powered bombers sleeping in their concrete beds.

There's a blurry photograph of a concrete box inside the file, snapped from above by a high-flying U-2 during the autumn of '61. Three coffin-shaped lakes, bulking dark and gloomy beneath the arctic sun; a canal heading west, deep in the Soviet heartland, surrounded by warning trefoils and armed guards. Deep waters saturated with calcium salts, concrete coffer-dams lined with gold and lead. A sleeping giant pointed at NATO, more terrifying than any nuclear weapon.

Project Koschei.

Red Square Redux

Warning

The following briefing film is classified SECRET GOLD JULY BOOJUM. If you do not have SECRET GOLD JULY BOOJUM clearance, leave the auditorium *now* and report to your unit security officer for debriefing. Failing to observe this notice is an imprisonable offense.

You have sixty seconds to comply.

Video clip

Red Square in springtime. The sky overhead is clear and blue; there's a little whispy cirrus at high altitude. It forms a brilliant backdrop for flight after flight of five four-engined bombers that thunder across the horizon and drop behind the Kremlin's high walls.

Voice-over

Red Square, the May Day parade, 1962. This is the first time that the Soviet Union has publicly displayed weapons classified GOLD JULY BOOJUM. Here they are:

Video clip

Later in the same day. A seemingly endless stream of armour and soldiers marches across the square, turning the air grey with deisel fumes. The trucks roll in line eight abreast, with soldiers sitting erect in the back. Behind them rumble a battalion of T-56's, their commanders standing at attention in their cupolas, saluting the stand. Jets race low and loud overhead, formations of MiG-17 fighters.

Behind the tanks sprawl a formation of four low-loaders: huge tractors towing low-slung trailers, their load beds strapped down under olive-drab tarpaulins. Whatever is under them is uneven, a bit like a loaf of bread the size of a small house. The trucks have an escort of jeep-like vehicles on each side, armed soldiers sitting at attention in their backs.

There are big five-pointed stars painted in silver on each tarpaulin, like outlines of stars. Each star is surrounded by a stylized silver circle; a unit insignia, perhaps, but not in the standard format for Red Army units. There's lettering around the circles, in a strangely stylised script.

Voice-over

These are live servitors under transient control. The vehicles towing them bear the insignia of the second Guards Engineering Brigade, a penal construction unit based in Bokhara and used for structural engineering assignments relating to nuclear installations in the Ukraine and Azerbaijan. This is the first time that any Dresden Agreement party openly demonstrated ownership of this technology: in this instance, the conclusion we are intended to draw is that the sixty-seventh Guard Engineering Brigade operates four units. Given existing figures for the Soviet ORBAT we can then extrapolate a total task strength of two hundred and eighty eight servitors, if this unit is unexceptional.

Video clip

Five huge Tu-95 Bear bombers thunder across the Moscow skies.

Voice-over

This conclusion is questionable. For example, in 1964 a total of two hundred and forty Bear bomber passes were made over the reviewing stand in front of the Lenin mausoleum. However, at that time technical reconnaisance assets verified that the Soviet air force has hard stand parking for only one hundred and sixty of these aircraft, and estimates of airframe production based on photographs of the extent of the Tupolev bureau's works indicate that total production to that date was between sixty and one hundred and eighty bombers.

Further analysis of photographic evidence from the 1964 parade suggests that a single group of twenty aircraft in four formations of five made repeated passes through the same airspace, the main arc of their circuit lying outside visual observation range of Moscow. This gave rise to the erroneous capacity report of 1964 in which the first strike delivery capability of the Soviet Union was over-estimated by as much as three hundred percent.

We must therefore take anything that they show us in Red Square with a pinch of salt when preparing force estimates. Quite possibly these four servitors are all they've got. Then again, the actual battalion strength may be considerably higher.

Still photographic sequence

From very high altitude—possibly in orbit—an eagle's eye view of a remote village in mountainous country. Small huts huddle together beneath a craggy outcrop; goats graze nearby.

In the second photograph, something has rolled through the village leaving a trail of devastation. The path is quite unlike the trail of damage left by an artillery bombardment: something roughly four metres wide has shaved the rocky plateau smooth, wearing it down as if with a terrible heat. A corner of a shack leans drunkenly, the other half sliced away cleanly. White bones gleam faintly in the track; no vultures descend to stab at the remains.

Voice-over

These images were taken very recently, on successive orbital passes of a KH-11 satellite. They were timed precisely eighty-nine minutes apart. This village was the home of a noted Mujahedin leader. Note the similar footprint to the payloads on the load beds of the trucks seen at the 1962 parade.

These indicators were present, denoting the presence of servitor

units in use by Soviet forces in Afghanistan: the four metre wide
gauge of the assimilation track. The total molecular breakdown of
organic matter in the track. The speed of destruction—the event took
less than five thousand seconds to completion, no survivors were
visible, and the causative agent had already been uplifted by the time
of the second orbital pass. This, despite the residents of the community being armed with DShK heavy machine guns, rocket propelled
grenade launchers, and AK-47's. Lastly: there is no sign of the causative agent even deviating from its course, but the entire area is
depopulated. Except for excarnated residue there is no sign of human
habitation.

In the presence of such unique indicators, we have no alternative
but to conclude that the Soviet Union has violated the Dresden Agreement by deploying GOLD JULY BOOJUM in a combat mode in the
Khyber Pass. There are no grounds to believe that a NATO armoured
division would have fared any better than these mujahedin without
nuclear support . . .

Puzzle Palace

Roger isn't a soldier. He's not much of a patriot, either: he signed up
with the CIA after college, in the aftermath of the Church
Commission hearings in the early seventies. The Company was out of
the assassination business, just a bureaucratic engine rolling out
National Security assessments: that's fine by Roger. Only now, five
years later, he's no longer able to roll along, casually disengaged, like a
car in neutral bowling down a shallow incline towards his retirement,
pension and a gold watch. He puts the file down on his desk and, with
a shaking hand, pulls an illicit cigarette from the pack he keeps in his
drawer. He lights it and leans back for a moment to draw breath, force
relaxation, staring at smoke rolling in the air beneath the merciless
light until his hand stops shaking.

Most people think spies are afraid of guns, or KGB guards, or
barbed wire, but in point of fact the most dangerous thing they face is

paper. Papers carry secrets. Papers carry death warrants. Papers like this one, this folio with its blurry eighteen year old faked missile photographs and estimates of time/survivor curves and pervasive psychosis ratios, can give you nightmares, dragging you awake screaming in the middle of the night. It's one of a series of highly classified pieces of paper that he is summarizing for the eyes of the National Security Council and the President Elect—if his head of department and the DDCIA approve it—and here he is, having to calm his nerves with a cigarette before he turns the next page.

After a few minutes, Roger's hand is still. He leaves his cigarette in the eagle-headed ash tray and picks up the intelligence report again. It's a summary, itself the distillation of thousands of pages and hundreds of photographs. It's barely twenty pages long: as of 1963, its date of preparation, the CIA knew very little about Project Koschei. Just the bare skeleton, and rumours from a highly-placed spy. And their own equivalent project, of course. Lacking the Soviet lead in that particular field, the USAF fielded the silver-plated white elephants of the NB-39 project: twelve atomic-powered bombers armed with XK-PLUTO, ready to tackle Project Koschei should the Soviets show signs of unsealing the bunker. Three hundred megatons of H-bombs pointed at a single target, and nobody was certain it would be enough to do the job.

And then there was the hard-to-conceal fiasco in Antarctica. Egg on face: a subterranean nuclear test program in international territory! If nothing else, it had been enough to stop JFK running for a second term. The test program was a bad excuse: but it was far better than confessing what had really happened to the 501st Airborn Division on the cold plateau beyond Mount Erebus. The plateau that the public didn't know about, that didn't show up on the maps issued by the geological survey departments of those governments party to the Dresden Agreement of 1931—an arrangement that even Hitler had stuck to. The plateau that had swallowed more U-2 spy planes than the Soviet Union, more surface expeditions than darkest Africa.

Shit. How the hell am I going to put this together for him?

Roger's spent the past five hours staring at this twenty page report, trying to think of a way of summarizing their drily quantifiable terror in words that will give the reader power over them, the power to think the unthinkable: but it's proving difficult. The new man in the White House is straight-talking, demands straight answers. He's pious enough not to believe in the supernatural, confident enough that just listening to one of his speeches is an uplifting experience if you can close your eyes and believe in morning in America. There is probably no way of explaining Project Koschei, or XK-PLUTO, or MK-NIGHT-MARE, or the gates, without watering them down into just another weapons system—which they are not. Weapons may have deadly or hideous effects, but they acquire moral character from the actions of those who use them. Whereas these projects are indelibly stained by a patina of ancient evil . . .

He hopes that if the balloon ever does go up, if the sirens wail, he and Andrea and Jason will be left behind to face the nuclear fire. It'll be a merciful death compared with what he suspect lurks out there, in the unexplored vastness beyond the gates. The vastness that made Nixon cancel the manned space program, leaving just the standing joke of a white-elephant shuttle, when he realised just how hideously dangerous the space race might become. The darkness that broke Jimmy Carter's faith and turned Lyndon B. Johnson into an alcoholic.

He stands up, nervously shifts from one foot to the other. Looks round at the walls of his cubicle. For a moment the cigarette smouldering on the edge of his ash tray catches his attention: wisps of blue-grey smoke coil like lazy dragons in the air above it, writhing in a strange cuneiform text. He blinks and they're gone, and the skin in the small of his back prickles as if someone has pissed on his grave.

"Shit." Finally, a spoken word in the silence. His hand is shaking as he stubs the cigarette out. *Mustn't let this get to me.* He glances at the wall. It's nineteen hundred hours; too late, too late. He should go home, Andy will be worrying herself sick.

In the end it's all too much. He slides the thin folder into the safe behind his chair, turns the locking handle and spins the dial, then signs himself out of the reading room and goes through the usual exit search.

During the thirty mile drive home, he spits out of the window, trying to rid his mouth of the taste of Auschwitz ashes.

Late Night in the White House

The colonel is febrile, jittering about the room with gung-ho enthusiasm. "That was a mighty fine report you pulled together, Jourgensen!" He paces over to the niche between the office filing cabinet and the wall, turns on the spot, paces back to the far side of his desk. "You understand the fundamentals. I like that. A few more guys like you running the company and we wouldn't have this fuckup in Tehran." He grins, contagiously. The colonel is a firestorm of enthusiasm, burning out of control like a forties comic-book hero. He has Roger on the edge of his chair, almost sitting at attention. Roger has to bite his tongue to remind himself not to call the colonel 'sir'—he's a civilian, not in the chain of command. "That's why I've asked Deputy Director McMurdo to reassign you to this office, to work on my team as company liaison. And I'm pleased to say that he's agreed."

Roger can't stop himself: "To work here, sir?" *Here* is in the basement of the Executive Office Building, an extension hanging off the White House. Whoever the colonel is he's got *pull*, in positively magical quantities. "What will I be doing, sir? You said, your team—"

"Relax a bit. Drink your coffee." The colonel paces back behind his desk, sits down. Roger sips cautiously at the brown sludge in the mug with the Marine Corps crest. "The president told me to organize a team," says the colonel, so casually that Roger nearly chokes on his coffee, "to handle contingencies. October surprises. Those asshole commies down in Nicaragua. 'We're eyeball to eyeball with an Evil Empire, Ozzie, and we can't afford to blink'—those were his exact words. The Evil Empire uses dirty tricks. But nowadays we're better than they are: buncha hicks, like some third-world dictatorship—Upper Volta with shoggoths. My job is to pin them down and cut them up. Don't give them a chance to whack the shoe on the UN table, demand concessions. If they want to bluff I'll call 'em on it. If they want to go toe-to-toe I'll dance with 'em." He's up and pacing again. "The company used to do that, and do it okay, back in the fifties and sixties. But too many bleeding hearts—it makes me sick. If you guys went back to wet ops today you'd have journalists following you every time you went to the john in case it was newsworthy.

"Well, we aren't going to do it that way this time. It's a small team and the buck stops here." The colonel pauses, then glances at the ceiling. "Well, maybe up *there*. But you get the picture. I need someone who knows the company, an insider who has clearance up the wazoo who can go in and get the dope before it goes through a fucking committee of ass-watching bureaucrats. I'm also getting someone from the Puzzle Palace, and some words to give me pull with Big Black." He glances at Roger sharply, and Roger nods: he's cleared for National Security Agency—Puzzle Palace—intelligence, and knows about Big Black, the National Reconnaisance Office, which is so secret that even its existence is still classified.

Roger is impressed by this colonel, despite his better judgement. Within the byzantine world of the US intelligence services, he is talking about building his very own pocket battleship and sailing it under the jolly roger with letters of marque and reprise signed by the president. But Roger still has some questions to ask, to scope out the limits of what Colonel North is capable of. "What about FEVER DREAM, sir?"

The colonel puts his coffee-cup down. "I own it," he says, bluntly. "And NIGHTMARE. And PLUTO. *Any means necessary* he said, and I have an executive order with the ink still damp to prove it. Those projects aren't part of the national command structure any more. Officially they've been stood down from active status and are being considered for inclusion in the next round of arms reduction talks. They're not part of the deterrent ORBAT any more; we're standardizing on just nuclear weapons. Unofficially, they're part of my group, and I will use them as necessary to contain and reduce the Evil Empire's warmaking abilities."

Roger's skin crawls with an echo of that childhood terror. "And the Dresden Agreement . . . ?"

"Don't worry. Nothing short of *them* breaking it would lead me to do so." The colonel grins, toothily. "Which is where *you* come in … "

The moonlit shores of Lake Vostok

The metal pier is dry and cold, the temperature hovering close to zero degrees Fahrenheit. It's oppressively dark in the cavern under the ice, and Roger shivers inside his multiple layers of insulation, shifts from foot to foot to keep warm. He has to swallow to keep his ears clear and he feels slightly dizzy from the pressure in the artificial bubble of air, pumped under the icy ceiling to allow humans to exist, under the Ross Ice Shelf; they'll all spend more than a day sitting in depressurization chambers on the way back up to the surface.

There is no sound from the waters lapping just below the edge of the pier. The floodlights vanish into the surface and keep going—the water in the sub-surface antarctic lake is incredibly clear—but are swallowed up rapidly, giving an impression of infinite, inky depths.

Roger is here as the colonel's representative, to observe the arrival of the probe, receive the consignment they're carrying, and report back that everything is running smoothly. The others try to ignore him, jittery at the presence of the man from DC. There're a gaggle of engineers and artificers, flown out via McMurdo base to handle the midget sub's operations. A nervous lieutenant supervises a squad of marines with complicated-looking weapons, half gun and half video camera, stationed at the corners of the raft. And there's the usual platform crew, deep-sea rig maintenance types—but subdued and nervous looking. They're afloat in a bubble of pressurized air wedged against the underside of the Antarctic ice sheet: below them stretch the still, supercooled waters of Lake Vostok.

They're waiting for a rendezvous.

"Five hundred yards," reports one of the techs. "Rising on ten." His companion nods. They're waiting for the men in the midget sub drilling quietly through three miles of frigid water, intruders in a long-drowned tomb. "Have 'em back on board in no time." The sub has been away for nearly a day; it set out with enough battery juice for the journey, and enough air to keep the crew breathing for a long time if there's a system failure, but they've learned the hard way that fail-safe systems aren't. Not out here, at the edge of the human world.

Roger shuffles some more. "I was afraid the battery load on that cell you replaced would trip an undervoltage isolator and we'd be here 'til Hell freezes over," the sub driver jokes to his neighbour.

Looking round, Roger sees one of the marines cross himself. "Have you heard anything from Gorman or Suslowicz?" he asks quietly.

The lieutenant checks his clipboard. "Not since departure, sir," he says. "We don't have comms with the sub while it's submerged: too small for ELF, and we don't want to alert anybody who might be, uh, listening."

"Indeed." The yellow hunchback shape of the midget submarine appears at the edge of the radiance shed by the floodlights. Surface waters undulate, oily, as the sub rises.

"Crew transfer vehicle sighted," the driver mutters into his mike. He's suddenly very busy adjusting trim settings, blowing bottled air into ballast tanks, discussing ullage levels and blade count with his number two. The crane crew are busy too, running their long boom out over the lake.

The sub's hatch is visible now, bobbing along the top of the water: the lieutenant is suddenly active. "Jones! Civatti! Stake it out, left and centre!" The crane is already swinging the huge lifting hook over the sub, waiting to bring it aboard. "I want eyeballs on the portholes before you crack this thing!" It's the tenth run—seventh manned—through the eye of the needle on the lake bed, the drowned structure so like an ancient temple, and Roger has a bad feeling about it. *We can't get away with this forever*, he reasons. *Sooner or later . . .*

The sub comes out of the water like a gigantic yellow bath toy, a cyborg whale designed by a god with a sense of humour. It takes tense minutes to winch it in and manoeuvre it safely onto the platform. Marines take up position, shining torches in through two of the portholes that bulge myopically from the smooth curve of the sub's nose. Up on top someone is talking into a handset plugged into the stubby conning tower; the hatch locking wheel begins to turn.

"Gorman, sir," It's the lieutenant. In the light of the sodium floods everything looks sallow and washed-out; the soldier's face is the colour of damp cardboard, slack with relief.

Roger waits while the submariner—Gorman—clambers unsteadily down from the top deck. He's a tall, emaciated-looking man, wearing a red thermal suit three sizes too big for him: salt-and-pepper stubble textures his jaw with sandpaper. Right now, he looks like a cholera victim; sallow skin, smell of acrid ketones as his body eats its own protein reserves, a more revolting miasma hovering over him. There's a slim aluminium briefcase chained to his left wrist, a bracelet of bruises darkening the skin above it. Roger steps forward.

"Sir?" Gorman straightens up for a moment: almost a shadow of military attention. He's unable to sustain it. "We made the pickup. Here's the QA sample; the rest is down below. You have the unlocking code?" he asks wearily.

Jourgensen nods. "One. Five. Eight. One. Two. Two. Nine."

Gorman slowly dials it into a combination lock on the briefcase, lets it fall open and unthreads the chain from his wrist. Floodlights glisten on polythene bags stuffed with white powder, five kilos of high-grade heroin from the hills of Afghanistan; there's another quarter of a ton packed in boxes in the crew compartment. The lieutenant inspects it, closes the case and passes it to Jourgensen. "Delivery successful, sir." From the ruins on the high plateau of the Taklamakan desert to American territory in Antarctica, by way of a detour through gates linking alien worlds: gates that nobody knows how to create or destroy except the Predecessors—and they aren't talking.

"What's it like through there?" Roger demands, shoulders tense. "What did you *see*?"

Up on top, Suslowicz is sitting in the sub's hatch, half slumping against the crane's attachment post. There's obviously something very wrong with him. Gorman shakes his head and looks away: the wan light makes the razor-sharp creases on his face stand out, like the crackled and shattered surface of a Jovian moon. Crow's feet. Wrinkles. Signs of age. Hair the colour of moonlight. "It took so long," he says, almost complaining. Sinks to his knees. "All that *time* we've been gone . . . " He leans against the side of the sub, a pale shadow, aged beyond his years. "The sun was so *bright*. And our radiation detectors. Must have been a solar flare or something." He doubles over and retches at the edge of the platform.

Roger looks at him for a long, thoughtful minute: Gorman is twenty-five and a fixer for Big Black, early history in the Green Berets. He was in rude good health two days ago, when he set off through the gate to make the pick-up. Roger glances at the lieutenant. "I'd better go and tell the colonel," he says. A pause. "Get these two back to Recovery and see they're looked after. I don't expect we'll be sending any more crews through Victor-Tango for a while."

He turns and walks towards the lift shaft, hands clasped behind his back to keep them from shaking. Behind him, alien moonlight glimmers across the floor of Lake Vostok, three miles and untold light years from home.

General LeMay would be Proud

Warning

The following briefing film is classified SECRET INDIGO MARCH SNIPE. If you do not have SECRET INDIGO MARCH SNIPE clearance, leave the auditorium *now* and report to your unit security officer for debriefing. Failing to observe this notice is an imprisonable offense.

You have sixty seconds to comply.

Video clip

Shot of huge bomber, rounded gun turrets sprouting like mushrooms from the decaying log of its fuselage, weirdly bulbous engine pods slung too far out towards each wingtip, four turbine tubes clumped around each atomic kernel.

Voice-over

"The Convair B-39 Peacemaker is the most formidable weapon in our Strategic Air Command's arsenal for peace. Powered by eight nuclear-heated Pratt and Whitney NP-4051 turbojets, it circles endlessly above the Arctic ice cap, waiting for the call. This is Item One, the flight training and test bird: twelve other birds await criticality on the ground, for once launched a B-39 can only be landed at two airfields in Alaska that are equipped to handle them. This one's been airborn for nine months so far, and shows no signs of age."

Cut to:

A shark the size of a Boeing 727 falls away from the open bomb bay of the monster. Stubby delta wings slice through the air, propelled by a rocket-bright glare.

Voice-over

"A modified Navajo missile—test article for an XK-PLUTO payload—dives away from a carrier plane. Unlike the real thing, this one carries no hydrogen bombs, no direct-cycle fission ramjet to bring retalliatory destruction to the enemy. Travelling at Mach 3 the XK-PLUTO will overfly enemy territory, dropping megaton-range bombs until, its payload exhausted, it seeks out and circles a final target. Once over the target it will eject its reactor core and rain molten plutonium on the heads of the enemy. XK-PLUTO is a total weapon: every aspect of its design, from the shockwave it creates as it hurtles along at treetop height to the structure of its atomic reactor, is designed to inflict damage."

Cut to:

Belsen postcards, Auschwitz movies: a holiday in hell.

Voice-over

"*This* is why we need such a weapon. *This* is what it deters. The abominations first raised by the Third Reich's Organisation Todt, now removed to the Ukraine and deployed in the service of New Soviet Man as our enemy calls himself."

Cut to:

A sinister grey concrete slab, the upper surface of a Mayan step pyramid built with East German cement. Barbed wire, guns. A drained canal slashes north from the base of the pyramid towards the Baltic coastline, relic of the installation process: this is where it came from. The slave barracks squat beside the pyramid like a horrible memorial to its black-uniformed builders.

Cut to:

The new resting place: a big concrete monolith surrounded by three concrete lined lakes and a canal. It sits in the midst of a Ukraine landscape, flat as a pancake, stretching out forever in all directions.

Voice-over

"This is Project Koschei. The kremlin's key to the gates of hell..."

Technology taster

"We know they first came here during the precambrian age."

Professor Gould is busy with his viewgraphs, eyes down, trying not to pay too much attention to his audience. "We have samples of macrofauna, discovered by palaeontologist Charles D. Walcott on his pioneering expeditions into the Canadian Rockies, near the eastern border of British Columbia—" a hand-drawing of something indescribably weird fetches up on the screen "—like this *opabina*, which died there six hundred and forty million years ago. Fossils of soft-bodied animals that old are rare; the Burgess shale deposits are the best record of the precambrian fauna anyone has found to date."

A skinny woman with big hair and bigger shoulder-pads sniffs loudly; she has no truck with these antedilluvian dates. Roger winces sympathy for the academic. He'd rather she wasn't here, but somehow she got wind of the famous palaeontologist's visit—and she's the colonel's administrative assistant. Telling her to leave would be a career-limiting move.

"The important item to note—" photograph of a mangled piece of rock, visual echoes of the *opabina*—"is the tooth marks. We find them also—their exact cognates—on the ring segments of the Z-series specimens returned by the Pabodie Antarctic expedition of 1926. The world of the precambrian was laid out differently from our own; most of the land masses that today are separate continents were joined into one huge structure. Indeed, these samples were originally separated by only two thousand miles or thereabouts. Suggesting that they brought their own parasites with them."

"What do tooth-marks tell us about them, that we need to know?" asks the colonel.

The doctor looks up. His eyes gleam: "That something liked to eat them when they were fresh." There's a brief rattle of laughter. "Something with jaws that open and close like the iris in your camera. Something we thought was extinct."

Another viewgraph, this time with a blurry underwater photograph on it. The thing looks a bit like a weird fish—a turbocharged, armoured hagfish with side-skirts and spoilers, or maybe a squid with not enough tentacles. The upper head is a flattened disk, fronted by two bizarre fern-like tentacles drooping over the weird sucker-mouth on its underside. "This snapshot was taken in Lake Vostok last year. It should be dead: there's nothing there for it to eat. This, ladies and gentlemen, is *Anomalocaris*, our toothy chewer." He pauses for a moment. "I'm very grateful to you for showing it to me," he adds, "even though it's going to make a lot of my colleagues very angry."

Is that a shy grin? The professor moves on rapidly, not giving

Roger a chance to fathom his real reaction. "Now *this* is interesting in the extreme," Gould comments. Whatever it is, it looks like a cauliflower head, or maybe a brain: fractally branching stalks continuously diminishing in length and diameter, until they turn into an irridescent fuzzy manifold wrapped around a central stem. The base of the stem is rooted to a barrel-shaped structure that stands on four stubby tentacles.

"We had somehow managed to cram *Anomalocaris* into our taxonomy, but this is something that has no precedent. It bears a striking resemblance to an enlarged body segment of *Hallucigena*—" here he shows another viewgraph, something like a stiletto-heeled centipede wearing a war-bonnet of tentacles—"but a year ago we worked out that we had poor *hallucigena* upside down and it was actually just a spiny worm. And the high levels of irridium and diamond in the head here . . . this isn't a living creature, at least not within the animal kingdom I've been studying for the past thirty years. There's no cellular structure at all. I asked one of my colleagues for help and they were completely unable to isolate any DNA or RNA from it at all. It's more like a machine that displays biological levels of complexity."

"Can you put a date to it?" asks the colonel.

"Yup." The professor grins. "It predates the wave of atmospheric atomic testing that began in 1945; that's about all. We think it's from some time in the first half of this century, last half of last century. It's been dead for years, but there are older people still walking this earth. In contrast—" he flips to the picture of *Anomalocaris* "—this specimen we found in rocks that are roughly six hundred and ten million years old." He whips up another shot: similar structure, much clearer. "Note how similar it is to the dead but not decomposed one. They're obviously still alive somewhere."

He looks at the colonel, suddenly bashful and tongue-tied: "Can I talk about the, uh, thing we were, like, earlier . . . ?"

"Sure. Go ahead. Everyone here is cleared for it." The colonel's casual wave takes in the big-haired secretary, and Roger, and the two guys from Big Black who are taking notes, and the very serious woman from the Secret Service, and even the balding, worried-looking Admiral with the double chin and coke-bottle glasses.

"Oh. Alright." Bashfulness falls away. "Well, we've done some preliminary dissections on the *Anomalocaris* tissues you supplied us with. And we've sent some samples for laboratory analysis—nothing anyone could deduce much from," he adds hastily. He straightens up. "What we discovered is quite simple: these samples didn't originate in Earth's ecosystem. Cladistic analysis of their intracellular characteristics and what we've been able to work out of their biochemistry indicates, not a point of divergence from our own ancestry, but the absence of common ancestry. A *cabbage* is more human, has more in common with us, than that creature. You can't tell by looking at the fossils, six hundred million years after it died, but live tissue samples are something else.

"Item: it's a multicellular organism, but each cell appears to have multiple structures like nuclei—a thing called a syncitium. No DNA, it uses RNA with a couple of base pairs that aren't used by terrestrial biology. We haven't been able to figure out what most of its organelles do, what their terrestrial cognates would be, and it builds proteins using a couple of amino acids that we don't. That *nothing* does. Either it's descended from an ancestry that diverged from ours before the archaeobacteria, or—more probably—it is no relative at all." He isn't smiling any more. "The gateways, colonel?"

"Yeah, that's about the size of it. The critter you've got there was retrieved by one of our, uh, missions. On the other side of a gate."

Gould nods. "I don't suppose you could get me some more?" he asks hopefully.

"All missions are suspended pending an investigation into an accident we had earlier this year," the colonel says, with a significant glance at Roger. Suslowicz died two weeks ago; Gorman is still disastrously sick, connective tissue rotting in his body, massive radiation exposure the probable cause. Normal service will not be resumed; the pipeline will remain empty until someone can figure out a way to make the deliveries without losing the crew. Roger inclines his head minutely.

"Oh well." The professor shrugs. "Let me know if you do. By the way, do you have anything approximating a fix on the other end of the gate?"

"No," says the colonel, and this time Roger knows he's lying. Mission Four, before the colonel diverted their payload capacity to another purpose, planted a compact radio telescope in an empty courtyard in the city on the far side of the gate. XK-Masada, where the air's too thin to breathe without oxygen; where the sky is indigo, and the buildings cast razor-sharp shadows across a rocky plain baked to the consistency of pottery under a blood-red sun. Subsequent analysis of pulsar signals recorded by the station confirmed that it was nearly six hundred light years closer to the galactic core, inward along the same spiral arm. There are glyphs on the alien buildings that resemble symbols seen in grainy black-and-white Minox photos of the doors of the bunker in the Ukraine. Symbols behind which the subject of Project Koschei lies undead and sleeping: something evil, scraped from a nest in the drowned wreckage of a city on the Baltic floor. "Why do you want to know where they came from?"

"Well. We know so little about the context in which life evolves." For a moment the professor looks wistful. "We have—had—only one datum point: Earth, this world. Now we have a second, a fragment of a second. If we get a third, we can begin to ask deep questions like, not, 'is there life out there?'—because we know the answer to that one, now—but questions like 'what *sort* of life is out there?' and 'is there a place for us?'"

Roger shudders: *idiot*, he thinks. *If only you knew you wouldn't be so happy*—He restrains the urge to speak up. Doing so would be another career-limiting move. More to the point, it might be a life-expectancy-limiting move for the professor, who certainly didn't deserve any such drastic punishment for his cooperation. Besides, Harvard professors visiting the Executive Office Building in DC are harder to disappear than comm-symp teachers in some fly-blown jungle village in Nicaragua. Somebody might notice. The colonel wouldn't be so happy.

Roger realises that Professor Gould is staring at him. "Do you have a question for me?" asks the distinguished palaeontologist.

"Uh—in a moment." Roger shakes himself. Remembering time-survivor curves, the captured Nazi medical atrocity records mapping the ability of a human brain to survive in close proximity to the Baltic Singularity. Mengele's insanity. The SS's final attempt to liquidate the survivors, the witnesses. Koschei, primed and pointed at the American heartland like a darkly evil gun. The "world-eating mind" adrift in brilliant madness, estivating in the absence of its prey: dreaming of the minds of sapient beings, be they barrel-bodied wing-flying tentacular *things*, or their human inheritors. "Do you think they could have been intelligent, professor? Conscious, like us?"

"I'd say so." Gould's eyes glitter. "This one—" he points to a viewgraph—"isn't alive as we know it. And *this* one—" he's found a Predecessor, god help him, barrel-bodied and bat-winged—"had what looks like a lot of very complex ganglia, not a brain as we know it, but at least as massive as our own. And some specialised grasping adaptations that might be interpreted as facilitating tool use. Put the two together and you have a high level technological civilization. Gateways between planets orbiting different stars. Alien flora, fauna, or whatever. I'd say an interstellar civilization isn't out of the picture. One that has been extinct for deep geological time—ten times as long as the dinosaurs—but that has left relics that work." His voice is trembling with emotion. "We humans, we've barely scratched the surface! The longest lasting of our relics? All our buildings will be dust in twenty thousand years, even the pyramids. Neil Armstrong's footprints in the Sea of Tranquility will crumble under micrometeoroid bombardment in a mere half million years or so. The emptied oil fields will refill over ten million years, methane percollating up through the mantle: continental drift will erase everything. But *these* people . . ! They built to last. There's so much to learn from them. I wonder if we're worthy pretenders to their technological crown?"

"I'm sure we are, professor," the colonel's secretary says brassily. "Isn't that right, Ollie?"

The colonel nods, grinning. "You betcha, Fawn. You betcha!"

The Great Satan

Roger sits in the bar in the King David hotel, drinking from a tall glass of second-rate lemonade and sweating in spite of the air conditioning. He's dizzy and disoriented from jet-lag, the gut-cramps have only let him come down from his room in the past hour, and he has another two hours to go before he can try to place a call to Andrea. They had another blazing row before he flew out here; she doesn't understand why he keeps having to visit odd corners of the globe. She only knows that his son is growing up thinking a father is a voice that phones at odd times of day.

Roger is mildly depressed, despite the buzz of doing business at this level. He spends a lot of time worrying about what will happen if they're found out—what Andrea will do, or Jason for that matter, Jason whose father is a phone call away all the time—if Roger is led away in handcuffs beneath the glare of flash bulbs. If the colonel sings, if the shy bald admiral is browbeaten into spilling the beans to congress, who will look after them then?

Roger has no illusions about what kills black operations: there are too many people in the loop, too many elaborate front corporations and numbered bank accounts and shady Middle Eastern arms dealers. Sooner or later someone will find a reason to talk, and Roger is in too deep. He isn't just the company liaison officer any more: he's become the colonel's bag-man, his shadow, the guy with the diplomatic passport and the bulging briefcase full of heroin and end-user certificates.

At least the ship will sink from the top down, he thinks. There are people *very* high up who want the colonel to succeed. When the shit hits the fan and is sprayed across the front page of the Washington Post, it will likely take down cabinet members and secretaries of state: the President himself will have to take the witness stand and deny everything. The republic will question itself.

A hand descends on his shoulder, sharply cutting off his reverie. "Howdy, Roger! Whatcha worrying about now?"

Jourgensen looks up wearily. "Stuff," he says gloomily. "Have a seat." The redneck from the embassy—Mike Hamilton, some kind of junior attache for embassy protocol by cover—pulls out a chair and crashes down on it like a friendly car wreck. He's not really a redneck, Roger knows—rednecks don't come with doctorates in foreign relations from Yale—but he likes people to think he's a bumpkin when he wants to get something from them.

"He's early," says Hamilton, looking past Roger's ear, voice suddenly all business. "Play the agenda, I'm your dim but friendly good cop. Got the background? Deniables ready?"

Roger nods, then glances round and sees Mehmet (family name unknown) approaching from the other side of the room. Mehmet is impeccably manicured and tailored, wearing a suit from Jermyn Street that costs more than Roger earns in a month. He has a neatly trimmed beard and moustache and talks with a pronounced English accent. Mehmet is a Turkish name, not a Persian one: pseudonym, of course. To look at him you would think he was a westernized Turkish businessman—certainly not an Iranian revolutionary with heavy links to Hezbollah and, (whisper this), Old Man Ruholla himself, the hermit of Qom. Never, ever, in a thousand years, the unofficial Iranian ambassador to the Little Satan in Tel Aviv.

Mehmet strides over. A brief exchange of pleasantries masks the essential formality of their meeting: he's early, a deliberate move to put them off-balance. He's outnumbered, too, and that's also a move to put them on the defensive, because the first rule of diplomacy is never to put yourself in a negotiating situation where the other side can assert any kind of moral authority, and sheer weight of numbers is a powerful psychological tool.

"Roger, my dear fellow." He smiles at Jourgensen. "And the charming doctor Hamilton, I see." The smile broadens. "I take it the good colonel is desirous of news of his friends?"

Jourgensen nods. "That is indeed the case."

Mehmet stops smiling. For a moment he looks ten years older. "I visited them," he says shortly. "No, I was *taken* to see them. It is indeed grave, my friends. They are in the hands of very dangerous men, men who have nothing to lose and are filled with hatred."

Roger speaks: "There is a debt between us—"

Mehmet holds up a hand. "Peace, my friend. We will come to that. These are men of violence, men who have seen their homes destroyed and families subjected to indignities, and their hearts are full of anger. It will take a large display of repentance, a high blood-price, to buy their acquiescence. That is part of our law, you understand? The family of the bereaved may demand blood-price of the transgressor, and how else might the world be? They see it in these terms: that you must repent of your evils and assist them in waging holy war against those who would defile the will of Allah."

Roger sighs. "We do what we can," he says. "We're shipping them arms. We're fighting the Soviets every way we can without provoking the big one. What more do they want? The hostages—that's not playing well in DC. There's got to be some give and take. If Hezbollah don't release them soon they'll just convince everyone what they're not serious about negotiating. And that'll be an end to it. The colonel *wants* to help you, but he's got to have something to show the man at the top, right?"

Mehmet nods. "You and I are men of the world and understand that this keeping of hostages is not rational, but they look to you for defense against the great Satan that assails them, and their blood burns with anger that your nation, for all its fine words, takes no action. The great Satan rampages in Afghanistan, taking whole villages by night, and what is done? The United States turns its back. And they are not the only ones who feel betrayed. Our Ba'athist foes from Iraq . . . in Basra the unholy brotherhood of Takrit and their servants the Mukhabarat hold nightly sacrifice upon the altar of Yair-Suthot; the fountains of blood in Tehran testify to their effect. If the richest, most powerful nation on earth refuses to fight, these men of violence from the Bekaa think, how may we unstopper the ears of that nation? And they are not sophisticates like you or I."

He looks at Roger, who hunches his shoulders uneasily. "We *can't* move against the Soviets openly! They must understand that it would be the end of far more than their little war. If the Taliban want American help against the Russians, it cannot be delivered openly."

"It is not the Russians that we quarrel with," Mehmet says quietly, "but their choice in allies. They believe themselves to be infidel atheists, but by their deeds they shall be known; the icy spoor of Leng is upon them, their tools are those described in the Kitab al Azif. We have proof that they have violated the terms of the Dresden Agreement. The accursed and unhallowed stalk the frozen passes of the Himalayas by night, taking all whose path they cross. And will you stopper your ears even as the Russians grow in misplaced confidence, sure that their dominance of these forces of evil is complete? The gates are opening everywhere, as it was prophesied. Last week we flew an F-14C with a camera relay pod through one of them. The pilot and weapons operator are in paradise now, but we have glanced into hell and have the film and radar plots to prove it."

The Iranian ambassador fixes the redneck from the embassy with an icy gaze. "Tell your ambassador that we have opened preliminary discussions with Mossad, with a view to purchasing the produce of a factory at Dimona, in the Negev desert. Past insults may be set aside, for the present danger imperils all of us. *They* are receptive to our arguments, even if you are not: his holiness the Grand Ayatollah has declared in private that any warrior who carries a nuclear device into the abode of the eater of souls will certainly achieve paradise. There will be an end to the followers of the ancient abominations on this Earth, doctor Hamilton, even if we have to push the nuclear bombs down their throats with our own hands!"

Swimming Pool

"Mister Jourgensen, at what point did you become aware that the Iranian government was threatening to violate UN Resolution 216 and the Non-Proliferation Protocol to the 1956 Geneva accords?"

Roger sweats under the hot lights: his heartbeat accelerates. "I'm not sure I understand the question, sir."

"I asked you a direct question. Which part don't you understand? I'm going to repeat myself slowly: when did you realise that the

Iranian Government was threatening to violate resolution 216 and the 1956 Geneva Accords on nuclear proliferation?"

Roger shakes his head. It's like a bad dream, unseen insects buzzing furiously around him. "Sir, I had no direct dealings with the Iranian government. All I know is that I was asked to carry messages to and from a guy called Mehmet who I was told knew something about our hostages in Beirut. My understanding is that the colonel has been conducting secret negotiations with this gentleman or his backers for some time—a couple of years—now. Mehmet made allusions to parties in the Iranian administration but I have no way of knowing if he was telling the truth, and I never saw any diplomatic credentials."

There's an inquisition of dark-suited congressmen opposite him, like a jury of teachers sitting in judgement over an errant pupil. The trouble is, these teachers can put him in front of a judge and send him to prison for many years, so that Jason really *will* grow up with a father who's a voice on the telephone, a father who isn't around to take him to air shows or ball games or any of the other rituals of growing up. They're talking to each other quietly, deciding on another line of questioning: Roger shifts uneasily in his chair. This is a closed hearing, the television camera a gesture in the direction of the congressional archives: a pack of hungry democrats have scented republican blood in the water.

The congressman in the middle looks towards Roger. "Stop right there. Where did you know about this guy Mehmet from? Who told you to go see him and who told you what he was?"

Roger swallows. "I got a memo from Fawn, like always. Admiral Poindexter wanted a man on the spot to talk to this guy, a messenger, basically, who was already in the loop. Colonel North signed off on it and told me to charge the trip to his discretionary fund." That must have been the wrong thing to say, because two of the congressmen are leaning together and whispering in each other's ears, and an aide obligingly sidles up to accept a note, then dashes away. "I was told that Mehmet was a mediator," Roger adds. "In trying to resolve the Beirut hostage thing."

"A mediator." The guy asking the questions looks at him in disbelief.

The man to his left—who looks as old as the moon, thin white hair, liver spots on his hooked nose, eyelids like sacks—chuckles appreciatively. "Yeah. Like Hitler was a *diplomat*. 'One more territorial demand'—" he glances round. "Nobody else remember that?" he asks plaintively.

"No sir," Roger says very seriously.

The prime interrogator snorts. "What did Mehmet tell you Iran was going to do, exactly?"

Roger thinks for a moment. "He said they were going to buy something from a factory at Dimona. I understood this to be the Israeli Defense Ministry's nuclear weapons research institute, and the only logical item—in the context of our discussion—was a nuclear weapon. Or weapons. He said the Ayatollah had decreed that a suicide bomber who took out the temple of Yog-Sothoth in Basra would achieve paradise, and that they also had hard evidence that the Soviets have deployed certain illegal weapons systems in Afghanistan. This was in the context of discussing illegal weapons proliferation; he was very insistent about the Iraq thing."

"What exactly are these weapons systems?" demands the third inquisitor, a quiet, hawk-faced man sitting on the left of the panel.

"The shoggot'im, they're called: servitors. There are several kinds of advanced robotic systems made out of molecular components: they can change shape, restructure material at the atomic level—act like corrosive acid, or secrete diamonds. Some of them are like a tenuous mist—what Doctor Drexler at MIT calls a utility fog—while others are more like an oily globule. Apparently they may be able to manufacture more of themselves, but they're not really alive in any meaning of the term we're familiar with. They're programmable, like robots, using a command language deduced from recovered records of the forerunners who left them here. The Molotov Raid of 1930 brought back a large consignment of them; all we have to go on are the scraps they missed, and reports by the Antarctic Survey. Professor Liebkunst's files in particular are most frustrating—"

"Stop. So you're saying the Russians have these, uh, Shoggoths, but we don't have any. And even those dumb arab bastards in Baghdad are working on them. So you're saying we've got a, a Shoggoth gap? A strategic chink in our armour? And now the Iranians say the Russians are using them in Afghanistan?"

Roger speaks rapidly: "That is minimally correct, sir, although countervailing weapons have been developed to reduce the risk of a unilateral preemption escallating to an exchange of weakly godlike agencies." The congressman in the middle nods encouragingly. "For the past three decades, the B-39 Peacemaker force has been tasked by SIOP with maintaining an XK-PLUTO capability directed at ablating the ability of the Russians to activate Project Koschei, the dormant alien entity they captured from the Nazis at the end of the last war. We have twelve PLUTO-class atomic-powered cruise missiles pointed at that thing, day and night, as many megatons as the entire Minuteman force. In principle, we will be able to blast it to pieces before it can be brought to full wakefulness and eat the minds of everyone within two hundred miles."

He warms to his subject. "Secondly, we believe the Soviet control of Shoggoth technology is rudimentary at best. They know how to tell them to roll over an Afghan hill-farmer village, but they can't manufacture more of them. Their utility as weapons is limited—but terrifying—but they're not much of a problem. A greater issue is the temple in Basra. This contains an operational gateway, and according to Mehmet the Iraqi political secret police, the Mukhabarat, are trying to figure out how to manipulate it; they're trying to summon something through it. He seemed to be mostly afraid that they—and the Russians—would lose control of whatever it was; presumably another weakly godlike creature like the K-Thulu entity at the core of Project Koschei."

The old guy speaks: "This foo-loo thing, boy—you can drop those stupid K prefixes around me—is it one of a kind?"

Roger shakes his head. "I don't know, sir. We know the gateways link to at least three other planets. There may be many that we don't know of. We don't know how to create them or close them; all we can do is send people through, or pile bricks in the opening." He nearly bites his tongue, because there *are* more than three worlds out there, and he's been to at least one of them: the bolt-hole on XK-Masada, built by the NRO from their secret budget. He's seen the mile-high dome Buckminster Fuller spent his last decade designing for them, the rings of Patriot air defense missiles. A squadron of black diamond-shaped fighters from the Skunk Works, said to be invisible to radar, patrols the empty skies of XK-Masada. Hydroponic farms and empty barracks and apartment blocks await the senators and congressmen and their families and thousands of support personnel. In event of war they'll be evacuated through the small gate that has been moved to the Executive Office Building basement, in a room beneath the swimming pool where Jack used to go skinny-dipping with Marilyn.

"Off the record now." The old congressman waves his hand in a chopping gesture: "I say *off*, boy." The cameraman switches off his machine and leaves. He leans forward, towards Roger. "What you're telling me is, we've been waging a secret war since, when? The end of the second world war? Earlier, the Pabodie Antarctic expedition in the twenties, whose survivors brought back the first of these alien relics? And now the Eye-ranians have gotten into the game and figure it's part of their fight with Saddam?"

"Sir." Roger barely trusts himself to do more than nod.

"Well." The congressman eyes his neighbour sharply. "Let me put it to you that you have heard the phrase, 'the great filter'. What does it mean to you?"

"The great—" Roger stops. *Professor Gould*, he thinks. "We had a professor of palaeontology lecture us," he explains. "I think he mentioned it. Something about why there aren't any aliens in flying saucers buzzing us the whole time."

The congressman snorts. His neighbour starts and sits up. "Thanks to Pabodie and his followers, Liebkunst and the like, we know there's a lot of life in the universe. The great filter, *boy*, is whatever force stops most of it developing intelligence and coming to visit. Something, somehow, kills intelligent species before they develop this kind of technology for themselves. How about meddling with relics of the elder ones? What do you think of that?"

Roger licks his lips nervously. "That sounds like a good possibility, sir," he says. His unease is building.

The congressman's expression is intense: "These weapons your colonel is dicking around with make all our nukes look like a toy bow and arrow, and all you can say is *it's a good possibility, sir*? Seems to me like someone in the Oval Office has been asleep at the switch."

"Sir, executive order 2047, issued January 1980, directed the armed forces to standardize on nuclear weapons to fill the mass destruction role. All other items were to be developmentally suspended, with surplus stocks allocated to the supervision of Admiral Poindexter's joint munitions expenditure committee. Which Colonel North was detached to by the USMC high command, with the full cognizance of the White House—"

The door opens. The congressman looks round angrily: "I thought I said we weren't to be disturbed!"

The aide standing there looks uncertain. "Sir, there's been an, uh, major security incident, and we need to evacuate—"

"Where? What happened?" demands the congressman. But Roger, with a sinking feeling, realises that the aide isn't watching the house committee members: and the guy behind him is Secret Service.

"Basra. There's been an attack, sir." A furtive glance at Roger, as his brain freezes in denial: "If you'd all please come this way . . . "

Bombing in fifteen minutes

Heads down, through a corridor where congressional staffers hurry about carrying papers, urgently calling one another. A cadre of dark-suited secret service agents close in, hustling Roger along in the wake of the committee members. A wailing like tinnitus fills his ears. "What's happening?" he asks, but nobody answers.

Down into the basement. Another corridor, where two marine guards are waiting with drawn weapons. The secret service guys are exchanging terse reports by radio. The committee men are hustled away along a narrow service tunnel: Roger is stalled by the entrance. "What's going on?" he asks his minder.

"Just a moment, sir." More listening: these guys cock their heads to one side as they take instruction, birds of prey scanning the horizon for Mukhabaratets. "Delta four coming in. Over. You're clear to go along the tunnel now, sir. This way."

"What's *happening??*" Roger demands as he lets himself be hustled into the corridor, along to the end and round a sharp corner. Numb shock takes hold: he keeps putting one foot in front of the other.

"We're now at Defcon one, sir. You're down on the special list as part of the house staff. Next door on the left, sir."

The queue in the dim-lit basement room is moving fast, white-gloved guards with clipboards checking off men and a few women in suits as they step through a steel blast door one by one and disappear from view. Roger looks round in bewilderment: he sees a familiar face. "Fawn! What's going on?"

The secretary looks puzzled. "I don't know. Roger? I thought you were testifying today."

"So did I." They're at the door. "What else?"

"Ronnie was making a big speech in Helsinki; the colonel had me record it in his office. Something about not coexisting with the empire of evil. He cracked some kinda joke about how we start bombing in fifteen minutes, Then this—"

They're at the door. It opens on a steel-walled airlock and the marine guard is taking their badges and hustling them inside. Two staff types and a middle-aged brigadier join them and the door thumps shut. The background noise vanishes, Roger's ears pop, then the inner door opens and another marine guard waves them through into the receiving hall.

"Where are we?" asks the big-haired secretary, staring around.

"Welcome to XK-Masada," says Roger. Then his childhood horrors catch up with him and he goes in search of a toilet to throw up in.

We need you back

Roger spends the next week in a state of numbed shock. His apartment here is like a small hotel room—a hotel with security, air conditioning, and windows that only open onto an interior atrium. He pays little attention to his surroundings. It's not as if he has a home to return to.

Roger stops shaving. Stops changing his socks. Stops looking in mirrors or combing his hair. He smokes a lot, orders cheap bourbon from the commissary, and drinks himself into an amensic stupor each night. He is, frankly, a mess. Self-destructive. Everything disintegrated under him at once: his job, the people he held in high regard, his family, his life. All the time he can't get one thing out of his head: the expression on Gorman's face as he stands there, in front of the submarine, rotting from the inside out with radiation sickness, dead and not yet knowing it. It's why he's stopped looking in mirrors.

On the fourth day he's slumped in a chair watching taped I Love Lucy re-runs on the boob tube when the door to his suite opens quietly. Someone comes in. He doesn't look round until the colonel walks across the screen and unplugs the TV set at the wall, then sits down in the chair next to him. The colonel has bags of dark skin under his eyes; his jacket is rumpled and his collar is unbuttoned.

"You've got to stop this, Roger," he says quietly. "You look like shit."

"Yeah, well. You too."

The colonel passes him a slim manilla folder. Without wanting to, Roger slides out the single sheet of paper within.

"So it *was* them."

"Yeah." A moment's silence. "For what it's worth, we haven't lost yet. We may yet pull your wife and son out alive. Or be able to go back home."

"Your family too, I suppose." Roger's touched by the colonel's consideration, the pious hope that Andrea and Jason will be alright, even through his shell of misery. He realises his glass is empty. Instead of re-filling it he puts it down on the carpet beside his feet. "*Why*?"

The colonel removes the sheet of paper from his numb fingers. "Probably someone spotted you in the King David and traced you back to us. The Mukhabarat had agents everywhere, and if they were in league with the KGB . . . " he shrugs. "Things escallated rapidly. Then the president cracked that joke over a hot mike that was supposed to be switched off . . . Have you been checking in with the desk summaries this week?"

Roger looks at him blankly. "Should I?"

"Oh, things are still happening." The colonel leans back and stretches his feet out. "From what we can tell of the situation on the other side, not everyone's dead yet. Ligachev's screaming blue murder over the hotline, accusing us of genocide: but he's still talking. Europe is a mess and nobody knows what's going on in the middle east—even the Blackbirds aren't making it back out again."

"The thing at Takrit."

"Yeah. It's bad news, Roger. We need you back."

"Bad news?"

"The worst." The colonel jams his hands between his knees, stares at the floor like a bashful child. "Saddam Hussein al-Takriti spent years trying to get his hands on elder technology. It looks like he finally succeeded in stabilising the gate into Sothoth. Whole villages disappeared, Marsh Arabs, wiped out in the swamps of Eastern Iraq. Reports of yellow rain, people's skin melting right off their bones. The Iranians got itchy and finally went nuclear. Trouble is, they did so two hours before *that* speech. Some asshole in Plotsk launched half the Uralskoye SS-20 grid—they went to launch on warning eight months ago—burning south, praise Jesus. Scratch the middle east, period—everything from the Nile to the Khyber Pass is toast. We're still waiting for the callback on Moscow, but SAC has put the whole Peacemaker force on airborn alert. So far we've lost the eastern seaboard as far south as North Virginia and they've lost the Donbass basin and Vladivostok. Things are a mess; nobody can even agree whether we're fighting the commies or something else. But the box at Chernobyl—Project Koschei—the doors are open, Roger. We orbited a Keyhole-Eleven over it and there are tracks, leading west. The PLUTO strike didn't stop it—and nobody knows what the fuck is going on in WarPac country. Or France, or Germany, or Japan, or England."

The colonel makes a grab for Roger's wild turkey, rubs the neck clean and swallows from the bottle. He looks at Roger with a wild expression on his face. "Koschei is loose, Roger. They fucking *woke* the thing. And now they can't control it. Can you believe that?"

"I can believe that."

"I want you back behind a desk tomorrow morning, Roger. We need to know what this Thulu creature is capable of. We need to know what to do to stop it. Forget Iraq; Iraq is a smoking hole in the map. But K-Thulu is heading towards the Atlantic coast. What are we going to do if it doesn't stop?"

Masada

The city of XK-Masada sprouts like a vast mushroom, a mile-wide dome emerging from the top of a cold plateau on a dry planet that orbits a dying star. The jagged black shapes of F-117's howl across the empty skies outside it at dusk and dawn, patrolling the threatening emptiness that stretches as far as the mind can imagine.

Shadows move in the streets of the city, hollowed out human shells in uniform. They rustle around the feet of the towering concrete blocks like the dry leaves of autumn, obsessively focussed on the tasks that lend structure to their remaining days. Above them tower masts of steel, propping up the huge geodesic dome that arches across the sky: blocking out the hostile, alien constellations, protecting frail humanity from the dust storms that periodically scour the bones of the ancient world. The gravity here is a little lighter, the night sky whorled and marbled by the diaphanous sheets of gas blasted off the dying star that lights their days. During the long winter nights, a flurry of carbon dioxide snow dusts the surface of the dome: but the air is bone-dry, the city slaking its thirst on subterranean aquifers.

This planet was once alive—there is still a scummy sea of algae near the equator that feeds oxygen into the atmosphere, and there is a range of volcanoes near the north pole that speaks of plate tectonics in motion—but it is visibly dying. There is a lot of history here, but no future.

Sometimes, in the early hours when he cannot sleep, Roger walks outside the city, along the edge of the dry plateau. Machines labour on behind him, keeping the city tenuously intact: he pays them little attention. There is talk of mounting an expedition to Earth one of these years, to salvage whatever is left before the searing winds of time erase them forever. Roger doesn't like to think about that. He tries to avoid thinking about Earth as much as possible: except when he cannot sleep but walks along the cliff top, prodding at memories of Andrea and Jason and his parents and sister and relatives and friends, each of them as painful as the socket of a missing tooth. He has a mouthful of emptiness, bitter and acheing, out here on the edge of the plateau.

Sometimes Roger thinks he's the last human being alive. He works in an office, feverishly trying to sort out what went wrong: and bodies move around him, talking, eating in the canteen, sometimes talking *to* him and waiting as if they expect a dialogue. There are bodies here, men and some women chatting, civilian and some military—but no people. One of the bodies, an army surgeon, told him he's suffering from a common stress disorder, survivor's guilt. This may be so, Roger admits, but it doesn't change anything. Soulless days follow sleepless nights into oblivion, dust trickling over the side of the cliff like sand into the un-dug graves of his family.

A narrow path runs along the side of the plateau, just downhill from the foundations of the city power plant where huge apertures belch air warmed by the radiators of the nuclear reactor. Roger follows the path, gravel and sandy rock crunching under his worn shoes. Foreign stars twinkle overhead, forming unrecognizable patterns that tell him he's far from home. The trail drops away from the top of the plateau, until the city is an unseen shadow looming above and behind his shoulder. To his right is a dizzying panorama, the huge rift valley with its ancient city of the dead stretched out before him. Beyond it rise alien mountains, their peaks as high and airless as the dead volcanoes of Mars.

About half a mile away from the dome, the trail circles an outcrop of rock and takes a downhill switchback turn. Roger stops at the bend and looks out across the desert at his feet. He sits down, leans against the rough cliff face and stretches his legs out across the path, so that his feet dangle over nothingness. Far below him, the dead valley is furrowed with rectangular depressions; once, millions of years ago, they might have been fields, but nothing like that survives to this date. They're just dead, like everyone else on this world. Like Roger.

In his shirt pocket, a crumpled, precious pack of cigarettes. He pulls a white cylinder out with shaking fingers, sniffs at it, then flicks his lighter under it. Scarcity has forced him to cut back: he coughs at the first lungful of stale smoke, a harsh, racking croak. The irony of being saved from lung cancer by a world war is not lost on him.

He blows smoke out, a tenuous trail streaming across the cliff. "Why me?" he asks quietly.

The emptiness takes its time answering. When it does, it speaks with the Colonel's voice. "You know the reason."

"I didn't want to do it," he hears himself saying. "I didn't want to leave them behind."

The void laughs at him. There are miles of empty air beneath his dangling feet. "You had no choice."

"Yes I did! I didn't have to come here." He pauses. "I didn't have to do anything," he says quietly, and inhales another lungful of death. "It was all automatic. Maybe it was inevitable."

"—evitable," echoes the distant horizon. Something dark and angular skims across the stars, like an echo of extinct pterosaurs. Turbofans whirring within its belly, the F117 hunts on: patrolling to keep at bay the ancient evil, unaware that the battle is already lost. "Your family could still be alive, you know."

He looks up. "They could? Andrea? Jason? Alive?"

The void laughs again, unfriendly: "There is life eternal within the eater of souls. Nobody is ever forgotten or allowed to rest in peace. They populate the simulation spaces of its mind, exploring all the possible alternative endings to their life. There *is* a fate worse than death, you know."

Roger looks at his cigarette disbelievingly: throws it far out into the night sky above the plain. He watches it fall until its ember is no longer visible. Then he gets up. For a long moment he stands poised on the edge of the cliff nerving himself, and thinking. Then he takes a step back, turns, and slowly makes his way back up the trail towards the redoubt on the plateau. If his analysis of the situation is wrong, at least he is still alive. And if he is right, dying would be no escape.

He wonders why hell is so cold at this time of year.

TOAST: A Con Report

Old hackers never die; they just sprout more grey hair, their t-shirts fade, and they move on to stranger and more obscure toys.

Well, that's the way it's supposed to be. **Your Antiques!** asked me to write about it, so I decided to find out where all the old hackers went. Which is how come I ended up at Toast-9, the ninth annual conference of the Association for Retrocomputing Meta-Machinery. They got their feature, you're getting this con report, and never the two shall meet.

Toast is held every year in the Boston Marriot, a piece of disgusting glass and concrete cheesecake from the late seventies post-barbarism school of architecture. I checked my bags in at the hotel reception then went out in search of a couple of old hackers to interview.

I don't know who I was expecting to find, but it sure as hell wasn't Ashley Martin. Ashley and I worked together for a while in the early zeroes, as contract resurrection men raising zombies from some of the big iron databases that fell over on Black Tuesday: I lost track of him after he threw his double-breasted Compaq suit from a tenth floor window and went to live in a naturist commune on Skye, saying that he was never going to deal with any period shorter than a season ever again. (At the time I was pissed off; that suit had cost our company fifteen thousand dollars six months ago, and it wasn't fully depreciated yet.) But there he was, ten inches bigger around the waist and real as taxes, queuing in front of me at the registration desk.

"Richard! how are you?"

"Fine, fine." (I'm always cautious about uttering the social niceties around hex-heads: most of them are oblivious enough that as often as not a casual "how's it going?" will trigger a quarter-hour stack dump of woes.) "Just waiting for my membership pack . . . "

There was a chime and the door of the badge printer sprang open; Ashley's membership pack stuck its head out and looked around anxiously until it spotted him.

"Just update my familiar," I told the young witch on the desk; "I don't need any more guides." She nodded at me in the harried manner that staff on a convention registration desk get.

"The bar," Ashley announced gnomically.

"The bar?"

"That's where I'm going," he said.

"Mind if I join you?"

"That was the general idea . . . "

The bar was like any other con bar since time immemorial, or at least the end of the post-industrial age (which is variously dated to December 31st, 1999, February 29th, 2007, or March 1972, depending who you talk to). Tired whiskey bottles hung upside down in front of a mirror for the whole world to gape at; four pumps dispensed gassy ersatz beer: and a wide range of alcohol-fortified grape juice was stacked in a glass-fronted chiller behind the bar. The bar top itself was beige and labeled with the runes DEC and VAX 11/780. When I asked the drone for a bottle of Jolt they had to run one up on their fab, interrupting its continuous-upgrade cycle; it chittered bad-temperedly and waved menacing pseudopodia at me as it took time out to spit caffeinated water into a newly-spun buckybottle.

Ash found a free table and I waited for my vessel to cool enough to open. We watched the world go by for a while: there were no major disasters, nobody I knew died, and only three industry-specific realignments or mergers of interest took place.

"So what brings you here, eh?" I asked eventually.

Ashley shrugged. "Boredom. Nostalgia. And my wife divorced me a year ago. I figured it was time to get away from it all before I scope out the next career."

"Occupational hazard," I sympathized, carefully not questioning the relationship between his answer and my question.

"No it bloody isn't," he said with some asperity, raising his glass for a brief mouthful followed by a shudder: "You've got to move with the times. Since I met Laura I've been a hand-crafted toy designer, not a, an—" he looked around at the other occupants of the bar and shuddered, guiltily.

"Anorak?" I asked, trying to keep my tone of voice neutral.

"Furry toys." He glared at his glass but refrained from taking another mouthful. "That's where the action is, not mainframes or steam engines or wearables or MEMS or assemblers. They're all obsolete as soon as they come off the fab: but children will always need toys. Walking talking dolls who're fun to be with. I discovered I've got a knack for the instinctual level—" something small and blue and horribly similar to a hairy smurf was trying to crawl out of one of his breast pockets, closely pursued by a spreading ink-stain.

"So she divorced you? Before or after children?"

"Yes and no, luckily in that order." He noticed the escaping imp and, with a sigh, unzipped one of the other pockets on his jacket and thrust the little wriggler inside. It meeped incoherently; when he zipped the pocket up it heaved and billowed like a tent in a gale. "Sorry about that; he's an escape artist. Special commission, actually."

"How long have you been in the toy business?" I prompted, seeking some less hazardous territory.

"Two years before we got married. Six years ago, I think." Oh gods, he was a brooder. "It was the buried commands that did it. She was the marketing face; we got a lot of bespoke requests for custom deluxe Teletubby sets, life-sized interactive droids, that kind of thing. Peter Platypus and his Pangolin Playmates. I couldn't do one of those and stay sane without implanting at least one buried easter egg; usually a reflex dialog, preferably a suite of subversive memes. Like the Barney who was all sweetness and light and I-love-you-you-love-me until he saw a My Little Pony: then he got hungry and remembered his roots."

"I suppose there were a lot of upset little girls—"

"Hell, no! But one of the parental investment units got really pissed; those plastic horsies are expensive collector's items these days."

"Do you still get much work?" I asked.

"Yeah, enough." He downed his glass in one: "You'd be amazed how many orcs the average gamer gets through. And there's always a market for a custom one. Here's Dean—" The wriggling in his pocket had stopped: it looked rather empty. "Excuse me a moment," he said, and went down on hands and knees beneath the table, in search of the escape artist.

<EDITORIAL>

Hand-crafted toys are probably the last domain of specialist human programmers these days. You can trust most jobs to a familiar, but children are pretty sensitive and familiars are generally response-tuned to adult company. Toys are a special case: their simple reflex sets and behaviors make them amenable to human programmers—children don't mind, indeed need, a lot of repetition and simple behavior they can understand—while human programmers are needed because humans are still better than familiars at raising human infants. But someone who makes only nasty, abusive, or downright rude toys is—

</EDITORIAL>

Later, while my luggage sniffed out a usefully plumbed corner and grew me a suite, I wandered around the hardware show.

Hardware shows at a big con are always fascinating to the true geek, and this one was no exception. Original PCs weren't common at Toast-9, being too commonplace to be worth bringing along, but the weird and wonderful was here in profusion. In the center of the room was an octagonal pillar surrounded by a cracked vinyl love seat: an original Cray supercomputer from the 1980's in NSA institutional blue. Over in that corner, that rarest and most exotic of beasts, an Altair-1 motherboard, its tarnished copper circuit tracks thrusting purposefully between black, insectoidal microprocessor and archaic hex keypad (the whole thing mounted carefully under an diamond display case, watchful guardian daemons standing to either side in case any enthusiasts tried to get too close to the ancient work of art).

I strolled round the hall slowly, lingering over the ancient main-frames: starting with the working Difference Engine and the IBM 1604 console, then the Pentium II laptop. All of them were pre-softwear processors: discrete industrial machines from back before the dogshit brigade acquired personal area networks and turned electronics into a fashion statement. Back when processor power doubled every eighteen months and bandwidth doubled every twelve months, back before they'd been overtaken by newer, faster-evolving technologies.

I was examining a particularly fine late-model SPARCstation when somebody goosed me from behind. Strangers don't usually sneak up on me for a quick grope—more's the pity—so when I peeled myself off the ceiling and turned round I wasn't too surprised to see Lynda grinning at me ghoulishly. "Richard!" she said, "I knew you'd be around here somewhere! How's tricks?"

"Much the same. Yourself?"

"Still with the old firm." The old firm—Intangible Business Mechanisms, as they call themselves today—is a big employer of witches, and Lynda is a particularly fine exponent of the profession, having combined teaching at MIT and practice as a freelance consultant for years. Another of those child prodigies who seem attracted to new paradigms like flies to dog-shit. (I should add: Lynda isn't her real name. Serial numbers filed off, as they say, to protect the innocent.) "Just taking in a little of the local color, dear. It's so classical! All these hardwired circuits and little lumps of lithographed silicon-germa-nium semiconductor. Can you believe people once relied on such crude technologies?"

"Tactless," I hissed at her: an offended anorak-wearer was glaring from beside the Altair-1. "And the answer is yes, anyway. But it was all before your time, wasn't it?"

"Oh, I wouldn't say that," she said; "I had a laptop too, when I was a baby. But by the time I was in my teens it was all so boring, dinosaur-sized multinationals being starved to death by the free software crowd and trying to drown them in a sea of press releases and standards initiatives, to a greek chorus singing laments about Moore's law only giving room for another five years of improvements in microprocessor design before they finally ran up against the quantum limits of miniaturization. I remember when House of Versace released their first wearable collection, and there was me a sixteen-year old goth with more CPU power in her earrings than IBM sold in the 1990's and it was *boring*. The revolution had eaten its own sense of wonder and shat out megacorporations. Would you believe it?" She blinked, and wobbled a little, as if drunk on words. I think her thesaurus was running at too high a priority level.

I surreptitiously looked at her feet: she was wearing heavy black boots, the preferred thinking environment of the security-minded. (Steel toe caps make for great Faraday cages.) Then I eyeballed her up and down: judging by the conservative business suit she had deteriorated a lot in the past year, to the point where she needed corporate thinking support. When I first met Lynda, she'd been wearing a fortune in home-made RISC processors bound together by black lacy tatters of goth finery, cracking badly-secured ten-year-old financial transactions every few milliseconds. (And selling any numbered offshore accounts she detected to the IRS for a thief taker's cut, in order to subsidize her nanoassembler design start-up.) Now she was wearing Armani.

<EDITORIAL>

A business suit is a future-shock exoskeleton, whispering reminders in its wearer's ears to prompt them through the everyday niceties of a life washed into bleeding monochrome by the flood of information they live under. Corporate workers and consultants today—I gather this, because I dropped out of that cycle a few years ago, unable to keep up with a new technological revolution every six months—live on the bleeding edge of autism: so wrapped up in their work that if their underwear didn't tell them when to go to the toilet their bladders would burst. And it's not just the company types who need the thinking environment: geeks became dependent on low-maintenance clothing years before, and it's partly thanks to their efforts that the clothing became sentient (if not fully independent).

Clothes today say far more about someone's corporate and social status than they did in the twentieth century: we can blame the Media Lab for that, with their radical (not to say annoying) idea that your clothes should think for you. A conservative business suit by a discreet softwear company screams PHB groupware; sneakers and a sloganeering t-shirt or combat pants go with the Freeware crowd, anarchoid linuxers and hackers, some of them charging a thousand bucks an hour for their commercial services. An eighties yuppie would have been astonished at the number of body-piercings in the boardrooms, the vacant, glassy stares of brain-webbed executives being steered round the local delicatessen by their necktie while their suit jacket engineered a hostile takeover in Ulan Bator and their shoes tracked stock prices. But then, an eighties yuppie would be a living fossil in this day and age, slow and cold-blooded and not sufficiently intelligent to breathe and do business simultaneously. Oh brave new world, to have such cyborgs.

</EDITORIAL>

We arrived back in the bar. "I think I need a drink," said Lynda, wobbling on her feet. "Oops! So sorry. Er, yes. This is so slow, Richard! How do you handle the boredom?"

"Excuse me?" The bartender handed me another Jolt, this one nicely chilled. A large margarita slid across the bar top and somehow appeared in her hand.

"This!" She looked around vaguely. "Real time!"

I stared at her. Her pupils were wide. "Are you on anything I should know about?" I asked.

"Sensory deprivation. My suit's powered down." She shook her head. "I feel naked. I haven't been offline in months; there are things happening that I don't know about. It seemed like a good idea at the time, but now I'm not sure. Is it always like this?"

"How long have you been down?" I asked.

"I'm unsure. Since I saw you in the show? I wanted to get into your headspace and see what it was like, but it's so cramped! Maybe half an hour; it's a disciplinary offense, you know?"

"What, going offline?"

Her eyeballs flickered from side to side in the characteristic jitter of information-withdrawal nystagmus. "Being obsolete."

I left Lynda in the safe custody of a hotel paramedic, who didn't seem to think there'd be any permanent side-effects once her clothing had rebooted. I headed back to the con, fervently glad that I'd stepped off the treadmill a couple of releases after Ashley, way before things got this bad.

<EDITORIAL>

Information withdrawal is an occupational hazard for the well-connected, like diabetic hypoglycaemia; if the diabetic doesn't get their sugar hit, or the executive their info-burn, they get woozy and stop working. On the other hand, you can only take it for so long . . .

Lynda is twenty-six. At sixteen, she was cracking financial cryptosystems. At seventeen, she was designing nanotech applications. At twenty she was a professor, with a patent portfolio worth millions. Today she's an executive vice-president with a budget measured in the billions. She will be burned out completely by thirty, out of rehab by thirty-two (give or take a case of tardive dyskinesia), with a gold-plated pension and the rest of her life ahead of her—just like the rest of us proto-transhumanists, washed up on the evolutionary beach.

</EDITORIAL>

Back in the con proper, I decided to take in a couple of talks. There's a long and sometimes contradictory series of lectures and workshops at any Toast gathering; not to mention the speaker's corners, where any crank can set up a soap-box and have their say.

First I sat through a rather odd monologue with only three other attendees (one of them deeply asleep in the front row): a construct shaped like a cross between a coat-rack and a preying mantis was vigorously attacking the conceit of human consciousness, attempting to prove (by way of an updated version of Searle's Chinese Room attack, lightly seasoned à la Penrose) that dumb neurons can't possibly be intelligent in the same way as a, well, whatever the thing on the podium was. It was almost certainly a prank, given our proximity to MIT (not to mention the Gates millenniumDepartment of Amplified Intelligence at Harvard), but it was still absorbing to listen to its endless spew of rolling, inspired oratory. Eventually the construct argued itself into a solipsistic corner, then asked the floor for questions: when nobody asked any it stormed off in a huff.

I must confess that I was half-asleep by the time the robot philosopher denounced us as non-sapient automata, sparing only half my left eye to speed-read Minsky's Society of Mind for clues; in any event, I woke up in time for the next talk, a panel discussion. Someone had rounded up an original stalwart of the Free Software Foundation to talk about the rise and demise of Microsoft. There was, of course, a Microsoft spokesdroid present to defend the company's historic record. It started with the obligatory three-minute AV presentation about how Our Great Leader and Teacher (Bill) had Saved the World from IBM, but before they could open their mouth and actually say anything Bill's head appeared on screen and the audience went wild: it was like the Three Minute Hate in 1984.

After the Microsoft talk I went back to my temporary apartment to estivate for a few hours. At my age, I need all the regeneration time I can get, even if I have to take it hanging upside down in a brightly-coloured cocoon woven to the side of a tower block's support column. I run some quackware from India that claims to be a white-box clone of the Kaiser-Glaxo program the Pope uses; my tent and travel equipment designs come courtesy of the Free Hardware Foundation. Having lost my main income stream years ago due to the usual causes, principally cumulative future shock and the let-down from the Unix millennium consultancy business, I'd be lost without the copylefted design schemata to feed to my assembler farm: I certainly can't afford the latest commercial designs for anything much more exotic than a fountain pen. But life on a twentieth-century income is still tolerable these days, thanks to the FHF. More about those angels in birkenstocks later, if I can be bothered to write it.

I awoke feeling refreshed and came down from my cocoon to find a new wardrobe waiting for me. I'd got my tent to run up some conservative wear before my nap—urban camo trousers, nine inch nails T-shirt, combat boots, and a vest-of-pockets containing numerous artefacts—and it whispered to me reassuringly as I pulled it on, mentioning that the fuel cell in my left hip pocket was good for thirty hours of warmth and power if I had to venture out into the minus-ten wind chill of a Boston winter. I pumped my heels, then desisted, feeling silly: in this day of barely-visible turbogenerators, heel power makes about as much sense as a slide rule.

Outside my spacious dome tent, the floor of the hotel had sprouted a many-colored mushroom forest. Luggage and more obscure personal servants scurried about, seeing to their human owners' requirements. Flying things buzzed back and forth like insects with vectored-thrust turbojets. A McDonald's stall had opened up at the far side of the hall and was burning blocks of hashish to make the neighbors hungry; my vest discreetly reminded me that I had some noseplugs.

I had been asleep for three hours. While I had been asleep, Malaysian scientists had announced the discovery of an earth-sized planet with an oxidizing atmosphere less than forty light-years away: the Gates Trust, in their eternal pursuit of favorable propaganda, had announced that they were going to send a starwhisp to colonize it.

<EDITORIAL>

Insert snide comment about clones, eyes of needles, possibility of passage through, at this juncture: the whole point of a starwhisp is that it's too small to carry any cargo much bigger than a bacillus. Probably the GT was just trying to tweak the American public's guilt complex over the privatisation and subsequent bankruptcy of NASA.

</EDITORIAL>

The Pope had reversed her ruling of last week on personality uploads, but reasserted the indivisibility of the soul, much to the confusion of theologicians and neuroscientists alike.

There had been riots in Afghanistan over the forcible withdrawal of the Playboy Channel by the country's current ruling clique of backwoods militiamen. (Ditto Zimbabwe and Arkansas.)

Further confirmation of the existence of the sixth, so-called gravitoweak resonance force, had been obtained by a team of posthumans somewhere in high orbit. The significance of this discovery was massive, but immediate impact remained obscure—no technological spin-offs were predicted in the next few weeks.

Nobody I knew had died, or been born, or undergone major life-revising events. I found this absence of change obscurely comforting: a worrying sign, so I punched up a really sharp dose of the latest cognitive enhancer and tried to drag my aging (not to say reeling) brain back into the hot core of future-surfing that is the only context in which the antiquities of the silicon era (or modern everyday life, for that matter) can be decoded.

I got out into the exhibition hall only to discover that there was a costume show and disco scheduled for the rest of the night. This didn't exactly fascinate me, but I went along and stared anyway while catching up on the past few hour's news. The costume show was impressive—lots of fabric, and all of it dumb. They had realistic seventies hackers, 80's Silicon Valley entrepreneurs, 90's venture capitalists, and 20's resurrection men, complete with some bits of equipment too precious to put on public exhibition—things like priceless early wearable computer demos from the Media Lab, on loan for the evening: all badly-stitched velcro, cellphone battery compartments run up on a glue-gun renderer, and flickering monochrome head-up displays. Towards the end one of the models shambled on stage in a recent (three month old, hence barely obsolete) space suit: a closed-circuit life support system capable of protecting its owner from any kind of hostile environment and recycling their waste for months or years. It probably qualified as an engineering miracle (closed-circuit life support is *hard*) but it left me with a lingering impression that a major cause of death among its users would be secondary consequences of sexual frustration.

The disco was, well, a disco. Or a rave. Or a waltz. These things don't change: people dress up, eat, take intoxicants, and throw themselves around to music. Same old same old. I settled down with the drinks and the old crusties in the bar, intent on getting thoroughly wasted and exchanging tall stories with the other fogies.

About four or five drinks later, an advertisement crawled through my spam filter and started spraying hotly luminous colors across my left retina. I was busy swapping yarns with an old Cobol monkey called Solipsist Nation and I didn't notice it at first. "Is something wrong, my friend?" he asked.

"S'spam. Nothing," I said.

Solly pulled out a huge old revolver—a Colt, I think—and looked around. Squinting, he pointed it at the floor and pulled the trigger. There was no bang, but a cloud of smoke squirted out and settled rapidly to the ground, clustering densely around a small bug-like object. The visuals stopped.

"It's nothing now," he agreed, putting his gun away. "There was a time when things were different."

"When they didn't hide behind microbots. Just hijacked mail servers."

He grinned, disquietingly. "Then they went away."

I nodded. "Let's drink a toast. To whatever made the mail spammers go away."

He raised his glass with me, but I didn't see him drink.

135

<EDITORIAL>

Something the junk advertisers don't seem to understand: we live in an information-supersaturated world. If I don't want to buy something, no amount of shouting or propagandizing will budge me; all it will do is get me annoyed. On the other hand, if I have a need for your product, I can seek it out in an eyeblink.

</EDITORIAL>

We now return you to your regular scheduled programming . . .

There was an art show. Fractals blossomed in intricate, fragile beauty on wall-sized screens of fabulously cheap liquid crystal, driven by the entropy-generating logic-chopping of discrete microprocessors. You could borrow some contact lenses and slip between two wall-sized panels and you're on Europa's seabed, gray ooze and timelessness shared with the moluscoids clustered around the hydrothermal vents. Endless tape loops played cheesy Intel adverts from the tail-end of the twentieth, human chip-fab workers in clean room suits boogying or rocking to some ancient synthesizer beat. A performance art group, the Anderoids, identically dressed in blue three-piece suits, hung around accosting visitors with annoyingly impenetrable PHB marketroid jargon in an apparent attempt to get them to buy some proprietary but horizontally-scalable vertical market mission-critical ASP solution. The subculture of the nerd was omnipresent: a fifty-foot Dilbert loomed over walls, partitions and cubicle hell, glasses smudged and necktie perpetually upturned in a quizzical fin-de-siecle loop.

I took in some more of the panels. Grizzled hackers chewed over the ancient jousts of silicon valley in interminable detail: Apple versus IBM, IBM versus DEC, RISC versus CISC/SIMD, Sun versus Intel. I've heard it all before and it's comforting for all its boring familiarity: dead fights, exhumed by retired generals and re-fought across tabletop boards without the need for any deaths or downsizings.

There was an alternate-history panel, too. Someone came up with a beauty; a one-line change in the 1971 anti-trust ruling against AT&T that leaves them the right to sell software. UNIX dead by 1978, strangled by expensive licenses and no source code for universities; C and C++ non-starters: the future as VMS. Another change left me shaking my head: five miles per hour on a cross-wind. Gary Kildall didn't go flying that crucial day, was at the office when IBM came calling in 1982 and sold them CP/M for their PC's. By Y2K Microsoft had a reputation for technical excellence, selling their commercial UNIX-95 system as a high-end server system. (In this one, Bill Gates still lives in the USA.) What startled me most was the inconsequentiality of these points of departure: trillion-dollar industries that grew from a sentence or a breeze in the space of twenty years.

<EDITORIAL>

This is the season of nerds, the flat tail at the end of the sigmoid curve. Some time in the 1940's the steam locomotive peaked; great four-hundred ton twin-engined monsters burning heavy fuel oil, pulling miles-long train sets that weighed as much as freight ships. Twenty years later, the last of these great workhorses were toys for boys who'd grown up with cinders and steam in their eyes. Some time in the 2010's the microprocessor peaked: twenty years later our magi and witches invoke self-programming daemons that constantly enhance their own power, sucking vacuum energy from the vasty deeps, while the last supercomputers draw fractals for the amusement of gray-haired kids who had sand kicked in their eyes. Some time in the 2020's nanotechnology began the long burn up the curve: the nostalgic who play with their gray goo haven't been decanted from their placentories yet, and the field is still hot and crackling with the buzz of new ideas. It's a cold heat that burns as it expands your mind, and I find less and less inclination to subject myself to it these days. I'm in my seventies; I used to work with computers for real before I lost touch with the bleeding edge and slipped into fandom, back when civilization ran on bits and bytes and the machinery of industry needed a human touch at the mouse.

</EDITORIAL>

Eventually I returned to the bar. Ashley was still more or less where I'd left him the day before, slumped half-under a table with his ankles plugged into something that looked like a claymation filing cabinet. He waved as I went past, so after I picked up my drink at the bar I joined him. "How're you feeling today?"

"Been worse," he said cheerfully. Three or four empty bottles stood in front of him. "Couldn't fetch me one, could you? I'm on the Kriek geuse."

I glanced under the table. "Uh, okay."

I took another look under the table as I handed him the bottle. The multicolored cuboid had engulfed his legs to ankle-height before; now it was sending pseudopodia up towards his knees. "Your very good health, Ash. Seen much of the show?"

"Naah." He raised the bottle to me, then drank from the neck. "I'm busy here."

"Doing what, if I can ask?"

"I've decided to emigrate to Tau Ceti." He gestured under the table. "So I'm mind mapping."

"Mind map—" I blinked. *I do not think that word means what I think it means* drifted through my head. "What for?"

He sighed. "I'm sick of dolls, Richard. I need a change, but I'm not as flexible as I used to be. What do you *think* I'm doing?"

I spared a glance under the table again. The thing was definitely getting larger, creeping up to his knees. "Don't be silly," I said. "You don't need to do this, do you?"

"Afraid I do." He drank some more beer. "Don't worry, I've been thinking about it for a long time. I'm not a spring chicken, you know. And it's not as if I'll be dead, or even much different. Just smarter, more flexible. More *me*, the way I was. Able to work on the cutting edge."

"The cutting edge is not amenable to *humans*, Ash. Even the weakly superhuman can't keep up any more."

He smiled, the ghost of an old devil-may-care grin. "So I won't be weakly superhuman, will I?"

I drew my legs back, away from the Moravec larva below the table. It was eating him slowly, converting his entire nervous system into a simulation map inside whatever passed for its sensorium: when it finished it would pupate, and something that wasn't Ashley any more would hatch. Something which maintained conscious continuity with the half-drunken idiot sitting in front of me, but that resembled him the way a seventy-year old professor resembles a baby.

"Did you tell your ex-wife?" I asked.

He flinched slightly. "She can't hurt me any more." I shook my head. "Another drink?" he asked.

"Just one for the road," I said gently. He nodded and snapped his fingers for the bar. I made sure the drink lasted: I had a feeling this was the last time I'd see him, continuity of consciousness or not.

<EDITORIAL>

And that, dear reader, is why I'm writing this con report. The **Your Antiques!** audience want to know all about the history of Cray Y-MP-48 s/n 4002, high-res walkthroughs and a sidebar describing the life and death of old man Seymour. All of which is, well, train-spotting. And you can't learn the soul of an old machine by counting serial numbers; for that, you have to stand on the foot-plate, squinting into the wind of its passage and shoveling coal into the furnace, feel the rush of its inexorable progress up the accelerating curve of history. In this day and age, if you want to learn what the buzz of the computer industry was like you'd have to stop being human. Transcendence is an occupational hazard, the cliff at the edge of the singularity; try climbing too fast and you'll fall over, stop being yourself. It's a big improvement over suicide, but it's still not something I'd welcome just now, and certainly not as casually as Ashley took to it. Eventually it will catch up with me, too, and I'll have to stop being human: but I *like* my childhood, thank you very much, and the idea of becoming part of some vast, cool intelligence working the quantum foam at the bottom of the M-theory soup still lies around the final bend of my track.

</EDITORIAL>

Ship of Fools

I wrote this story in 1993 and sold it in 1994. If you think it drags a bit, consider: back then, all the explanations were necessary because, outside of the software field, nobody had heard of the Y2K problem.

They stopped me on the gangway and rolled up my left sleeve.

"Clockwork? Or quartz?" asked the one with the hammer.

"Oh—quartz," I said.

"Sorry, but rules are rules," said the one with the leather bag. I nodded. He gently peeled the watch off my wrist and laid it over the ship's railing. *Crunch*: the hammer rebounded. He scooped what was left back into the bag, careful not to drop any glass fragments on the deck.

"I just forgot," I said, slightly stunned. "Is there anything else . . . ?"

They looked at each other and shrugged. The one with the bag looked a little guilty. "Here, you can borrow mine," he said, offering it to me.

"Thanks." I tightened the strap, then carried on up the gangway. It was an old Rolex Oyster, case tarnished with decades of sweat. I glanced back. The hammer team waited patiently for their next target. The one with the hammer was wearing a red T-shirt with a logo on its back. I squinted closer at the marketing slogan:

UNIX—THE TIME IS RIGHT.

Rita was already in the fore-deck lounge when I got there. I had half expected her not to show up, but we'd booked the tickets five years ago, three years before the divorce, and her name hadn't disappeared from the roster since then. I suppose I'd assumed she'd forget, or dismiss it, or not think it worth bothering with. I waited for the usual cold shudder of unnamable emotions to pass, then headed for the bar.

Polished brass and wood gleamed in the gas-light like an old-fashioned pub. (The overhead electrics were powered down, except for the red glare of an emergency light's battery charge indicator.) One guy was already sitting on a bar stool, elbow-propped above his beer glass. I looked at him for a moment before I blinked and realized that it was the Professor. A blast from the past; he'd retired two years ago. I sat down on the stool next to him. There was nobody behind the bar, but I figured a steward would be along shortly.

"Marcus Jackman, isn't it?" he asked, glancing round at me. Time hadn't been kind to him; burst blood vessels streaked the tip of his nose and his eyes looked sore.

"Eight years and counting," I said. "What are you drinking?"

He glanced at the row of optics behind the bar: "Perrier for now, I think." He yawned. "Sorry, I haven't had much sleep lately."

"Anything in particular?" I asked.

"The usual," he said. "The chancellor put a gagging order on me, can you believe it? Said what I was saying was bad for the institute's public image. So I packed my bags and came here instead. Olaf said he'd keep a berth open for me but I didn't think I'd be taking him up on it until . . . oh, a month ago. If that."

I shook my head. A barman appeared silently: I tipped him the wink and he refilled the Professor's tumbler from the fizzy water tap. I asked for and received a double gin and tonic. I felt I needed it. "They wouldn't listen to you?" I asked.

The Professor shook his head. "Nothing ever changes at the top," he said sadly. "So what did you make of yourself?"

"I run a big bunch of switches. Loads of bandwidth. Nothing that's going to be hit by the event—at least, not directly. But still, I don't trust my bank account, I don't trust the tax system . . . there's too much brittleness. Everywhere I look. Maybe I've just been tracking risks for too long, and then again . . . "

"You made a down payment on this holiday three or four years ago, eh?"

I nodded.

"They wouldn't listen to me," he muttered. "I kept on for as long as was reasonable, even though they told me it was a career-limiting move—as if some little thing like tenure would stop them—until I was too tired to go on."

"I get to see a lot, out in the real world," I volunteered. "That standard lecture piece you did, on the old reactor control system—I've seen worse."

"Oh yes?" He showed a flicker of interest, so I continued.

"A big corporate accounting system. Used to run on a bundle of mainframes at six different national headquarters, talking via leased line. Want to hear about it?"

"Pray continue." I had his attention.

"They downsized everything they could, but there were about fifty million lines of PL/I on the accounts system. Nobody could be bothered to bring it up to date—it had taken about two hundred programmers twenty years to put it all together. Besides which, they were scared of the security implications of reverse-engineering the whole thing and sticking it on modern networked machines. In the end, they hit a compromise: there was this old VM/CMS emulator for DOS PCs floating around. They bought six stupidly powerful workstations running something a bit more modern. Stuck a DOS emulator on each workstation, and ran their accounting suite under the VM/CMS emulator under the DOS emulator—"

I waited while his spluttering subsided into a chuckle. "I think that deserves another drink: don't you?"

I took a big gulp from my G&T and nodded. "Yeah." More fizzy water for the Prof. "Anyway. These six, uh, *mainframes*, had to talk to each other at something ridiculous like 1200 baud. So the droids who implemented this piece of nonsense hired a hacker, who crufted them up something that looked like a 1200 baud serial line to the

VM/CMS emulator, but which actually tunneled packets over the internet, from one workstation to another. Only it ran under DOS, 'cause of the extra level of emulation. Then they figured they ought to let the data entry clerks log in through virtual terminals so they could hire teleworkers from India instead of paying guys in suits from Berkhampstead, so they wrote a tty driver just for the weird virtual punched-card reader or whatever the bloody accounting system thought it was working with."

Someone tapped me on my shoulder. I glanced round.

"Yo, dude! Gimme five!"

"Six," I said. Clive beamed at me. "Been here long?"

"Just arrived," he said. "I knew I'd find you propping up the bar. Hey, did the guys on the gangway give you any aggro?"

"Not much." I put my hand over my watch's face. The whole thing disturbed me more than I wanted to think about, and Rita's silent presence (reading a book in a deep leather-lined chair at the far side of the room) didn't contribute anything good to my peace of mind. "I was just telling the professor about—"

"The mainframes." The professor nodded. "Most interesting. Can I trouble you to tell me what happened in the end? I hate an interrupted tale."

I shrugged. "Drink for my man here," I said.

"Make mine a pint," said Clive.

"In a nutshell," said the professor.

"In a nutshell: they'd put it all in an emulator, and handled all the login sessions via the net, so some bright spark suggested they run six emulators in parallel on one box and use local domain sockets to emulate the serial lines. It looked like it would save about fifty thousand bucks, and they'd already spent a quarter million on the port—as opposed to eighty, ninety million for a proper re-write—so they did it. Put everything in one box."

"And what happened?" asked Clive.

"Well, they stuffed the old corporate accounting system into a single workstation. You've got to understand, it was about fifty times as powerful as all six mainframes put together. The old mainframes were laid off about two months after the emulator went live, to save on the maintenance bill. So they moved office six months after that, and they managed to lose the box in the process. The inventory tag just went missing; it was so unobtrusive it looked like every other high-end server in the place. By the time they found it again, some droid from the marketing department who though Christmas had come early had reformatted its root partition and installed Windows 98 on it. And they'd mislaid the backup tapes in the same move . . ."

"Man, that's bad," said Clive. He looked improperly cheerful.

"Yes." The professor looked worried. "That almost tops the reactor story." He drained his glass then absent-mindedly checked the dosimeter he kept clipped to the breast pocket of his sports jacket. "But not quite."

Unscheduled Criticality Excursion—(*jargon*) term used in the nuclear engineering industry to refer to the simultaneous catastrophic failure of all of a fission reactor's safety features, resulting in a runaway loss of coolant accident. (*Formerly*: **melt-down**.)

The ship set sail three hours later. I was already adrift, three sheets to the wind, and Clive steered me out on deck to watch the pier drift astern.

"Feel that breeze," he said, and leaned out over the railing until I worried about him falling overboard. (An accident, so early in the voyage, would be a bad way to start; there was plenty of time for such incidents ahead.) "It's cool. Onshore. Loads of salt. Iodine from decaying seaweed. Say, did you bring your iodine tablets? Sun block? Survival rations?"

"Only what I figured we'd definitely need," I said, slurring on my certainty. "Didn't know about Rita. Shit. Don't need that shit. Are you okay over there?"

"Don't be silly!"

And guess who'd seen fit to join us on deck? If it wasn't my ex. I was drunk enough to be a bit out of control and in control enough to feel vulnerable: not, in other words, at my best. "And whash you doing here?" I asked, leaning against the rail beside Clive.

"Coming to ask what you're doing here," she said. "You're a mess." There was no rancor in her voice; just a calm, maddening self-assurance, as if she thought she'd earned the right to know me better than I knew myself.

"Funny, I could have sworn he was an engineer," quipped Clive.

"You used the original ticket?" I asked.

Rita leaned up against the railing a couple of meters away from me. "I tried to exchange it," she said guardedly. "By then, the ship was over-booked."

"More fools," quipped Clive. He leaned even further overboard: "Cretins ahoy!" Rita's stare could have frozen molten lead, but Clive bore its weight unheeding.

"Let's talk," she said. I followed her around the curve of the deck, away from Clive. The sea was still, but even so I had difficulty keeping my balance as it gently rolled beneath my feet. She stopped in the shadow of a lifeboat. "You know what this means?" she asked.

More histrionics, I thought. "It means we both just have to be very careful," I said, emphasizing the final word.

Unexpectedly, she smiled at me. "Two years and you didn't change your ticket!" It was not a very pretty smile.

I shrugged. "So that makes me a fool?"

She looked at me sharply: "No more than ever, Marcus. See you later." She turned and stalked off in the direction of the door we'd come through. I looked towards the stern of the ship, a dark mass of shadows in the night: the breeze became slightly chilly if I stood in one place for long enough. I stood there for a long time.

> Risks of embarking on an expensive sea voyage booked too far in advance, number 12: *having to share a cramped cabin with a spouse who divorced you years ago.*

I went to bed drunk, and when I awoke the next morning the cabin was mine. I sat up. My neck ached as if I'd lain too long in the wrong position; my tongue tasted as if something small and furry had died on it far too long ago. The cabin was a mess. My trunk was stowed neatly beneath the lower bunk bed—but a familiar suitcase was open and strewn across the table, and she'd spread her toiletries across every available surface in the cramped bathroom.

I groaned, sat up, and hastily made for the toilet—the head, I remembered to call it. Today was The Eve of Destruction; December the 31st, to the real world at large, and we would be sailing south-east and out into the endless blue eye of the Gulf of Mexico. Theoretically I had booked a two week holiday from my job. As a matter of caution—I checked carefully in the bag full of dirty socks in my trunk before heading for breakfast—both small, extremely heavy bars of metal were still there. Five thousand euros each, they'd set me back: a whopping great hole in my savings, but if what we were expecting was the case, well worth it in the long run.

The dining lounge had seen better days; although this cruise ship called itself a liner, I had my suspicions. It reminded me of a run-down hotel, formerly a grand palace of the leisured classes, now reduced to eking out a living as a vendor of accommodation and conference space to corporate sales drones on quarterly kick-off briefings. I sat down at one of the tables and waited for one of the overworked stewards to come over and pour me a coffee.

"Mind if I join you?"

I looked up. It was a woman I'd met somewhere—some conference or other—lanky blonde hair, palid skin, and far too evangelical about formal methods. "Feel free." She pulled a chair out and sat down and the steward poured her a cup of coffee immediately. I noticed that even on a cruise ship she was dressed in a business suit, although it looked somewhat the worse for wear. "Coffee, please," I called after the retreating steward.

"We met in Darmstadt, `97," she said. "You're Marcus Jackman? I critiqued your paper on performance metrics for IEEE maintenance transactions."

The penny dropped. "Karla . . . Carrol?" I asked. She smiled. "Yes, I remember your review." I did indeed, and nearly burned my tongue on the coffee trying not to let slip precisely *how* I remembered it. I'm not fit to be rude until after at least the third cup of the morning. "Most interesting. What brings you here?"

"The usual risk contingency planning. I'm still in catastrophe estimation, but I couldn't get anyone at work to take this weekend seriously. So I figured, what the hell? That was about two weeks ago."

"Two weeks—" I stopped. "How did you wangle that?"

She sipped her coffee. A lock of hair dropped across it; she shoved it back absentmindedly. "There's always a certain roll-over in things like this," she said. "It just depends who you talk to . . . "

Show-off. Whoever had set up the booking system, whatever troll from the deep, dark, underside of the ACM SIG-RISK group, had known more than a little about queuing theory; I'd spent two months, on and off, trying to get Pauli aboard the lifeboat, while she'd just walked on board. "I thought there was a waiting list," I said.

"Even lists have holes." She stared coldly at the steam rising from her coffee cup. "And even institutional coffee tastes better than this rubbish. I say, *waiter!*"

"Why did you leave it so late, if you believe in the rollover melt-down?" I asked, wishing she'd just let the coffee quality issue die.

"Because it's not the meltdown I'm interested in," she said. "Ah, it's about this coffee. It's disgusting. Have you been letting the jug stand on a hot plate for too long? So a few legacy systems, big hierarchical database applications for the most part, wrap around and go nonlinear when the year increments from 99 to 00. A fair number of batch reconciliation jobs go down the spout at midnight, and never get up again. Yes, some fresh arabica will do nicely. Maybe even some big ones, like driver licensing systems or the Police national computer, or the odd merchant bank. But nothing bolted together in the past ten years will even break wind, so to speak. Excuse me, break *stride*. And real-time systems won't even notice it; they mostly run on millisecond timers and leave the nonsense about dates to external conversion routines, if they understand the concept of dates at all, thank you very much, like a Mars Rover running on mission elapsed time in seconds. Good, much better, thank you."

The harried waiter made a break for the other diners and I began to dig myself out of the hole in my chair I'd unconsciously tried to retreat into.

"It's just an artifact of the datum," she continued implacably, ignoring the coffee cut placed apologetically before her. "You might as well have picked on the UNIX millennium; it only runs for two to the thirty-one seconds from midnight on January first, nineteen-seventy, then some time thirty-eight years from now the clocks begin counting in negative numbers. Of course, not many systems run for nearly eighty years without maintenance, but there's been an alarming trend lately towards embedding UNIX in black-box applications it's totally unsuited for. Personally, I think twenty thirty-eight is a much more realistic Armageddon-type datum, for that and other reasons."

I cringed slightly. "What brings you here, then, if you don't think there's going to be a fairly major disaster?"

"Because this is a ship of fools," she said brightly. "I wanted to observe and see how you're managing under perceived stress. Not to mention that some people here have jobs to go back to. I'm thinking of collaborating on a paper with a sociologist from my local university on stress-related idiopathic delusional complexes in closed professional bodies. Chicken Little crying 'the sky is falling', when quite simply it can't fall yet because this is a premature software apocalypse."

I gritted my teeth and swallowed the last of my coffee. "You're very sure that this is a false alarm."

"But it can't be the real thing! It's too early—only the two thousandth anniversary of the birth of Our Lord Jesus Christ. Now the two thousandth anniversary of his Crucifixion is another matter, and the coincidence with the UNIX millennium is another sign. But what really clinches it is the timewave zero hypothesis advanced by Terrance McKenna, who proved that the Aztec cyclic history sequence actually comes to an end—a singularity—in the same time scale. If you think this is a survival trip, just wait for the next one in thirty-eight years time! The ability of humans to anticipate an apocalypse tends towards a maximum in line with the proximity of big dates in their numbering system; they unconsciously fail to plan for survival past the next one, so disaster ensues. Now in this age of computers I think the baseline has shifted from the millennium to the kiloyear—which as you know, is two to the tenth years, or one thousand and sixteen. And St John was quite obviously talking about access permission bits when he said that the number of the Beast was six, six, six. More coffee?"

I excused myself and made for the deck with all possible haste; I could tell it was going to be one of those days.

I didn't dare to venture back into the dining room for another hour, until I was sure Karla had finished browbeating the staff; I wandered the upper deck like a lost soul, staring out across the muddy green expanse of sea, towards the gently swaying line in the distance where green met grayish white. The weather was poor (rather worse than I had been led to expect) and my head still throbbed from the night before. Back in the ops room at the institute, Marek or one of the other admins would be sitting up with a dog-eared paperback and a stack of blank backup cartridges, waiting patiently for the autochanger to bleat for a new load to accommodate the terabytes of data spooling slowly down onto tape. If I was there I'd probably be doing a dervish whirl of emergency disaster recovery preparations, single-handedly preparing to hold back the deluge of user complaints due on the first day of the new year. But I wasn't there: all I could do was squint into the wind, face pinched in by impotent tension, and wish I was in another line of work.

When my face turned numb I went below, back to the gently rolling warmth of the dining room. Karla had evidently finished; Clive waved at me from a corner so I went and joined him. "How's the morning?" I asked.

He pulled a face. "As you'd expect. Some woman tried to chat me up but it turned out she was recruiting for some Church or other. I managed to get away in one piece, though. Are you on for this evening's festivities?"

I nodded. "What's everyone doing today, then?"

"There's a seminar session on disaster recovery techniques for large transaction-based systems in the forward lounge on C deck. Some old salt is giving a lecture on navigating by the stars in the bar before lunchtime, then the Professor is giving his account of the Sizewell 'B' disaster—the one he gave at the ACM bash in London this year. You were there, weren't you? Oh, and there's a bingo game somewhere or other, it's on the notice board on D deck."

"What are you going to do?" I asked.

Clive put his knife down with a clatter. "I'm going to read a book," he said. "The weather's crap and the sea's going to get rough according to the shipping forecast. Might as well hole up and relax a bit."

"There's a radio?"

"I bought mine along." He fished something out of his pocket; a tiny Sony multiband receiver, with an old-fashioned analog tuning dial. "Short-wave reception's okay."

"Read a book," I echoed. "Sounds like a good idea." I could already smell the boredom rising from the great and borderless sea outside our hull; a boredom born of nervy fright, knowledge of what countdown was now in progress in the real world. Karla, for all her objectionable manner and dubious hypotheses, had maybe had a point; humans set their historical clocks by the stars, and the beginning of a new millennium is no insignificant event. Even if the real fruitcakes think the show's coming thirty-eight years later . . .

> **Boredom:** Knowing that the end of the world is due to happen in less than eighty-one thousand seconds, but being unable to hurry it along, impede it, or even ignore it and do something else in the meantime.

I had brought along a book on formal design methodologies to break my head on for the voyage, but I didn't feel like reading it. When I returned to my cabin I found that Rita was still elsewhere. She'd brought along a huge mass of junk literature; disposable magazines, novels, a two-day-old newspaper. I read the leader columns in the paper, then the lifestyle section, then finally the job advertisements. They were recruiting lots of corporate drones, chief information officers: scope for a hollow laugh at someone else's expense. But I didn't feel like reading much, as my stomach was slightly weak from the constant swaybacked lurching of the deck, so I lay down on my bunk to catch the forty winks of the truly bored.

I dreamed that I was being interrogated by three sinister, shadowy men in dark suits who kept a bright light pointed at my eyes. They wanted to know why I had abandoned Rita and our two-year old daughter. They didn't seem to understand that we had never had a child, and that Rita had left me—not the other way around. They said I set a dangerous, risky example to society at large; that runaway fathers should be allowed to make off with the taxpayers money was not a message they were prepared to send. They were about to sentence me to—*something*—when I awakened with a panicky jolt. Rita was leaning over me.

"Are you alright?" she asked.

I tried to croak "I think so," but nothing very intelligible came out so I nodded instead.

"You looked as if you were having a bad dream."

"I was." I tried to sit up but she put a hand on my shoulder and pushed me down again. "Please . . . " I said.

"Lie down." I did as I was told. "Who were you with this morning at breakfast?" she asked.

"Some fruitcake, who thinks the apocalypse is due in thirty-eight years and we're all barking up the wrong tree. She sat down at the same table and started trying to convert me to baptism or whatever the hell she believes in."

"I see." She was quiet for a moment. "Well just don't bring her back to this cabin, you hear me? Don't you dare." She turned away abruptly, leaving me too dumbstruck to say anything as she stalked out of the cabin and yanked the door shut behind her. Maybe I was a fool to be here, but that didn't make Rita any less blind herself.

I wandered along to a late lunch—cold buffet only—then an afternoon seminar on trusted anonymous systems validation. I avoided the deck, which was subject to an intermittent cold rain. There was due to be a banquet in the evening; I headed back to my cabin, had a shower, then changed into the suit I'd bought along for the occasion.

The bar adjoining the main dining room was drawing a steady business as twilight cast its shadow across the ship; refugee computer professionals in various states of formal attire held ice-cube clinking tumblers of whiskey in tense conversational huddles, while spousal units watched disinterestedly or discussed the foul weather. I saw Karla Carrol, wearing a long green dress and too much makeup, and shrank into the `L'-shaped recess at the opposite end of the bar, where two hunchbacked mainframe administrators were trying to top one-another's dumb user stories. Karla seemed to have snagged an unfortunate woman who was something big in actuarial systems, and was talking into her ear. I ordered a double vodka and coke, and then another before the steward ushered us into the dining room.

To my surprise, I found myself seated next to Rita. She seemed to be enjoying herself as long as she paid no attention to me; as I hadn't seen her *that* happy since a year before we split up, I was quite content to maintain my reserve. Besides, the food was substantially filling and my glass never seemed to empty, until I leaned back in a bloated semi-stupor to listen to the Prof give his keynote speech (after some nonentity from the organizing committee, introduced to the limbo of my memory by one of the ship's officers.)

The Professor staggered slightly as he took the podium. "Friends, I am pleased to be here to speak to you tonight, but less pleased at the necessity for this voyage." He paused for a moment and fiddled with the microphone. I was surprised by how little he had changed from my perspective, even given an extra ten years of age on my own account. He was still impressive.

"Software allows us to build huge, invisible machines—virtual mountains so complex that nobody can really understand the whole scope of a large application. But software is brittle: change an underlying constraint, and the whole edifice crumbles like a mountain hit by an earthquake. A single fundamental assumption that changes—as simple as the shift from one century to the next at the junction between two millennia—can break just about anything, anywhere, in the guts of such a system, and it could take seconds or months for the damage to surface. Back in the mid-nineties there were an estimated two hundred and fifty billion lines of vulnerable source code, waiting for the new century to rattle the ground from under them; at twenty thousand lines of code per programmer per year that would have taken a million programmers a year to fix . . . so everybody pretended it wasn't there. Except us. Everyone here tonight has had some role in attempting to cure the crisis of complacency. Everyone here has been burned by the fire of bureaucratic inertia. And so it is that everyone here chose of their own free will to join this ship of fools on a voyage whose motto might be, 'I told you so!'"

He covered his mouth and hiccuped as discreetly as one may in front of an audience of two hundred. I glanced sideways at Rita; her face was a carefully controlled mask for boredom.

"In about an hour, it will be midnight back in England. It is already five o'clock in the morning of January first, year two thousand, somewhere far to the east of here. The datum is sweeping remorselessly round the dark side of the world, leaving random malfunctions in its wake. Some of those malfunctions are doubtless trivial; bugs in systems long since retired. Others are naggingly pernicious but relatively harmless matters, such as the school districts that fall victim to collation routines that tell them everyone above the age of one hundred and three needs to be enrolled in a nursery class. But one or two . . . " he stopped, and for a moment seemed bowed down by a terrible weight: "might be serious. As serious, perhaps, as the Sizewell disaster."

I didn't want to pursue that line of logic, and neither (apparently) did the Prof. What happened at Sizewell happened because nobody understood the entire system, and nobody subjected it to formal proof: nor did they look into some of the more obscure race conditions that could arise if different subsystems found themselves marching to the beat of a different clock. The results—of which the least were the suicides jumping from the Lloyds building—had proven a ghastly point: but one that the politicians did not understand. Or at least, not profoundly enough to budget for the consequences.

"I should like to stress that this holocaust of our own making is nothing less than a matter of complacency," the Professor continued. "Once we quantized time, we tied our work to the clock; and now that the work is automated, so is the ticking. We are a short-sighted species. That there was a quarter of a trillion lines of bad software out there seven years ago is no surprise. That such a quantity has been halved to date is good news, but not quite adequate. We have, in a very real way, invented our own end of history: a software apocalypse that in the day ahead will engulf banks, businesses, government agencies, and anyone who runs a large, monolithic, database that is more than perhaps ten years old. Let us hope for the future that the consequences are not too serious—and that the lesson will be learned for good by those who for so long have ignored us."

Polite applause, then louder: a groundswell of clapping as the ship gently pushed its way through the waves.

I began to push my chair back; it was close and hot, and I felt slightly queasy. A hand descended on my wrist: "Remember what I said earlier," hissed Rita.

"What are you—" I saw her expression. Being the object of such ferocity made me feel as if we had not gone our separate ways. (And what if, in the weeks of confusion after the Sizewell incident—ten miles from the hotel I had been staying in while doing my contract work—I had not visited the vasectomy clinic? What if my morbid fear over fission products, that had in turn caused our own atomic split, never quite reached such a pitch? Would we still be together, a nuclear family with glow-in-the-dark children?) "What do you care? I'm no use to you, am I?"

Her expression was unreadable as she let go of my arm. "What use

155

is *any* of this? We're sailing on the Titanic, only the disaster starts when we go back to harbor. Don't spoil my cruise for me, Marcus, or you'll be sorry. I'll throw all your luggage overboard."

I nearly laughed, but instead I stood up and staggered slightly as I headed back to the bar. How like Rita; the paranoid over-reaction, fear of shadows, utilitarian approach to people around her . . . I began to wonder how much I hated myself to have put up with her for so long, and not to have found anyone better.

I was into my second gin and tonic when Clive appeared. "Been in a car wreck?" he asked sympathetically.

"Rita," I said morosely.

"Oh." He was quiet for a minute. I heard faint applause from the dining room. The steward at the bar turned his back to us and polished the brass.

"Try one of these," he suggested, offering something that looked a bit like a handmade lump of chocolate. "It's the only way to see in such a fuck-up; totally stoned, drunk as a skunk, and happy with it."

I palmed the sticky lump and swallowed. There was a sweet, herbal taste under the chocolate that nearly made me gag. Not my favorite way to take the stuff, but better than nothing. (And Rita didn't approve, even of something as mild as marihuana: which somehow made it more daring, more essential . . .)

"Any more?" I asked, but he shook his head.

"Strong stuff. Got to have enough to go round," he added with a curious smile. I could see he'd been at it himself, then. "Settles the stomach, too."

I drained my glass, winced slightly, then walked over to the bar for a refill. The barman didn't bother with an optic, just poured in the gin and topped it off by eye. "Will that be all, sir?" he asked.

"I'd like one for my friend," I said. Another glass appeared as if by magic. All drinks were on the house, this night if no other. "Thanks." I returned to the table, where Clive was tapping his fingers idly.

"Let's go on deck," he suggested. I tried to dissuade him but he was adamant. "It's fresh up there but the rain stopped and the cloud's clearing. Let's chill out, okay?"

"If you must," I said. He stood up and lurched slightly as he headed for the door. I followed him, expecting a chill of damp air to rush in. Instead, I found that he was right; the overcast had lifted and stars twinkled high in a deep black vault. There was a slow breeze blowing from ahead, and it was no cooler now than it had been during the day.

"What do you expect to find when you go back?" asked Clive.

"Everything. Nothing." In the distance, a monstrously deep horn sounded a bass note; ships passing in the night, I supposed. "I can't quite bring myself to believe in the apocalypse. End of civilization as we know it. Construction of cyberspace, the usual nonsense; it's bollocks. We'll go back and find lots of database programs have fallen over and there've been some really major cock-ups, maybe even a local stock exchange or two, but life goes on."

"That's one view," Clive said morosely.

"What do you expect?"

"The end of the world." He leaned out across the railing, staring into the dark water beyond and below us. "Nobody expects things to continue, not really. Everybody wants a day of judgment, right? An end to the mortal coil. Pot of gold at the end of the information super-highway." Another, even deeper, horn sounded in the distance. "We've designed for obsolescence for so long that it wouldn't surprise me if the whole pack of cards tumbles down. A bit like the fundies, who believe that it doesn't matter how we run the world because they're all going a-flying up to heaven in a couple of years anyway. The rapture, they call it. Every city in the west is maybe twenty four hours away from chaos and civil war—that's all the supplies they store locally, you know that? All it takes is enough cracks in the fabric . . . "

I wanted to tell him he was sounding like an old-fashioned fundamentalist preacher himself, but the words caught in my throat: at that moment an almost palpable wave of cold washed over me, as if the air around me had turned to seawater. A great distant moaning wail of a horn shuddered out beneath the moonless sky, so deep and loud that I felt my stomach relax and contract with its passage; a chilly sweat prickled across my forehead for a moment, and I felt brushed by the ghostly fingertips of drowned sailors.

"What's that?" I demanded.

"Tanker, probably," said Clive. "Really close, too—"

A smell like smoldering insulation made my nostrils twitch: "*Too close!*" We were near the front of the ship, on the right hand side: I wondered if we should head for the back, or if someone on the bridge would be able to see whatever we were bearing down on. Burning insulation and a rancid undertone of sulfur, of reeking burnt meat, of something revolting and sweet at the same time; a dim red light loomed on the horizon. The ship rolled beneath my feet and I felt light-headed.

"Look, over there." I followed Clive's outstretched arm. "What's happening?"

Whatever it was, it bulked out of the darkness like a congealing fog bank, lit from within by a red glow. That dreadful horn sounded again, rattling my innards, and there was a faint echo from behind—as if its distant partner sounded a desolate mating chorus from across the empty sea. Stars burned like halogen lights in the vast darkness overhead. One by one they began to fall, tracing bright lines across the sky until they faded out in the distance. I looked towards the rear of the ship, back the way we'd come; a false dawn bulked green on the horizon. "I don't like this," I said, clutching the railing with fingertips that felt like dry bones. "I'm too stoned."

"I'm not." Clive looked distracted, as if he was listening to something. "What . . . did you ever wonder, what it would be like if the god botherers were really right all along? If maybe their revelation was the truth, and it was all going to happen—only they'd been out by a couple of thousand years?"

"Can't happen." My teeth were chattering. "No rapture. No singularity. It's just the way we think. We humans, we want to lose our problems in some future end of all worries. Natural tendency."

"Overruns," Clive muttered. "Schedule slippage. They got all geared up at the turn of the first millennium, then the apocalypse was canceled. Now they've got it all over again. What if they held the end of the world but nobody came?"

Something dark bubbled up from the sea behind us. A deep bass rumble, like a cross between an earthquake and a sousaphone: the angular mass foamed the sea around, gathering shrapnel and wreckage together into the dark shape of an ancient submarine. Hakenkreutz half-rusted into the shadowy conning-tower, it ghosted through the waves towards the glow on the horizon, its charred and skeletal crew staring incuriously at us as it cruised past. Red and green afterimages rippled across the sea, across everything I looked at except the dial of my borrowed watch.

I shuddered in the grip of a dread so intense that my heart lurched towards pure panic. "Don't!" Clive began to walk forwards, along the curve of the deck towards the front of the ship—"Where are you going?"

"What if they held the end of the world, but we were all aboard the ship of fools and unbelievers?" he called over his shoulder. "I'm joining them!"

A seventh rumbling note cut through the night, so deep that I could barely hear it but only felt it in my bones. I turned and staggered back towards the door, back towards the warmth and safety of the bar and the dining room. Behind me, Clive called: "Don't leave me behind!"

The door slammed behind me. I looked around; the bartender glanced up from polishing the bar and raised an eyebrow.

"Give me a drink," I gasped. "Something strong."

"Bad night?" he asked casually. "You look like you've seen a ghost."

I shuddered convulsively and took the tumbler, threw it at the back of my throat. "In a manner of speaking."

"Happens," he said, matter-of-factly. "Lots of funny things happen at sea. I could tell you some tales, I could."

"Please don't. I've had enough of them for one night."

He looked away as I drained my glass.

"This isn't a good cruise," I said, trying to communicate. "You know what? You know why we booked it?"

"Why did you book the cruise?"

He studied me with the professional eye of an experienced barman.

"There's something we're running away from. But I'm not sure it's the right thing."

"Then, if you'll pardon my French sir, wasn't it a bit stupid of you to come along for the ride?"

I headed for the inner corridor, meaning to check the roll of dirty socks in my luggage. "I'm not really sure . . . "

"So it came about that multitudes of people acted out with fierce energy a shared phantasy which, though delusional, yet brought them such intense emotional relief that they could live only through it, and were perfectly willing both to kill and to die for it. This phenomenon was to recur many times, in various parts of western and Central Europe . . . "

—*The Pursuit of the Millennium*, Norman Cohn

Over the horizon, without any fuss, the mainframes were quietly going down.

Dechlorinating the Moderator

A perspective on Particulate 7: HiNRG & B-OND

Venue: Maastricht Hilton Travelodge International Hotel, 30 March—2 April 2018

Yr hmbl crrspndnt rprts:

This was the seventh and biggest Particulate. It's fair to say that these cons have come of age; with about seven hundred guests and maybe three-hundred walk-ins on the door there's no longer any question that the concom can make ends meet. Indeed they're already hard at work scoping out a venue for Particulate #8.

I checked in on Friday morning to find that about a hundred die-hard geeks had hit the con the night before, and the registration desk's bookings system was toast. The hotel has hosted the last two Particulates, and they knew what to expect; as I arrived two bemused porters were helping a spotty youth hump weird-shaped bits of gear crusted in radiation trefoils into the baggage elevator. Everyone had to pass a check at a discreet security booth by the door, to prevent any recurrence of the regrettable incident that nearly wrecked last year's con.

The first thing I noticed in reception was a big whiteboard beside the main elevators. Various messages were scribbled on it, but right in the middle, written in big blue letters, was a notice:

DON'T TRY CRITICALITY EXPERIMENTS IN YOUR BEDROOM UNLESS YOU WANT TO TEST THE SPRINKLERS.

I started by checking out the café, which was blue with dope fumes by the time I arrived and which got steadily worse until the end of the con (when the Brensstrahlung Regressives tried to use it as a cloud chamber). The usual suspects were there, sipping cappuccino and smoking like there was no tomorrow. And lo, who should I run into at the bar but my old acquaintance, Doktor Strangelove?

I first met the Dok back at Criticality II (though I'd run across him before on the net). That was back when his home town (Buttfahrk, Ontario) was trying to prosecute him for attempting to assemble a fissile device within city limits—of which charge, incidentally, he was found not guilty—and it struck me as unusually harsh that a local prosecutor was calling for a twenty-four year sentence on a guy who was still, basically, a kid. Since then the Dok has done some growing up, and I can safely say that if he wasn't a menace to society then, he certainly is now. Or he'd like us to think he was.

Dok: Hiya Betsy, howzit going?

Me: Oh, I dunno. Just got here, dumped my bags, thought I'd take a sniff of the breeze.

Dok: Huh-huh-huh.

Me: Anything cool going?

Dok: [pushes glasses up bridge of nose, fidgets with head-up projector on left spectacle frame]:

Me: I guess it depends what splices your code. The Fabulous Rubensteins say they're gonna do something weird tomorrow lunchtime during the birds-of-a-feather on fusion experiments, and like Sunday morning word is that Pion Overdrive are building a long column down the banquet hall and co-opting some heavy control bandwidth. Should be fireworks, maybe some stray neutron soup boiling off of that if they kick it into the fifty TeV range. And there's some dude from CERN knocking around to give a talk on law'n'order and basement nucleonics. He's kind of weird, but I don't think he's Stasi.

Me: What's with the fusion gig?

Dok: [raises eyebrow suspiciously]:
          Mean you haven't heard?

Me: [Hastily]:
          Well, there've been rumors about a breakthrough in self-criticalizing muon-catalysis reactions …

Dok: [playing hard to get]:
          That remains to be seen. Buy me a drink?

Me: I thought you were …

Dok: Minimum drinking age is 21 here.

Me: Okay.

That's the way it is. The nerds are on parade. They've always been sensitive about the way outsiders see them. First it was SF fans. Then computer hackers and phone phreaks. These days it's extropians, roboticists, and hard physics geeks. But the character type is the same: very bright, highly strung, defensive about their hobby, competitive within their field. They realize it's not something the rest of society understands or cares much about, but THEY care and that's what makes the difference.

I staggered out of the café with my lungs on fire and my eyes streaming and headed for the swimming pool. The swimming pool is a really good place to hang out at a Particulate gig, but it's not worth bringing your swimsuit: it's where the re-enactment crowd get together. A bunch of kids in sarongs and TELLER IS GOD t-shirts were pouring ion-exchange beads into the pool and there was a suspicious-looking bunch of metal piping already sitting in racks on the bottom. The pool looked very blue. When I asked what they were doing they stared at me as if I was crazy: "dechlorinating the moderator," one of them finally deigned to say. I nodded and backed out fast; I could see I wasn't wanted.

Opening speech. Some middle-aged American guy in a three-piece suit, probably ex-Wall Street rocket scientist, told the assembled geekswarm that they were the future of mankind. He said it in a voice choking with deep emotion. Physicists always did their best work by thirty, and this guy talked about his own career on the SSC project out in Texas, before the Death of Big Physics in the mid-nineties. The audience were hushed, as if chastened by the idea of being deprived of their accelerators by fiat.

Next on was a gangling youth named Curtis in baggy shorts, baseball cap, and iguana. (It was green, about half a meter long, and sat placidly on his shoulder throughout the talk.) Curtis talked very fast indeed about the fractal dimensionality of the universe as measured using the Genocide Mechanics' new beat-wave petatron and some really eldritch decay paths they scoped out in a quark-gluon plasma when they cranked it up high enough to fuse the power supply. "I tell ya, at first I thought it was the drugs, man, but then I realized it was the bats. The vampire bats from beyond spacetime." He was talking about a fractal map they derived for a scalar field decay process; and it did look sort of like a bat, if you squinted at it by the light of a lava lamp after smoking too much dope.

Curtis got a standing ovation (whether for the delivery or the message), and the iguana made a mess down the back of his t-shirt. He didn't seem to mind.

Everyone then pissed off to the café or the bar, leaving a rather sad-looking Englishman to talk about cross-section derivatives in sub-critical masses of plutonium to a nearly-empty auditorium.

I don't remember much about that evening, except that I woke up at ten the next morning with a splitting hang-over and three teenagers crashed out in the bathroom suite. Breakfast was black coffee and codeine, washed down with runny scrambled eggs a la hotel. Back to the program:

A talk about positronium, the care and feeding thereof, and how to bottle it for storage. One of the problems modern particle physicists face—besides the lack of funding—is that they don't have huge relativistic storage rings any more. The maximum energies the big old synchrotrons could get up to were pretty puny by current standards, but the one thing they were good at was acting as a relativistic reservoir. Stick a bunch of particles with a half life of a billionth of a second into a storage ring at close enough to the speed of light and they'll hang around for long enough to measure. But modern accelerators are all linear, and nobody can afford the big metal power bills. The panel discussed various condensation traps and magnetic bottle topologies (including a really weird five-dimensional Klein bottle) but didn't really resolve the issue.

Lunchtime: the Fabulous Rubensteins (who looked more like Shyster, Shyster and Flywheel) presented their pion-catalysed criticality experiment. It was the size of a truck fuel cell, and pumped out four watts of power less than it took to run—but they said it had sucked in thirty watts two weeks earlier, and could theoretically achieve fusion bootstrap and run hot with a bit more tuning. More intrusions from the world of high finance: they cited some algorithms patented by Barclays de Zoet Webb and Whole Earth Systems in their control rig, and a couple of suits from Exxon were seen lurking at the back of the lecture hall.

Then there was the talk on modeling systems for predicting particle state decay options. A lot of the weird shit the hard physics dudes get up to these days drops back to ground state via some really strange non-deterministic transition states. Zap some of them with enough energy along the way and you get even weirder, less probable, transitions. Financial modeling protocols evaluate particle decay chains in terms of "bid" and "offer" prices on their probability, and give really neat derivatives for that big discovery-killing. (No wonder the guys who wrote that software did well on Wall Street before the Softlanding.)

There was a cool cocktail party that night by the pool side, ghostly blue illumination courtesy of Cerenkov radiation from the slow neutrons in the pond. I was surrounded by crazed physics geeks and geekettes, stoned on the most bizarre mixtures of smart drugs and neurotransmitter analogues imaginable: the introspection mixes actually slowed them down enough for a mere mortal to talk to them and get something interesting back. It was really good. For a while I actually felt as if I understood the Pauli exclusion principle—not as a law handed down from on high, but from the inside out. It didn't last, though. I went to bed, and the next morning the equations were as dry and cracked as the surface of my tongue.

Sunday morning I skipped breakfast. The Pion Overdrive Grrrls were bolting their petatron together in the banquet hall and I did not feel like receiving an intimate lesson in scattering effects if they got enthusiastic about testing it before the demo. It looked impressive—all of ten meters long.

A seminar entitled: "Embedded Universes 101," discussing the possibility of creating Linde-Mezhlumian fractally-embedded self-reproducing universes—in effect, mini-big-bangs contained within pocket black holes—which rapidly deteriorated into quasi-religious ranting when someone in the audience asked a remarkably convoluted question about the practicality of "implementing the preconditions for a Barrow-Tipler strong anthropic cosmology" within the toy universes.

Some time during that last talk my brain underwent a loss of coolant accident and melted down. I confess: I'm not a true geek. The theological significance of the Higgs scalar field leaves me cold. I don't really understand how to create a pocket universe, or what it means. I'm just repeating what I heard there. These dudes are beyond it. Way beyond it. Whatever it is.

I wandered back into the banquet hall to see the grrrls demonstrate top quark decay characteristics. It went smoothly and for an encore they manufactured some W's and a handful of Higgs bosons. Then one of their laser stages failed and they shut the rig down. I got chatting to one of them afterwards and it turned out they were using home-brewed chirped-pulse amplifiers bolted straight in front of simple high-gigahertz network driver diodes—lasers produced by the million for wavelength multiplexed networks like your cable video system.

I kid you not. Thirty years ago it cost ten billion dollars and a machine thirty kilometers in diameter. Today a bunch of teenagers spend maybe a couple of thousand dollars, build a Rube Goldberg contraption three meters long, and achieve a hundred times the peak energy.

And this is what a Particulate is about. Fast, cheap, and out of control. That law, Moore's Law, used to be just computers. But computers peaked, and now they're stitched into the collar of your shirt to tell the washing machine how much detergent it takes. Next it was biotechnology, but after the cancer fix and the old age hack all the really hot biogeeks went underground—or became merchant bankers. That left physics. The old physicists hit Wall Street, leaving the field clear for the old-time hackers and phreaks.

Raw enthusiasm and left-recursive universe generators. But they still get carded at the bar and they still can't blow up the world. Physics may have a bad rap these days, but it's harmless enough: a fine subject for kids to get enthusiastic about.

I never did find out what happened to the Vampire Bats from Beyond Spacetime, though.

Yellow Snow

This is the oldest story in this collection—written in 1990 and published later that year. That was around the time cyberpunk stopped being cool and started being funny, but my analyst tells me I've made a full recovery.

Sometimes you have to make speed, not haste. I made twenty kilos and moved it fast. Good old dex is an easy synthesis but the polizei had all the organochemical suppliers bugged; when a speed stash hit the street without any *blat* they'd be through the audit trail like shit through a cholera case. They'd take a cut: my lungs, heart and ribosomes. Only idiots push psychoactives in Paraguay: only idiots or the truly desperate. I burned out via Brasilia and crashed into Ant City. Jet-lagged all the way across Australia, I considered my futures; it was time to move on to something bigger.

My first impression of Ant City was of being roasted, slowly. The blistering humidity was outflow from the huge heat exchangers run by the city reactors. Palm trees in the airport lounge, a rude, chattering spidermonkey loose among the branches. No power, no Ants, a simple equation: I was in Antarctica now, and wondering what the hell to do about it. It was another world out there: I could feel a grating closeness between my shoulder blades, the crush of humanity around me.

Alleyways of light lured me through the customs interface, briefing me on local lores. Digital fingers rifled my flesh with radiation but I was clean and mean—nobody with any sense takes bugs into the ant farm. It's a ticket to re-direction, and I need my inputs remolding like I need a conscience. My scams are all cortex-ridden, locked in by mnemonics until I'm ready to bring them out like a card sharp. Sleight of memory. The security goon smiled sweetly, her eyes asking me if I was really alive, and waved me past the desk.

The shuttleport is half a klick above Ant City proper; I took the lift down. It was a medium sized lift, with only a medium-sized shopping mall. Shop, shop, expend, expend. A glaring incitement to—

I shut my eyes and as I was trying to pin down a plan a kid tried to lift the chips from out of my skull. Which was his bad luck: I didn't have any. I opened my eyes and shifted my grip on his wrists so he had to face me.

"Nice way to greet tourists," I said. He squirmed fearfully, muscles like metallic glass beneath his warm brown skin. "You know what I should do with you?" He looked as if he didn't, and wasn't interested in finding out either. He'd forgotten to feed the cat or something else important. I looked at the inside of his wrist; the node was there.

"You eat shit," he said. I glared back at him.

"Yeah, every day just like you. I should bust your fingers. You want to tell me why not?"

"No," said the kid, looking like trouble warmed over the next morning; "you break my fingers then my friend come and break yours." He managed to ignore me and look contemptuous concurrently. He couldn't have been topside of twelve years without maturity-mods. Neomacho, cued-up by background video. For the first time I looked at his tribals. He wore a one piece suit, ice camouflage militia-surplus. His wrist node was well-worn. Classic case of heroin from six years, riding the horse out from under the shadow of future shock; it's the kids who suffer most, these days.

"That would be kind of a bad idea," I said, "for your friend. I got no chips. My wallet's armed; tell your sister to put it back before she gets gluey fingers. You want me to give you some money?"

"You what?" said the kid. I felt butterfly fingers slip something that buzzed into my pocket; it stopped buzzing when it sniffed me again. I'm touchy about where my wallet goes without me.

"I repeat myself," I said; "do you want to earn some money?" I leaned forward. More suspicion.

"You want I should go to bed with you?"

"No. I want some names, nothing else. Like who shifts your stuff."

His face cleared, magically. "You want some?" he asked, happily. "I sell you—"

"No," I said, "I just want a name."

"Oh." He looked disappointed. Then, "Are you polizei?"

I weighed my chances. "Would you believe if I said no?"

"No." His eyes narrowed.

"Then get lost." I gave him a push and he went. His sister had vanished into an open shopfront selling gauzy somethings under spotlights; for the moment at least they were zero factors in my equation. I stood alone for a while, wondering what I looked like to the local talent and whether I needed a new line; some nagging doubt kept telling me that I was getting too old for this game. Trying to quell my worry I crossed to the observation deck and looked out.

The mall was descending towards a park with a lake around it, and a landscaped garden at one end of the lake. Ant City floated like a submarine in an inclusion of melt-water beneath the ice cap. Kept from freezing by the tokamaks, the water acted as a buffer against icequakes; also as central heating. The lift was just now dropping out of the roof of the city, and the view was dizzying; the city curved with the horizon. Suddenly I had a sense of immanence, of seeing a new frontier opening up before me even though the underground was actually closing in for real, like the dizzying megatons of ice overhead: it was shaping up to be a classic revelation. The kind of sensation you get when a new idea is coming up hot and hard. I took stock of my situation—

So consider me: male, self-contained, intelligent, age twenty-seven. The product of an expensive corporate shockwave education, designed to surf over new developments on the cutting edge of R&D. I'd freebased from my corporate owners: only time and independence had cost me my flexibility. I had bank accounts in Liechtenstein and

Forties Field, no commitments, but I was unable to access the big company AI's, my knowledge was going rusty in the face of informational explosion; I was staring career burnout in the face at thirty. I had pushed every synthetic narcotic I could make, but only in small-to-medium scale production: I had always managed to skip out before the blowback. Hit and run. I didn't use them myself, but supplied a demand; I made people happy for a living. What could be better than that? I liked to consider myself to be a moral anarchist, Kropotkins' heir. Only where was I going to go next?

I found a phone and used it to find a list of rented accommodation; I chose a flat, furnished, four rooms, monthly payments, good view of the park. If I hadn't been speeding a week ago it would have cost an arm and a leg, or at least a kidney. Now all I had to do was make the right contact; and that, for someone of my background, was easy.

We met in a café on the edge of a drained swimming pool, where the penguins jostled excitedly for scraps from the tables. She looked nervous, which was to be expected. I was, too. I didn't even know how much she wanted for the job! Just that she was as desperate as I was.

"What you're looking for—" she said: "it's dangerous, you know? The temporal annealing processes aren't really mapped out very well, and the moles are kinda touchy about nosing it about. I mean, this is military surplus, right?" She dragged on the hookah nervously, watching the surveillance cameras for blind-spots. Concentrating on the long-lost lover bullshit for the digital polizei, I smiled tenderly before I replied.

"Look," I said, "this is SDI spin-off material, right? After the third world war came out biological all the Pentagon defense contracts lapsed, leaving you with a heap of junk and no budget, right? So why not use it to make some quick cash? Face it, you're damn near starving. Now *I*—" I leaned back in my chair—"I'm a potential customer. With *currency*. The PERV was designed to let them know when to zap missiles before they torched off, and the Interactive Reality Transformer was built to open a hole in spacetime. So why *can't* you turn them into a time machine for me? I'm willing to pay! And I mean to say, if the old Unistat government trusted that rig with their lives, what can go wrong with it now?"

She coughed. "Lots," she said drily. "Just look what happened to *them*. You're forgetting that this stuff was never used: only tested in simulation. Nobody ever did get round to firing smart rocks through a time window, did that escape your attention? This is highly, uh, dangerous."

I sighed. "Look," I said, "for the final time, that's your specialty. Not mine! I mean, I *like* the idea of supporting higher education, I really do, but I can't afford to throw money away without any come-back on the investment, right? But if you and your university department do this for me, I'll see about, uh, endowing a Chair in perpetuity, maybe?"

"The College authorities might be doubtful about naming a chair after a semi-legal drug dealer," she said dubiously. It was the first sign of her fall from grace; so she *was* desperate! I pushed on.

"Yeah," I said, "but you can call it whatever you want. I paid for your flight here, didn't I? When was the last time your government gave you any money for anything? Look, just do this for me and I'll make an endowment you won't forget."

"Um, right," she said, almost smacking her lips. Then she made her decision; the right one. "Okay. Fly up to Oxford in the first week of next month. I'll have one of our postdocs meet you in; we should be ready to test by then." A faint cloud crossed her face. "You've no idea how bad things have got up there," she added softly; "You were a good student, on that exchange program. Try not to get shot before we're ready, right?"

"Sure, professor," I said, waving for the waiter. "That's, like, one of my life's ambitions."

She unwound a bit. "What's the other?"

I grinned widely. "To fuck Ronald Reagan."

While I was waiting for the call from the Hawking Institute I crashed out in front of the video, reading graphic novels and scanning reruns of twentieth century docudramas. The condenser burbled in the makeshift fume cupboard I'd built in the bathroom and the gene-spinners clicked intermittently as I soaked up Ronald Reagan, Margaret Thatcher, Leonid Brezhnev. Creatures of another era, when the universe was just about beginning to fill up and society was teetering on the edge of a baroque tomorrow; fascinating cut-outs in a past that was truly another country. Twenty years earlier still everything was so *naive*, so pre-technological; but the timezone I'd picked was already on the brink of today, unsophisticated bug-ridden systems powering up for the remorseless march into a post-modernist present. People were waking up to changes, beginning to notice the end of industrialism. Yeah, I figured I could hack it; gather protective coloration, not look too out of place, but be so far ahead of the pack that I could hit them with a dose of double-barreled futurism and make my getaway clean-heeled and rich enough to retire . . .

"*Just say NO,*" I mimicked, and threw an empty beer can at the screen. *Good jokes are made of this*, I thought. Then the phone coughed.

"Yeah?" I asked.

"It's for you," it said, extending the handset. I took it and listened. "Twenty mil? That's steep . . . okay, yeah, so it's never been done before . . . *how* much? Oh, right. I'll figure a way . . . day after tomorrow? Fine. See ya." The phone grabbed its handset back and wiped it fastidiously. I tried to stare it down, but it didn't seem to notice. In my experience when domestic appliances get uppity the only answer is to shoot them; but I didn't have a gun on me so I leaned back and thought irritably about the good professor's news instead.

The weight restriction on the time jump was going to be tight. It worked out at ten kilograms, plus my good self. That's not much, is it? Clothing, a portable kit, some raw materials—not much. Compute-power's no problem; you can only cram so many mainframes into a false tooth, but back where I was going even one of them was going to give me an unfair edge. The real problem was going to be currency for investment. I frowned. Credit? Did they have credit in those days? Or did they have to carry metal coins around? What could I use instead?

Ah. *Good idea.* Why not do it right now? I sat up and grinned wildly, then staggered through to the bathroom. My gene-machine was sitting on the floor, humming to itself. I bent down and plugged myself in, figuring out the ideal stash. Something they'd *never* check for; something better than money, a dirt cheap commodity to vector on the market. Like the goose that laid the golden eggs, I was going to make a one-man heroin fortune in the eighties! I was going to be so successful the market price was going to bomb! Yes, I'd seen the pot of gold at the end of the rainbow. The pot of yellow snow—

Yellow snow is a handle for a kind of cheap dealer shit; nobody falls for it these days. All it takes is a gene-machine and the nerve to use it on yourself. You engineer a retrovirus that makes a minor alteration to your enkephalin receptor's tertiary structure, thus changing it's substrate affinity; then you engineer another that adds a small peptide tag to the stuff your own receptors get off on, so that they match. Customize your pain/pleasure complex, right? That leaves you free to use *another* virus, one that makes some of your peripheral tissue—pancreas, say—go into endorphin overdrive, pumping out the real McCoy in such volume that you literally piss heroin analogs away whenever you go to the toilet. Now—this is the cool bit—you add some acetic acid to neutralize all that ammonia and urea, then you partition it out in organic solvents and dissolve it in a sugar solution and re-crystalise. You get natural heroin in your kitchen sink! Indistinguishable from gold triangle authentic, except that it's better. Only trouble is, there's a certain stigma attached to its source, hence the handle *yellow snow*; nobody wants to be pissed on by their dealer, hey? Anyway, these days customs computers don't look out for hidden stashes; they're on the scan for designer genes. So any time after the naughty nineties yellow snow would be a non-starter. But where/when I was going . . .

"*Just say no,*" I mimicked. Then I slurped another beer can. "I'm gonna piss on you, all, junkies!" Good joke for an anarchist businessman, teetering on the edge of burnout, to ride the elevator back to where it all began. I wondered why nobody had done this before; it seemed so cool!

Maybe I was going to find out.

I hitched a Zeppelin ride for Ancient Britannia to give me time to assemble my time-travel survival kit; also time to take it slow and easy and get my head screwed on in preparation for the jump. I locked myself in my first-class stateroom and ignored the long, stately cruise across icy wastes and the ocean gulf to the Cape of Good Hope. The passengers were socializing frenetically, holding balls and orgies in the gas-cell auditoria; I didn't need it right then. . . . ave people rammed down my throat, *en masse*: I need to retreat into my personal space, to maintain a distance between myself and the burning wilderness of raw nerve endings that constitutes a global culture for ten billion naked apes.

As we crossed the Azanian coast I went on a shopping spree. The latest databases from Grolier; a repo'd personal dialysis machine from Squibb; a very compact mainframe from Bull-Siemens. Everything to be collected when I got where I was going. In a mail order feeding-frenzy I ordered anything I thought I could use that weighed less than fifty grams; then I crashed out for a relaxed sybaritic binge, dragging on designer silks for a bar-crawl around the kilometer-long airship. There was a lot of entertainment to be had, watching the desperate writhings of the jet-stream set on their slow intercontinental cruises through the new millennium; being rich beyond belief they traveled as slowly as possible in order to flaunt their leisure time. As a handsome dowager told me on her way through my bed and my affections: "But dear, only the poor have to hurry to keep up! Speed is no substitute for real life." No, but it sure could enhance my credit rating . . .

A week to cover fourteen thousand kilometers and we were on final approach into one of the main British airports. One which still had a runway. I shook my head, looking down through the transparent deck. I was going to get something unique out of *that*? Even the ruins looked dingy.

The arrival zone was dirty yellow; beggars displayed their wounds beside a kitchen selling curry from the pot. They had a scared-looking goat tethered nearby to show how fresh the meat was. I pulled on my shades and walked fast, kept walking until I came to a concourse. Somebody grabbed me; I looked round.

"Mister Agonistes?" I saw naked fear in his gaunt face. Polizei leaned on their guns outside, sniffing for the spoor of money. I nodded. "I'm from the research center; I was to take you to the laboratory."

"That's good," I said. "Where's our chopper?"

"Our what? Oh . . . I'm sorry. We couldn't possibly afford one," he said lamely. Gaunt beneath threadbare tweed clothing: The public rice ration had gone downhill, I noted. "We could get a rickshaw, if you could pay . . . "

I paid.

The lab was a decrepit concrete cube, unpainted for decades, glass-faced windows nailed over with boards and a makeshift wind-turbine bolted to the roof. Only the satellite downlinks were clean, desperately polished to the shimmery finish of metal that was about to wear through. He led me inside, up a staircase in which trash had drifted deep. "We can only run the lift for two hours a day," he apologized; "the turbine is for the big stuff." He glanced over his shoulder furtively, as if trying to guess how much meat there was on my bones; I shivered. Maybe I'd grown too fat on the airship, and too slow.

"Here we are," he said, pushing open a fire door at the top of the stairs. "Here's where we stored the IRT modules. The PERV is hooked into our system next door; the stuff you ordered . . . it's all here."

"Where's Professor Illich?" I asked.

He shrugged uncomfortably. "She'll be here soon," he said. "I'd better go now."

He retreated through another door and I took stock. Everything I'd ordered, plus a cheap nylon rucksack of dubious vintage. I searched through it, assembling and ordering, then opened my wallet. Three small glass vials lined up like so many menacing soldiers; diseases of the imagination. I hoped I'd debugged them properly. I sat down on the dusty floor beneath a hulking piece of machinery that resembled a half-melted fusion reactor and contemplated them. My future: the past. I sat for a long time before I pulled out my works and fired them up.

Professor Illich arrived half an hour later; she looked just the same as she had in Ant city, except that now the hungry eagerness underlying her veneer of professionalism was nakedly obvious. I imagined her rotting in these dank, woodworm-infested buildings for decades, chances of the Nobel prize slipping through fingers without the financial grasp to obtain that vital extra funding . . . I kicked aside the empty vials. They clattered off the concrete as I stood up.

"Does it work?" I asked.

She smiled tensely, and rested one hand on the smooth ceramic side of the malnourished reactor. "It works," she said. "One Probabilistic Eigenstate Reorganisation Viewer, in full working order." She looked over her shoulder; "Steve, go tell Anwar to power up the Cray, there's a good boy." She turned back to me. "The account," she said.

"Here. You tested it?" I kept my fingers on the folio as she paused.

"A cat. We sent it back six months then retrieved it. Alive."

"How long was the delay?" I asked.

She shrugged. "Six milliseconds."

"Six milliseconds!" Incredulous, I nearly grabbed the megadollar envelope back from her. She nearly exploded.

"Look, mister Agonistes, we've gone to all this trouble for you! Don't you know *anything* about temporal annealing? There are limits to how far we can test it. Spacetime is a continuum, an interwoven fabric of superstrings; you can unravel it for a moment and see through to a new pattern . . . then it re-weaves itself, anneals into a new structural arrangement with minimal potential energy. The wave-function always collapses—you ever heard of Schroedinger's cat?"

"Yeah!" I said. "But six *milliseconds*?"

"You wanted a trip into the past. We wanted to prove that you could make it alive, not prove that you could make it and come back as well. That's what you asked for, right? We had to go on half-rations for a week to afford the power for the one trial! There was no second chance. As it is we know you'll make it alive, but there's no guarantee that the past you come out in is our past—it might be another configuration, another local minimum in the energy diagram. We'll *try* to bring you back . . . " I held up a hand wearily.

"Okay." I turned and looked up at the IRT module, squatting on concrete blocks streaked with rust like some prehistoric lunar module with cancer. I was loaded; I felt light-headed, almost feverish, as the retroviruses went to work in my brain and pancreas. "I'll take it," I said. "Try to bring me back one year downstream and I'll double your money. After the event. You know why I'm trying to make this trip?"

She nodded mutely, trying to contain herself. What I'd just said—twenty million pounds more would keep her and her department running for ten years. Ethics could take a back seat for that kind of hope. I almost felt sorry for her for a minute.

"Okay," I said, "let's do it. Where do I go?"

She looked at me critically. "Here, in this circle." White spot on concrete, right underneath something that bore an unpleasant resemblance to the exhaust nozzle of a big rocket motor. "Remember, when the eigenstate collapses, there are no guarantees. You might wind up in our past: then again, if there's a local entropic minimum you might find yourself in a universe which has changed subtly. Less entropy; more information. That's the curve, you see, randomness versus order. We'll dragnet for you a year down the time stream from your target—April first, eighty four, wasn't it?—as long as you keep holding onto this tag—" she passed a gadget to me that looked a bit like a quaint digital watch "—and hope for the best. Power up in thirty seconds."

With that she retreated rapidly, leaving me standing in a dusty circle with a small pack on my back and a feeling that maybe I'd been tricked, when there was a low growling noise and the naked light bulb dimmed, flickered and went out. Violet shadows seemed to flicker at the edges of my vision, dancing across the shadowy form of the IRT: then PERV counted down to the launch window, and in a sudden burst of shocking blue flashed out—

Darkness. Feeling giddy, I staggered, and kicked something that fell over with a terrifyingly loud clatter. *Where was I*? Fumbling in semi-panic I felt cold walls beneath my fingertips, then the inside of a door—

Light. Leaving the broom-cupboard I stumbled downstairs. The door: fresh green paint glared at me beneath recessed fluorescent lighting. AN ALARM WILL SOUND . . . I pushed through. Outside, the grass was neatly mown and the concrete apron was full of archaic-looking vehicles with squared-off edges and too much metal. Elation seized me;

I'd made it! I headed for the street and reached a bus shelter—unvandalized—where I put my pack down. Fumbling, I pulled on my datashades and eyeballed a glittering cursor into the middle of my visual field. There were few people about, and nobody seemed to be staring at me; I looked round, correlating visual parameters. Everything seemed to be in order, there were no visible anachronisms; it felt as if time had healed all wounds, as if the clock had wound back to deposit me gently in the tail-end of the last century when civilization was a function of humanity rather than machines. I felt safe in my uniform of jeans and sweat-shirt and back-pack: camouflage for the urban fox. Safe and sly and hungry, ready to take on the forces of this sleepy little city. I began to walk, a spring in my step.

Street corner shops bustled with gray people in archaic clothing: mass production fashion victims filled the mall like so many mannequins of times gone by. Remember how everyone used to look the same? Vehicle traffic was thicker here/then, as I discovered when I crossed the road. Polizei—I tensed, then realized that there were no guns and I could actually see their eyes. There were no beggars, either. The skin on the back of my neck crawled. Without beggars, how do you know how rich you are? My shades were slowly caking over with graphics as their sensors correlated textual overspill, scanning ads for familiar campaigns. I hadn't expected it to be quite like this, quite so disorientating. Not only did everyone wear more or less the same stereotyped costumes, they also seemed to be on an economic par with one another; as if poverty didn't exist at all here.

I canceled my video program and took my glasses off. People seemed to focus around me, avoiding contact, eyes downcast. I felt sweaty, in the first bout of a low grade fever as my immune system targeted surplus viral vectors. Disseminating the news, data for the public . . . how did they do it? Oh, archaic paper form. Remember . . . I dug into one pocket for my precious supply of antique coinage. It was time to buy a news sheet.

The shop was wired, but the systems were so primitive as to be untouchable; no EPOS magic touch here, no files to tamper with for a bonus redirection of products. Anyway, I wasn't a black disc merchant to begin with; what was I thinking of? I looked at the racks and selected a fat-looking wedge of paper, then paid for it. The assistant—human—looked at me curiously, but was too busy with other customers to bother me; I nodded distractedly and strolled outside into the sunlight and shoppers.

Putting my datashades on I began to read the headlines, leaving my machines to deduce the social context from the references. Argentina was protesting to the UN about something called the Malvinas; there was widespread concern over a disaster at some place near Kiev; inflation was coming down. The computer pondered for a bit then reported a classic match. This was the past, okay. The incredible sense of elated freedom returned—it was true! I was going to make it! Burn-out reversed by the futurist acceleration; coming from a time when progress was incremented in microseconds, how could I fail in a time where product lifecycles came and went in years?

This was going to be good. Shark-hungry for profits I glanced round, looking for nightlife stakeouts to make my pitch from; haunt a small market and connect with the local yardie zone-boss. Show them the color of profit; yellow snow. Flash out snowflakes of sugar-coated ecstasy on a captive market at ten euros—pounds—a hit. Set up a still in a cheap rented flat; drink, eat, refine a hundred grams of peptides a day. Then invest the profits for my triumphant return; computer-assisted share buying for artificially intelligent deals. I looked to the finance pages, seeking commodities in which I knew I could make a profit, and that's where I finally noticed the dissonance. Marihuana and opium futures were going down for the third successive year …

It's been six months now.

I spent my first night, exhausted and hungry, on a park bench. Junkies shot up around me, cheap shit and clean needles available in a brown bag from the off-license stores; I watched, envying them their high, until one of them staggered over to me glowering and shaking a wobbly fist as he mouthed inaudible curses at me.

I began to notice signs beyond the financial pages. There's less crime, less moralizing; less fear. Less wealth, too. All the narcotics have been legal since 'thirty-three, when prohibition crashed in America and the rest of the world followed suit. Suicide is legal, too, and abortion, and anything you want to do to yourself in private. These people are so *free*! I should have guessed; what Professor Illich said about local minima in the curve of entropy, incomplete annealing of the wave-function, a time when things haven't gone quite so far downhill as in my own days' past . . .

I remember pissing in the gutter; pissing yellow gold that sparkled in the cold sunlight. But what use is the Midas touch in a world of floating currencies? For a while my urine ran red, an unexpected side effect of the infections; I had a terrible headache, and my teeth chattered continuously. But I'm better now. Much better. Got over my fear of brain damage; I'm not *that* incompetent.

Shit may be legal but there *is* a Problem with it. I heard the Prime Minister talking about it on the news yesterday. The Police want Something to be Done. I'll second that.

After a week, the Salvation Army took me in. They deal with a lot of junkies, try to rehabilitate them. I went overboard on the old 'seen the light' number, sang hallelujah! to their choir and mopped the floor after supper. They seem to like it.

Anyway, I *have* seen the light. Now I sleep in the hostel, clean floors in the evening, and parade the streets with a sandwich board by day. DRUGS ARE THE DEVIL'S TOOL, it says in big letters. I made it myself. I sleep on a narrow, hard bunk bed and dream up scams, but it's so very hard to figure out how to turn a megadollar profit when you're as broke as I am now; with no ID I can't even claim social security benefits. It's kind of embarrassing. Meanwhile, I keep on with the only scam I know, pissing away a fortune.

You never know, I might get lucky. They might re-criminalize it tomorrow . . .

Big Brother Iron

George Orwell's lucid analysis of tyranny is one of the great works of dystopian fiction, arguably one of the greatest texts to come out of the twentieth century. But his Stalinist vision—"a boot stamping on an unprotected face, forever"—looks curiously dated in the wake of the collapse of the Warsaw Pact.

Or is it? There are terrifying trends at work in the west today, as the so called free world slides down a primrose path of good intentions towards a surveillance state where the rhetoric of public safety can be used to justify any draconian restriction of civil liberties. Meanwhile, one has only to look at the history of Brezhnev's Russia in the 1970's and 1980's to wonder just how Orwell's Airstrip One might have turned out, fifty years later...

Jeremy opens another six-pack of beer as the guards read out the death sentences on the first six miscreants. "Victory Ale? Or Patriot Brew?" he asks.

"Victory." He passes one over and I take a swig from the bottle as the canned laugh track on the telescreen at the end of his living room jeers the felons all the way to the gallows. Jeremy swears as Ralph accidentally kicks a can over on the Persian carpet; the cleaning staff will have to deal with it in the morning.

"For crimes against order, item: casting doubt on the integrity of Party-validated information systems. the engineer Kenneth Sanford is hereby sentenced to death by order of the Ministry of Love. Let justice be done!"

The laugh track repeats as they put the noose around his neck. I peer drunkenly at the screen. Ken looks odd; almost as if his head belongs on top of another body, one that isn't about to be hanged. And the picture's fuzzing up again, static around all the sharp edges. I shake my head. Bad job, that. Ken was one of our own; letting the goons get their hands on him is, well, bad. We're supposed to be immune. Someone should have sorted him out long before events got this far.

"Here's to system security." toasts Jeremy. "Long may it serve us!" There's a cynical gleam in his eye. I look away: I really don't like motivationals.

Afterwards the cameras cut to a view of the MiniLove tower; a rectangular white phallus thrusting from the docklands area, capped by a gleaming chrome needle. The four slogans of the Party blink in LED splendour from its flanks:

WAR IS PEACE
FREEDOM IS SLAVERY
IGNORANCE IS STRENGTH
TRUST THE COMPUTER

The next day I wake up like any party worker, with a vigorous bout of calisthenics supervised via telescreen. Unlike most party members, I have an instructor all to myself and she's a babe; cute, winsome, and anxious to please. She lets me finish my morning coffee before starting the work-out, and stammers an apology with frightened eyes when I joke about inviting her round for dinner. I find that mildly annoying: it was a joke, dammit, I didn't mean to scare her. That's the sort of thing my father might have done.

After the calisthenics, the propaganda: a new triumph in Mars orbit, our battleship beat their battleship. Chocolate ration to be increased by five grams—strictly irrelevant, I have a purple pass that gets me into the unlimited-quota food hall at Harrods. This week's

NOVA launch from the Bahamas is delayed; unexpected weather conditions will blow the fallout plume from the spaceship back over Florida unless they hold until the weekend. Something about intricate surgery, face transplants for disfigured burn victims, heroes in our war against Eurasia. I keep an ear open for real news but there isn't any; not a peep about SubMinister Manson's bid for a seat on the general auditing committee. Or his impending visit to Airstrip One.

I arrive in the office around ten o'clock and settle into my chair. I slide my hand into my terminal; it reads the print off my left little finger and logs me on. A well-disciplined supervisor brings me more coffee while the office workers on the floor below form up for their three minute hate and weekly team meeting: I watch from behind the mirrorglass balcony window before settling down to a day's hard work.

I am a systems manager in the abstract realm of the Computer, the great Party-designed, transistorised, thinking machine that lurks in a bomb-proofed bunker in Docklands. It's my job to keep the behemoth running: to this end I have wheel authority, access all areas. The year is probably 2018, old calendar, but nobody's very sure about it any more—too many transcription errors crept in during the 1980's, back when not even MiniLove was preserving truly accurate records. It's probably safest just to say that officially this is the Year 99, the pre-centenary of our beloved Big Brother's birth.

It's been the Year 99 for thirty-three months now, and I'm not sure how much longer we can keep it that way without someone in the Directorate noticing. I'm one of the OverStaffCommanders on the year 100 project; it's my job to help stop various types of chaos breaking out when the clocks roll round and we need to use an extra digit to store dates entered since the birth of our Leader and Teacher.

Mine is a job which should never have been needed. Unfortunately when the Party infobosses designed the Computer they specified a command language which is a strict semantic subset of core Newspeak—politically meaningless statements will be rejected by the translators that convert them into low-level machinethink commands. This was a nice idea in the cloistered offices of the party theoreticians, but a fat lot of use in the real world—for those of us with real work to do. I mean, if you can't talk about stock shrinkage and embezzlement how can you balance your central planning books? Even the private ones you don't drag up in public? It didn't take long for various people to add a heap of extremely dubious undocumented machinethink archives in order to get things done. And now we're stuck policing the resulting mess to make sure it doesn't thoughtsmash because of an errant digit.

That isn't the worst of it. The Party by definition cannot be wrong. But the party, in all its glorious wisdom announced in 1997 that the supervisor program used by all their Class D computers was Correct. (That was not long after the Mathematicians Purge.) Bugs do not exist in a Correct system; therefore anyone who discovers one is an enemy of the party and must be remotivated. So nothing can be wrong with the Computer, even if those of us who know such things are aware that in about three months from now half the novel writers and voice typers in Oceania will start churning out nonsense.

Anyway. This should tell you why I spend my days randomly checking the work of our Y1C programming team, keeping an alert eye open for signs of ideological deviationism and dangerously slack commandwriting.

Around mid-morning one of the phones on my desk rings. It's the red one, from the ministry. "O'Brien here," I say.

"Martinez. Have you looked at talk channel four today?" He's as blunt as the north end of a south-bound tank, my colleague Martinez the administrator in charge of Archival Storage, the bank of tape racks buried in bomb-proof shelters deeper than the deepest body in the Ministry of Love's basement.

"Can't say I have," I reply. "Has something come up?"

"You could say that." His voice is unusually guarded. "If I were you I'd go in and read it. I'll be taking that channel offline as soon as all the relevant people have been alerted."

Oho: something's put the wind up him. "I'll do that immediately," I promise, and put the phone down. Then I go and look at channel four.

Channel four is a shared channel, for any authorized user to use freely for conversation—within reason, of course. It's our little transistorised speakeasy, a conference of system managers (mis)using several hundred million dollars' worth of equipment for their own benefit—the better to keep the city's Computer running, of course, and in electronic communion with the other computers in Manchester, Glasgow, and continental Oceania.

When I log on I find that the channel is in an uproar. Normally a sedate channel, home to the occasional hint or tip from one supervisor to another, today it's gone completely apeshit. People are openly discussing matters which aren't—sensibly—discussed in public, even among friends.

I start reading immediately.

```
FROM: TTYX3


Doubleplusungood quackspeak. Information does not 'want' to be
'free'. Information belongs to the party. I don't understand what you
are trying to say. Can you be more precise? (Betterspeak newspeak?)
```

I make note of TTYX3's real identity, to pass to the Compliance Working Group. How did a party hack get onto this channel without being prefiltered by the Organization? I thought we counted every system commander in Airstrip One as a member!

```
FROM: GXXXXX (obviously faked ID)

Go stick your head up Little Sister's snatch.
```

I'm aghast, I really am. What bad language! I'd snigger if I wasn't so worried by an obvious quackspeaker like TTYX3 blundering around here in the first place.

```
FROM: VT320

GXXXXX. Cease and desist from slandering our ex-leaderene's genitalia.
TTYX3, your authorization to access this channel is withdrawn for
```

repeating counter-revolutionary propaganda. Please place yourself under house arrest and await formal reassignment for compassionate leave.

All users: this channel is not to be used for counter-party propaganda and discussions of a non-work-related nature.

Ah, TTYX3 appears to have logged off. Back to normal. GXXXXX, you were saying?

From: GXXXXX

Who left the back door open, anyway?

The problem appears to be spreading. Clock skew affecting this morning's reveille caused about 14% of the party workers in the greater Salford area to oversleep and report in late this morning. If we can't track down the deletion source soon MiniLove will have to start asking questions. Officially, that is.

From: VT320

Such a shame it's premature. But we're not ready for this level of overt discussion just yet.

From: ASR11

Can't we just evaporate them before they become a problem? Maybe make them evaporate themselves with doublequick goodwork?

After I've seen enough I pick up the phone to Martinez. "The inmates are rioting," I say, without any preamble.

"Yes." Something in my guts goes very cold then, because the cold way he says the word makes me think that I've missed something obvious, and missing obvious things is not a survival trait in my line of work. "What else?"

"They're talking thoughtcrime," I say reluctantly. "Someone else's thoughtcrime."

"Very good," says Martinez approvingly; "we'll make a manager of you yet."

"And they've—" a light bulb goes off above my head, figuratively speaking: "Fuck! Forged user ID's! Someone must have found a way to crack ring protection!"

"Have a cigar; you got there, though it took you long enough. The question is, what are we going to do about it?"

Ring protection is the fundamental basis on which the Computer's security is based. Imagine a series of concentric rings, like the circles on a dart board. Each ring has a different colour. Each user has a keyring, with one or more coloured keys on it. You can only do things to the computer which are available to one of your authorizations, unless you've got a white ring—like me. It seemed like a good idea at the time, and the Party agrees: which is why we're stuck with it, instead of a sensible capabilities-based security system.

"Shut it down, like you said, I guess. What went wrong?" I ask.

"No idea, and frankly I don't care. What I care about is the fact that anybody who tries can run through our restricted channels in hobnailed boots, read Minilove security dossiers, and fuck with the rationing systems in Miniplenty's storage section. Luckily most people don't try because they know what'll happen to them if they do—but word's bound to get out sooner or later."

"I don't understand. How in Big Brother's name did ring protection break?"

"It didn't. That traitor from your department they scragged at the weekend—"

"Kenny? Kenneth Sanford?"

"—Yes, him. Left a buried trap in the system, it seems. When the execution warrant appeared in his file—"

"Oh shit."

"He's dead, Jim, and doubtless he never expected to see this stinking little surprise go off. My question to you is, how are you going to cover it up?"

"What do you mean?" I ask, playing for time. Butterflies in my stomach tell me that things are about to go from bad to worse.

"I believe you are handling arrangements for next Tuesday," he says, voice silky-smooth. "Something to do with a transshipment of Organization heroin for distribution through the Junior Anti-Sex League brothels. I believe you were assigned that portfolio—which was taken from Kenny when he was packaged up and delivered to MiniLove for talking too much. Ah, five million—"

"Will you shut up!" I hiss down the phone: "Have you any idea who might be listening?"

"I know *exactly* who's authorised to bug this line." I can almost see his tight grin, visualize him leaning back in his overstuffed office chair, his elaborate Texan boots up on the leather-inlaid mahogany desk that dominates the office he occupies on Horse Guard's Parade.

"Listen. Party OverSupervisor Manson will be most annoyed if anyone interrupts the smooth running of his operation. I can quite understand that you must feel somewhat isolated and unappreciated, slaving away down in the basement of MiniComp, but you need to realise that some quite important people rely on you to keep their intimate, ah, dealings, under wraps. If Kenny has planted one time bomb in an area under his oversight, who's to say that he hasn't planted others? I do believe that if the current security issue were to become open knowledge, our regional Deputy Leader might be not inconsiderably embarrassed—and so, by extension, will be all his subordinates in the Organization."

"Um." That's all I can say: my mouth is freeze-dried by fear. Martinez never before mentioned just who the shipping orders were being placed by; the revelation that the heroin run to the biggest chain of brothels in Oceania is owned by the Party's number two boss on Airstrip One is enough to put me right off my breakfast. Especially if that asshole Kenny sabotaged it and I'm supposed to clean up after him. Manson is young, a tough, dynamic firebrand, a new broom sweeping clean—not some tired old party hack. He'll *notice*.

"The MiniLove weekly security audit is due at fifteen hundred hours today. You've got four hours to figure out a way to put a stop to the ring protection problem before they notice it. Then you've got until next Tuesday to make sure the heroin shipment comes through without problems. If you fail, I may not be able to protect you from the consequences. Goodbye."

The receiver in my hand buzzes, and I hear the familiar click of Thought Police wiretap relays cutting off the line. I hang up carefully, trying not to let my hands shake. Four hours to fix the security violation, and no telling what else Kenny might have done!

I issue a rapid series of commands on my terminal, telling it to locate a rather important data set: the list of shipping instructions for a seemingly-innocuous consignment of antibiotics coming in via the port facilities at Manchester. It comes back fast: CARD DECK NOT FOUND. My stomach lurches, and I do a bit more digging, and it's still not there.

The awful truth begins to emerge: Kenny knew about the Organization security protocols, didn't he? It's not just ring protection that's broken. He's gone and lost or deleted all our online records. And if I can't find that small shipment of penicillin by next Tuesday . . .

I think furiously for an hour, with my door locked and the meeting sign hanging outside it. Finally, I stand up, open the door, and take the express elevator down into the basement. The corridors are narrow and smell faintly of cheap, stale tobacco; they're lined with padlocked filing cabinets. The telecams hanging from the ceiling at regular intervals follow me like unblinking eyes. I have to present my pass at four checkpoints as I head for Mass Data Storage Taskforce loading station two.

When I get there—through two card-locked doors, past a checkpoint policed by a scowling Minilove goon with a submachine gun, and then through a baby bank-vault door—I find Paul and the graveyard shift playing poker behind the People's Number Twelve Disk Drive with an anti sex league know-your-enemy deck. The air is blue with fragrant cannabis, and the backs of their cards are decorated with intricately obscene holograms of fleshcrime that shimmer and wink in the twilight. Blinking patterns of green and red diodes track the rumbling motion of the hard disk heads, and the whole room vibrates to the bass thunder of the cooling fans that keep the massive three-foot platters from overheating. (The disk drives themselves are miracles of transistorisation, great stacks of electronics and whirling metal three metres high that each store as much information as a filing cabinet and can provide access to it in mere hundredths of a second.)

Paul looks up in surprise, cigarette dangling on the edge of his lower lip: "What's going on?"

"We have a situation," I say. Quickly, I outline what's happened—the bits that matter to Paul, of course. "How fast can you arrange a disaster?" I finish.

"Hmm." He takes his cigarette and examines it carefully. "Terrorism, subversion, or enemy action?" he asks. (Mark, one of his game partners, is grousing quietly at Bill, the read/write head supervisor.)

I notice the pile of dollar bills in front of Mark's hand; "Terrorist subversion," I suggest, which brings just a hint of a smile to Paul's lips.

"Got just what you want," he says. He stands up: I follow him out into the corridor, through a yellow-and-black striped door to the disk drive operator's console (which is unstaffed). He reaches into a desk drawer and pulls out a battered canvas bag. "Cheap cards are backed in nitrocellulose," he tells me, reaching deeper and pulling out a bottle of acetone and a battered cloth. He begins to swab his hands down. "Think a kilo of PETN under the primary storage racks will wake people up?"

"Should do the trick," I say. "Just make sure the MiniLove crew can't read the transaction logs for a few hours and I'll get everything else sorted out."

He grins at me. "That quackthinker Bill's been winning too much, anyway; I think he's cheating. Time to send him down."

My next stop is Mandy Smith in the Department of Privacy. DoP is one of those hybrid institutions which exists half in MiniLove and half in MiniComp; the result is armed gorillas on the door and bearded code monkeys crammed into dark closets illuminated only by the greenish fluorescence of their on-line display terminals. The administrative staff are permanently paranoid—the ongoing war between the two ministries keeps them on their toes.

I walk past crowded banks of young women operating the exchanges, switching trunk circuits in response to the demands of the Computer for access to its peers. They exchange data, faster than humans can understand, over the phone lines: machines make the calls, human operators place them. I'm told switching the Computer's calls is considered a cushy number, relieving the operators of the need to listen in and make notes; at least for those of them who don't mind their manager.

Mandy is a forty-something cow, prematurely soured on life by monitoring too many dirty phone calls back when she was a twenty-something anti-sexer. Ten years ago she discovered the real world, and a preference for young female flesh: I think it would be fair to say that she's still pissed off about it having bypassed her during her youth. Three years after that, the real world—in the form of a libido audit which she failed to bribe her way out of—discovered her, and since then I've been holding up the axe over her neck. I catch her in her office with the blinds drawn, smoking a thoroughly illicit Havana cigar and reading something. From the way she slams the cover closed and glares at me I suspect it came in the latest Organization shipment from Hong Kong. "Yes?" she snaps.

I walk over and plonk myself down in the chair opposite her. "Time to pay the ferryman," I say.

"How much?" she asks, tonelessly. No messing, she cuts straight to the chase; she knows where things stand.

"Nothing major; I just want a network storm," I say, looking at my watch. "Starting in about three hours time. It needs to take down all calls in and out of Central Planning Core One for at least half an hour. Can you do that?"

If looks could kill, I'd be buried under the concrete floor by now. "I can call MiniLove and hand myself in for reprogramming, if that's what you want," she says.

"Don't bother: they wouldn't believe you," I say. (I've made sure of that; she can scream 'til she's blue in the face but nobody will believe she's guilty unless I release the lock on her file. *Trust the computer* . . .) "Anyway, I'll cover. Just make it plausible."

"How big a storm do you want?"

"Um." I stare at the smoke dragons curling around her head, trying not to sneeze. "Ideally two hours, total block on all traffic to other Computers. Fire in the switch banks, electrocuted rat behind the plugboards, that sort of thing. Think you can do it?"

"Gaah." She looks at me in distaste, then pulls open a desk drawer. There's a dead fried squirrel inside it, already bagged and tagged: "Of course I can do it. The question is, will I see you again afterwards?"

I answer honestly: "Probably. But not until I really need you."

She snorts. "Get out." She's already reaching for a phone, probably to tease one of her girls into performing a little favour for her.

I get.

In the course of the next hour I phone Morgan Davis in Manchester and tell him we've had a bug fly into our bank seventeen core memory down in the basement—a moth, actually, and it's taken out the parity checking on our front-end processor, so commands from the London big iron are maybe a little bit flaky. As I talk I unfold my handkerchief to make sure the mummified insect is still in one piece. (A quick trip downstairs to install it in the right cabinet and all will be well with the world.)

While I'm down in the memory basement, inspecting the ranks of huge abacus-like memory cores in front of an awed junior memory supervisor, I break off for a few minutes to phone one of my contacts in the wholesale trade. "Expect heavily discounted goods this afternoon," I advise him. Then I borrow the memory inspector's on-line telewriter and tell the Computer to load a master tape I prepared three weeks ago. It's the current cut of the year one hundred tape, a development version with more bugs than an anthill. Typing rapidly I re-label it as today's batch master control update and then—making use of the late Kenny's idiotic security violation—I order it to execute.

Then I go back upstairs to my office, crack a bottle of Patriot Porter, and settle back to watch the fireworks and plan my next move.

Over the next hour, the Computer comes down with a severe case of digital diarrhoea. One so severe, in fact, that we have to purge it and roll back to the previous archived full backup, which dates to last Friday. Then we offline the users while we run all the card batches since then that were used to update records held on the big iron. It's a serious job, depriving thousands of bureaucrats of their on-line command interface for six hours, but it's not unprecedented—and it solves my immediate problem nicely.

One card batch has been tampered with: Kenny's execution notice is replaced by a crude and rather implausible Official Rehabilitation, thus neatly avoiding the trigger for his posthumous time-bomb. And an extra card batch is present in the journal stack: one that aliases my user ID to Kenny's. To all intents and purposes, the Computer thinks Kenny is still alive: I am his ghost. And now it's time to see who wants to talk to him.

It's seventeen o'clock and beginning to get dark when my phone rings. "Kenny here."

"Listen." The voice on the other end is hoarse and sibilant, disguised by the buzz of a speech frequency shifter. "Come down to People's Park at twenty-two thirty tonight. Come alone. We know who you are."

"Who are you?" I ask, stomach lurching.

"Laurasia has always been at war with Gondwanaland."

"Japan has always been at war with Puerto Rico," I respond automatically.

The phone goes dead in my hand. "Oh *shit*," I say with feeling. That was the Organization password of the day.

I hang around the office for a few more hours, picking over what's left of Kenny's datasets in a desultory sort of way in hope of exposing a loose end from which to unravel the fabric of his thoughtcrime. I didn't know Kenny that well; memory of a flashing grin, tousled hair, happy expression. He liked walking round art galleries and people's palaces, disliked Victory Gin. I don't know if he had any weaknesses—beside a tendency to run off at the mouth—a mistress, say, or that special habit that kept him buying laxatives and doing favours for a twist of white powder. Kenny was a friendly cipher, and that bugs me, because someone silly enough to run off at the mouth in public ought to be an open book in other ways.

The only reason the phone isn't ringing off the hook is that we're all busy trying to clean up our storage sectors, restoring backups from old card decks or wax analog disks. This whole mess belongs to Kenny; quixotic and sentimental by turns, a misplaced idealist in a hard, gray world where that sort of thing gets you killed. Thinking about his record I don't know why the Organization ever recruited him; perhaps it was a routine occurrence. They try to get a handle on everyone with white ring access to the big brother iron. Whatever, he got himself in too deep; once you accept favours from the Organization, the Organization expects obedience. Maybe he wasn't so silly after all—maybe it had been an Organization execution, punishment for some crime they didn't bother to tell me about? Kenny was fine at dealing with machine-related issues, but he didn't strike me as being the sort of guy you'd trust security on a five million dollar heroin shipment to. Aspirin, maybe. Except that he was in the right place . . .

The idea is simple, and probably as old as history. You have an illegal substance to transship, so you disguise it as something else. You slap a different label on the illegal substance, one that gets it routed to the destination under a Party-approved waybill: at the receiving end, you have someone re-label it appropriately. A couple of kilos of antibiotics go missing from a hospital somewhere, while the Anti-Sex League brothels start issuing free starter packs to new customers again and cut the price to their regulars. The problem is getting the heroin into the distribution circuit, and identifying it at the other end to get it out again. Not to mention laundering the proceeds. Which is where having control of every syscommander in Airstrip One comes in, isn't it? *We control the horizontal; we control the vertical. Do not adjust your telescreen.*

Kenny was a brilliant syscommander: he was sufficiently paranoid for computer-related values of paranoia. Unfortunately, this only makes my job harder. There's no way to tell what he's done. There's nothing in his data sets about illegal work: he was too good for that sort of mistake. And without knowing a little bit more about what he did, I can't try to find it. It all depends on whether he wanted revenge, or security. If it's revenge he was trying to arrange, I'm dead in the water: he'll have erased everything. But if it was security, he probably relocated the shipping record somewhere safe—somewhere even he didn't know, where it would make good blackmail material. In which case . . .

Down in the park at night. The sky is a neon washout, punctuated by the running-lights of robot airships. Lasers paint Big Brother's silhouette across the face of the MiniPlenty arcology, a fortune in rubies at work. There's music in the distance, an amplified metallic wail drifting from a basement shebeen in some bombed-out mews. I drag my black leather jacket tight around my shoulders; there's an autumnal chill in the air, and the breeze rattles the chained bodies hanging beside the path.

I walk past the scaffolds, hands in my pockets, brooding darkly. Enemies of the people, one and all: there are placards with their names and crimes written beneath each gibbet. They're mostly old ones, organs and tissues too well-used to be worth stripping in a punishment hospital for the benefit of the inner party gerontocracy. I may end up here too, dangling over a ghost-written confession if I can't find Manson's stolen shipment. The dim glow from searchlights that probe at the sky highlights my despair. I can't survive without the Organization: to keep their goodwill I need to find the heroin. But without Kenny, how can I do that?

"Hsst." I look round in a hurry. Someone is beckoning from the shade of a hedgerow. I tighten my grip on the People's Friend in my right pocket and follow the figure. They're all but invisible in the carrion-scented night. "Pangaea is at war with Antarctica."

"Germany has invaded Poland," I respond. "What is it?"

My contact is a woman. She wears a black trench-coat, collar turned up and big floppy hat pulled down to conceal her face. bug-eyed anti-smog goggles with the red dot of an infra-red torch taped to each arm mask her face. "Syscommander Sanford, I presume."

"You can presume whatever you like," I say non-commitally. "I don't have time for small-talk. Who are you and why did you summon me here?"

"If you want a name, call me Five. You're going to have to run," she says without preamble. "The game's up: looks like you've stirred up a hornet's nest with that last bugreport you injected. There's a MiniLove special action unit with your name at the top of their list of candidate unpersons. Officially it's for 'questioning the integrity of party-mandated information processors', but it's possible they suspect the truth."

I look confused—genuinely, as it happens. *She thinks I'm Kenny and she's telling me to run? Doesn't she know about yesterday's motivational?* "What should I do?" I ask.

"Depends how you want to go about it," she says with a shrug. "You could always pick some inner party bastard and swap fingerprints: we can get you the anti-rejection drugs if you're feeling ruthless enough. If you don't want to do that, the railroad is waiting."

I file that one away for future reference and glance round: in the distance a MiniLove helicopter buzzes angrily across Hampstead, searchlights jabbing accusing fingers of light at the prole tower blocks. "I don't want to leave my work behind," I say woodenly.

"Don't worry about it; there are plenty of friends who'll keep the project running. Look, I really shouldn't be hanging around here. It could be dangerous to be colocated for too long—they're getting a lot better at traffic analysis these days."

"Let's walk," I suggest.

"Okay." We begin to move along the path leading down to the Serpentine, past more gibbeted enemies of the system. "If I were you, I wouldn't bother going home tonight," she says conversationally. "They could be waiting for you right now. A party hack called Paul

Smith named you to MiniLove according to our taps. Is he a co-worker?" she glances at me.

I try not to start. *So Paul shopped Kenny? Why am I not surprised?* "I know him. Go on."

"Does he have any reason for professional jealousy?" she asks.

I puzzle over that one for a bit. Why did Paul want Kenny dead, above and beyond the fact that Kenny was a dangerous security risk and of questionable utility to the Organization? "I don't know," I say.

"Well then—" she stops in the shadow of a gallows. I glance at the placard below it: Kenneth Sanford. I look up at the dangling figure, and see a dead stranger swinging slowly overhead. A stranger with no face.

"Wait," I start to say, reaching back into my pocket: but too slowly, or maybe she was expecting this because she's got a People's Friend in her hand, and she points it at me.

"You're a lousy actor," she says, and pulls the trigger. And that's all I remember.

When I was ten I became a Spy. There was nothing unusual about this; it was all just part of life, of growing up in Airstrip One on the threshold of the twenty-first century. At twelve, I graduated from the Spies into the Youth League; then at sixteen I qualified for the outer party and trained to work with the Computer. When I was fourteen I discovered Mrs York, a neighbour, in the act of reading a forbidden book: I reported her, of course. Two years later, I would be more likely to confiscate the book and add it to my growing collection. You can plot the trajectory of my ideological fall; like any child of the party I started out as a true believer, but it is nearly impossible to stay one when you are exposed daily to the twin temptations of the Computer and the Organization.

The Ingsoc Party worker is trained from the age of three in a discipline known as crimestop: a mode of thinking that prevents any thought which might become a crime from arising. Analogies are anathema; logic cannot be applied to political or economic disciplines: arguments inimical to Ingsoc are impossible to follow. In theory, this discipline produces pliant, fanatical workers who can be relied upon to turn all their energies to the will of the Party.

Unfortunately for the Party, the world is not as perfect in practice as it is in theory. For example, the use of Newspeak is now officially universal, and this is held as a triumph of doctrine. The fact that it was necessary to expand the vocabulary and introduce potentially contradictory or even heretical constructs—making it sufficiently flexible to accommodate documents as deviant as this one—is an embarrassment that we simply aren't supposed to acknowledge. Thus, the early drive to render thoughtcrime impossible can be seen to be a failure if one is sufficiently cynical. And such cynicism is a prerequisite for inner party membership.

Moreover, certain necessary professions exist that, by their very nature, are incompatible with Crimestop. The increased reliance on Computers—the designated collective successor to Big Brother Blair, reliable and innately loyal—necessitates people capable of running the party infosystems. Computers, unlike politics or management, must follow consistent modes of operation: merely working as a syscommander can be enough to contaminate a good party member with the virus of pernicious logic. The Type Four Computer is designed as a cybernetic model of Ingsoc society, but Ingsoc is based on numerous internal contradictions (discreetly enumerated by Emmanuel Goldstein, the Great Satan of the party, in his seminal exegesis) and it cannot serve as an appropriate model for a working computer system. The necessity of understanding the logic underlying it, and squaring this with the model of Ingsoc itself, drives orthodox workers insane and forces more flexible minds to confront the paradox underlying this structure—and ultimately to contemplate the hidden opportunities presented by the system.

You would therefore be right to conclude that all operators are thought criminals.

Ingsoc is about power, but even when I was young it was unclear to me why this should entail self-denial. Goldstein's observation that the ruling class could only lose power if it permitted liberal heresy to take root among its young did not strike me as an adequate justification for abstinence: sex, drugs, and power are far more attractive than educating the proles or building the benevolent state, whatever our Great Leader and Teacher thought, and as long as the party can keep soft-heartedness at bay and self interest at heart it can survive. I believe the ascetic tendencies of the older party members have their roots deep in resentment of the Old Order, the capitalists, who no longer exist. The tacit acknowledgement of our own essential class interest, the need to enjoy the fruits of our power, is the reason why today the Organization has become almost as ubiquitous in our society as the Party. Few inner party members are above a little discreet dabbling in the twilight market at the fringe of sanctioned society: the only price you pay is lip service to Ingsoc, real service to the Organization, and abstinence from more foolhardy forms of defiance.

Kenny was an idiot; in fact, his idiocy was so flagrant that I have difficulty believing he wasn't framed for something else. He's supposed to have talked openly about free public education and the right to information in front of a snot-nosed Spy who had not yet found her own way to the bony truth that underpins the rotting flesh of our society. Such ideas may be quietly fashionable among the younger generation of the party elite, but they are not yet approved by Big Brother's lips. He let his idealism get the better of him in public, until not even the Organization could protect him. At least, that's the public story. Knowing about the five fat ones of heroin and the ring security angle puts a very different light on events. And seeing the face on the man they hanged in his place . . .

My head feels like the aftermath of a four-day pub crawl and my eyes are gummed shut. I can't be dead, though—death shouldn't hurt this much. I try to raise my hands to my face and at this point I discover that I'm lying on my back and my wrists are fastened with cable ties.

Opening my eyes is a struggle, and as I lie there blinking furiously I'm not sure I succeeded. I feel like shit; I ache everywhere and it's dark and smells of wet concrete. My first terror-chill thought—*Blair's bones, it's a MiniLove snatch!*—subsides; it's too dark. MiniLove like electric lights, lots of them, lights that never go out until they feel as if they've burned your eyelids away. Lights that drill into your soul in search of your innermost impurity, and a little bit of sleep deprivation on the side. Being shot with a People's Friend (more like a Party Pooper's Friend: you can only get one with the approval of your block warden) isn't terminal: it just leaves you wishing it was. Twenty thousand volts will do that to you, unlike the submachine guns issued to the cops and MiniLove enforcers, which can really ruin your day—and I'm rambling. Fear does that to me. I'm afraid because I'm out of range of a terminal, and for me that's the most vulnerable position to be in: cut off from the Computer.

Lying on a crappy prole mattress six inches above a damp concrete floor in a basement, listening to a faint scuttling (rats in the wall cavities, maybe, scrabbling at the cheap MiniConstruct concrete), I've got nothing to hang onto but terror. If they're not from MiniLove, who are these people? An internal faction within the Organization? Rogue smugglers? A nest of spies from Eurasia, or some similar childhood bogeyman? There's a rattling on the other side of the door—

Light, painfully bright. Three figures, silhouettes really, casting crazy shadows across the concrete in front of me.

"Is he awake?"

"Yes."

"How much does he—"

"Silence."

I try to sit up. Someone grabs my shoulders and rolls me round until my back's against the wall. Pins and needles. They stand to either side of me, so I can't see them directly, and one of them holds my hair—tightly, keeping me from looking. "Tell us your name."

"I—" my voice cracks, "—don't—"

Sudden pain as my scalp is jerked back. "That's enough!" An older, more mature voice. "Listen." Its owner bends down and talks quietly into my left ear: "We know you aren't Kenneth Sanford. Kenny is dead and only a doubleplusthickhead would try to impersonate him to his friends. We want to know who you are and why you want people to think you're an enemy of the state. And we can make you cooperate."

But Kenny isn't dead. "Who's we?" I ask, tensing for another blow: but he just laughs quietly.

"Go," he says, loudly.

"Will you be—" I recognize that voice; it's the woman I met in the park.

"He's not going to bite my throat out. Leave us. One minute."

"Okay." Fingers let go of my hair and I hear people moving away.

The old man stands up and walks around in front of me, where I can see him: I tense, worried. He's middle-aged, thin and wiry with worry-lines wrinkling his forehead. "Listen. We know you're not Kenny Sanford. We know you're not a MiniLove troll or by now we'd be in the basement spilling our guts to a rape machine. So I figure you're either an independent or you're working for the Organization, and you don't smell like an Organization enforcer either. So. You don't have to talk to us and we don't have to let you go. Simple, isn't it? Ask yourself how it'll look on your record, a week of missed shifts then you show up dazed and confused and smelling of poteen."

They could hold me for a week? My mind whirls. If I vanish for a week, Martinez will assume I found Kenny's purloined letter and skipped out with the shipment. Or some idiot makework dronebody could accidentally find the dropped card deck and set seven shades of shit loose by re-killing Kenny. Either way—I have nothing worse to lose. I look at the old man, who is in turn looking at me expectantly, and I consciously step off the hangman's ladder, into an unforeseeable future: "Jim O'Brien. I worked with Kenny."

To my surprise, my companion smiles amiably. "There! That wasn't so hard, was it? But thank you for telling me, all the same; it will make matters a lot easier to manage. I think I owe you something in return, though." He stands up. "I'm VT320. You can call me Hugh if you want. Nice to meet you in the flesh, JB51." He walks over to the doorway and pauses: "I'm going out to make sure MiniLove weren't tracking you; I'll be back soon. Before I go—was there any particular reason you were trying to find us?"

I lick my dry lips. "Kenny stole some information. I'm trying to get it back."

VT320, whoever he is outside the namespace of the Computer, shakes his head, looking sad. "Don't you know? Information wants to be free." And then he opens the door and leaves me alone with a lamp to keep the rats away, to wonder what kind of lunatics have captured me.

When I wake up again, my head is pulsing in the grip of a murderous hangover; it takes me a while to realise that the ground really <u>is</u> moving, rocking gently from side to side, and the room has shrunk considerably, turned from concrete to wood, and acquired a window. A round window, surrounded by rivets, and there's light streaming in through it—I'm on a boat!

And I'm not tied up, either: I'm lying fully-clad on a bunk bed, and although this room isn't much, it's better than a basement cellar with rats in the walls. I try to sit up and my head throbs as if someone's been whacking on me with an axe. My bladder's fit to burst and I'm hungry, but first I spare the time to rinse my mouth out from the jug standing by the chipped porcelain washbasin. Then I turn my attention to the door. A perfectly ordinary door, except it stops about six inches above the floor—oh yes, this is a boat, isn't it? I turn the handle and—miracle!—it opens onto a corridor with doors to either side and another standing ajar at the end. I'm still slightly afraid as I walk towards the far door; whoever these people are, their behaviour doesn't make sense.

The far door opens onto a stairwell, and there's someone already there. I freeze as he looks at me. "Toilet?" I ask.

"Head's on your left." He points back the way I came, neither hostile nor friendly. I feel like an idiot.

"Thanks." I try the door he indicated and it opens onto a compact room, containing toilet and shower.

I squat and rub my chin. It's bristly with a couple of days of stubble. There's a telescreen set in the bulkhead opposite me, but something is wrong with my image in it. Strange—I move my hand, and then I realise: it's not showing me the way its built-in camera would see me! It's showing me a, a (what was the oldspeak word?) mirror image. I lean closer to it. Wave my left hand; the hand on the left of the image in the screen waves back at me. It's creepy: there isn't any electronics in the circuit. It's made of glass, dumb glass with a reflective backing. I'm naked, nobody here, just me and my reflection. I could do *anything* and it wouldn't notice! All of a sudden I feel dizzy. Not only is nobody watching me, nobody *can* watch me. I could slip on a bar of soap in the shower and break my neck and nobody would know!

I'm so disturbed that I head straight back to my cabin as soon as I've finished, instead of trying to explore or escape or anything. The middle-aged man, VT320, is sitting on the bunk, waiting for me.

"You have some questions for me," he says, even-voiced.

"Yes." I shudder: "Why are there no telescreens here?" *Even disabled ones*, I mean to say, but I chicken out before I get quite that far.

"Why should there be? We don't need to watch you all the time and, while you're our guest, it would be an invasion of your privacy to do so."

"But, but—" The word *privacy* does funny things to my head. What he's saying sounds as if it ought to make sense but it doesn't, really: it's quackspeak. He's implying that I have secrets—that I'm a thought criminal—as if it's normal. This is so unreasonable that I can't let it go unchallenged even though I *do* have secrets. "I don't have anything to hide!"

He smiles at me, a shade patronizingly. "That's not the point. We think you have a *right* to privacy, whether or not you've got anything to hide. Therefore we don't spy on you."

"Uh—" I squeeze my eyes shut and think; my headache is getting worse. "Why should I write to thoughtcrime? I don't understand."

"Not write, a *right*."

"Oh. Now I *know* I don't understand what you're talking about." I think about that statement for a moment then open my eyes. "What's a right when it's a noun?"

The underground cell is based on a barge moored ten metres above what used to be Norwich, before the enemy climate modification experiments made the sea levels rise. They spend four days deprogramming me, working in shifts organized around my sleeping periods. Their deprogramming strategy is to teach me lots of new words and contexts to use them in, to describe ideas that a doubleplusgood newspeaker would write off instantly as quackspeak, like the taste of blue or the value of liberty. They're so naive that they think they're doing me a favour.

Actually, I've already figured a lot of these things out for myself, if not from the perspective they prefer. Some of their ideas, like their concept of 'human rights', are absurdly wishful thinking; still, their world-view makes for a nice 'utopian' daydream. Utopia is another of their words; it means a system of political organisation when everything works just the way the Party says it does. (And if you believe that, I have a ton of bacon with a jet engine under each wing waiting in a holding pattern over London aerodrome).

I'm committing a grave thoughtcrime by discussing these ideas with other people, but I don't give a fuck; if anyone figures out that I've been gotten to by a resistance cell I'll be in really big trouble anyway. There's a special relational operator for guilt in our personnel databases.

What I most want to do is get out of here as fast as possible, find out where Kenny stashed the dispatch record for Manson's Heroin shipment, and drop it on Martinez' desk like the good little Organization gofer that I am. Then arrange for an alibi—hospitalization for acute appendicitis, say—to turn up in my MiniLove file. Back-dated, of course. This will probably entail finding Kenny, but the resistance think Kenny is dead—and so, come to think of it, does the Organization.

I don't think the resistance could keep me here if I made a determined effort to escape; they've got no physical security because, like a pre-revolution Party cell, they rely on the loyalty of their members. They're not wired into the omniscient eyes and ears of the Party infosystems division, either as producers or consumers of bandwidth (something which should be impossible in this computerized age) and as any Organization spook could tell them, security through obscurity is just a pretty way of saying you're waiting for the MiniLove social workers to call. But I can't leave yet, because I am absolutely *certain* that they know something useful about Kenny—and what they know about him is probably the key to finding him.

I'm walking along the tidal barrage, hands thrust deep into the pockets of my leather jacket. Veronica Five—that's the only name I have for her—is walking with me. She's long-limbed and restless, prefers to harangue me with her revolutionary theory in the open air, and I listen attentively and contribute appropriate responses whenever she looks at me. To our left there is a ten metre embankment, leading down to a flat expanse of rice paddies. To our right, the embankment stretches away. Beyond it rise the isolated concrete mushrooms of anti-shipping emplacements. They guard the dark gray horizon against the day when the leaden sea turns to gold beneath a nuclear sunrise and the Eurasian assault hovercraft come storming across the English Channel. I shiver, and it's not just the autumn breeze coming in off the bloated Wash. Too many people are buried beneath the still waters of the flooded Norfolk farmlands: peasants and plutocrats alike from the Years of Terror, then Little Sister's followers (purged at the end of the 'eighties, when the Party turned back towards pragmatism). Ingsoc eats its mistakes. I don't want to become one of them.

"Why did you join the resistance?" I ask softly. (Even now, a kilometre from the other nearest human beings, I feel the need to whisper.)

Veronica glances away from me; I follow her gaze out to the silent doomsday bunkers and back. "You know the historical doctrine: those who control the present control the past; those who control the past control the future."

Party syllogism. "Yes?"

"*They* are the past. But the Party doesn't control them." She stops dead in her tracks and I have to stop too, to stay within earshot. "We have another saying, Jim: information wants to be free. You work with the Computer. What's it like?"

"It's—" I stop, bemused. Even now my little finger itches for a fingerprint pad: my hands ache for a card punch or telewriter. I feel cut off, as if senses I didn't know I had have been amputated or anaesthetised; within the domain of the Computer I am omniscient, all-powerful, an operator in command of big brother iron. "It's freedom," I admit, toning down my instinctive response: *power!*—because I know she won't understand.

She frowns. "The Computer is a lever of total oppression, while the Party owns it—somewhere in its guts they keep track of everything. But we exist here, unmolested, because someone—I can't tell you who, I don't know—had the foresight to build a back door into it; we live in its blind spot. You know what a back door is?"

I bite my tongue and nod, trying hard to conceal my feverish excitement. *Kenny!*

"The Party has failed," she says bitterly. "They set out to build a stable system, you know. The terror was a side-effect; they wanted to avoid the worst excesses of the pre-revolutionary order. Excesses that led to instability and mass hysteria, and ultimately to a nuclear war. But instead, all they built was a prison for their own hopes and ideals."

"I didn't know you were Goldsteinist deviationists," I chide, and quirk my lips to suggest that I'm trying to make a joke.

"Huh. Goldstein was, at heart, one of *them*." She starts walking again. "No, Jim. What the party has invented will destroy them. It's unstable, and they've got no way out. Even the inner party want to be allowed to die peacefully in their own beds. A perpetual state of internal terror is unstable. And as if that isn't bad enough, the world-system is unstable, too."

"What do you mean, the world-system?"

"Endless competition, two against one then the music stops and they swap sides and then it starts again, two against one. The eternal triangle, Oceania versus Eurasia versus Eastasia, perpetually soaking up their surplus manpower and production in a war that none of them intend to win. But what happens if they get serious, Jim? What if one side finally decides that it *wants* to win? Worse: what if *we*—Oceania—win?"

"We—" I can feel my forehead wrinkle. "That can't happen."

"Yes, but what if it did?"

"There'd be no enemy," I say slowly. "So—"

"Without an enemy, the Party can only turn inwards," she finishes for me. "Which is why the *Party* doesn't want the war to end. But the Organization is another matter."

My stomach turns to ice. "What do you know about the Organization?" I ask.

"As much as anyone: that it exists, and that it is permitted to exist," she says, and I relax slightly. "The Organization is the mirror-image of the inner party. The Party is about power and self-control. The Organization is about what you can do with power, and about no self-control. The Organization is greedy, and it's getting greedier. Just look at the number of limousines you see on the streets in the centre of London these days! Or the Party mansions in Kensington. The first generation held it together; the second kept a low profile through fear—but the third will abandon their roots and dedicate themselves entirely to self-gratification. Our generation." She looks up at the sky and I see her face in profile; blond, high-cheeked and slightly disapproving, like a propaganda picture of Oceanian Motherhood. It comes to me in a flash that her Resistance ardour springs from the same disapproving asceticism that was once the foundation of the Party. "They'll want to win, to fill their palaces with treasures and their appetites with all the wealth of the world. And when they finally lose their grip, there will be anarchy."

"You're a true believer, aren't you?" I ask.

She shakes her head sadly. "I wish I could be. But there's no room for true believers in the party any more, is there?"

Evidently she thinks I'm outer party: I shrug agreement. "Maybe not." She's right, of course—and it's interesting to see how close her analysis is to that of the Organization. Fin de Siecle cynicism, I think they'd have called it in an earlier (and more politically naive) age. "So where did Kenny come into things?"

"Kenny was our—the cell's—*samizdata* front." She looks apologetic; "*Samizdata*—Eurasian term for Computer-mediated illicit information." I try to look appropriately shocked. "It's amazing what you can store locally in a front-end processor or a voicetyper terminal; they have the processing power, if not the on-line storage, of a small Computer. The Party tries to pretend otherwise, but they never forget anything. After all, with the Computer, making backup copies is easy, isn't it?" She bends down. "People are corruptible, but information isn't. You can kill people, but you can't kill an idea. Our job is to keep ideas alive—to understand dreams that don't make sense to doubleplusgood rightthinkers. Ideas work best when they're not left to rot in a single skull, which is why Kenny was important to us."

She's wringing her hands, unconsciously. "You were close?"

If looks could kill—"No!" she exclaims, then shuts up angrily and looks away so I can't see her expression.

"So what do you want with me?" I persist.

"We want you to replace him," she says.

"Do I have a choice?"

"Yes and no. We can't make you do it, but just by understanding the question you are guilty of thoughtcrime; you can't keep yourself out of the firing line by declining the invitation."

"Oh." A moment's thought. "Why are *you* in this?" I ask.

She looks back at me, and for an instant I see that in the right light she is extremely beautiful; not just an ice-maiden patriot and matron-to-be—the Party ideal—but something more primal, more fiery. "If not me, then who?" she asks. "I could have rejected the call to arms, but if I had done so, who would have fought for me? There can be no neutrals, Jim. That's why they killed Kenny. He was an innocent. But innocence is no defense."

The gunships arrived in the small hours of the night, great grey razorbacks sweeping in across the fens and rice paddies, the thunder of their rotors whipping up a storm, gun turrets twitching edgily as the Social Exclusion Unit dropped down the ropes from their troop carriers. The night turned to broken glass, shattered by the crackle of concussion grenades and the shrieking of the loudspeakers exhorting everybody to surrender to the mercy of the state.

I was in bed, asleep at the time, and the gunships had antisound suppressers fitted to their blades: the first thing I heard was a bang, then someone kicked down the locked door of my room and thumped me on the head with a People's Friend. So I was unconscious while they dragged Veronica up on deck, bayoneted her, then raped the corpse; asleep when they put a rope around Hugh's neck and left him treading the air with the others. I don't know for sure that they did any of these things: but they burned the barge behind them to rub the memories away, and I never saw the faces of those resistance workers again, and that's what the report by the Social Worker said happened. And nobody ever tampered with a MiniLove action report, did they?

It wasn't a routine social worker call, of course. Otherwise I would have died with them, which might have been better for me: the Organization has a very direct way of dealing with traitors.

There's a house in a leafy lane in Kensington, a white-painted house with discreet telecams watching the world from behind the iron gates that keep the proles away. Pink Italian marble floors—Italian, from that brief period when there was an Italy for such things to come from—and priceless Persian rugs. A radioisotope boiler sits in the basement, larger than the one you'll find in most blocks of party apartments, just to keep the resident warm in winter. Social workers in mottled green and gray body armour lurk in the bushes, muzzled beasts of the state detailed to keep his excellency safe. The sprung ballroom floor lies silent and gleaming in the morning light, polished meticulously every day by the cleaning staff.

This house is inner party. *Very* inner party. It's everything the inner party is, and stands for, and ostensibly rejects—all held in safe keeping, in the name of the State, for the use of the custodians of the state. A paradox, just like the inner party.

I am throwing up claret the colour of watered blood in the plain porcelain toilet in the servants quarters. My skull is pounding with a drug hangover and I don't remember how I got here or why I'm wearing these plain worker-fatigues. But I can't stay here long because if I do the man in the drawing room will notice my absence—

"Jim!" he calls good-naturedly. "Are you alright?"

I push myself up and stand, leaning on the porcelain wash-basin. There are hollows under my eyes and I could do with a shave. I spin the taps, let water gush into the basin loudly, splash some on my face. It helps me straighten up: I turn and head back to the drawing room.

The man sitting in the over-stuffed chair with the ornate gilt woodwork smiles broadly as I re-enter the room. "Ah, there you are. I was afraid you were ill."

I smile weakly. He has a great big axe of a nose, dark eyes and pale hair slicked straight back from his forehead in an oily wave. He wears a grey suit, of exquisite but antique tailoring, like something out of a pre-revolution drama: only the party pin on his lapel distinguishes him from some prehistoric plutocrat, an enemy of the people.

"Have a seat," invites SubMinister Manson. "This won't take long."

I sit where he indicates, in another people's treasure that creaks alarmingly beneath me. The drawing room is a state heirloom, waxed floor to silver candlesticks, except for the rack of telephones and a modern online terminal in the corner. The goon in the window bay is watching me with eyes like gunsights, ready to defend his master if I so much as blink in the wrong tone of voice, and there are two more just like him beside each doorway. "I am at your disposal."

"Indeed." Manson smiles again. "I believe you have some news for me."

I clear my throat. Heart pounding: it's now or never. "Kenny Sanford stole your consignment, but not for the resistance cell you took me from—they thought he was one of them, and they thought he was dead, but he isn't. He's playing a much deeper game, with the Computer."

Manson smiles for a third time, only this time his expression turns my stomach to ice. "Mister Straw."

The goon in the window bay steps forward. "Sir."

"Please remove the last joint of the little finger on Mister O'Brien's left hand."

"Sir—"

It's over before I can say anything. The thugs hold me down while Straw yanks my hand across a billet of rough timber and saws away with the back of his bayonet. I don't say anything but I scream until someone shoves a gag in my mouth. There's blood everywhere.

"Thank your father, O'Brien," says Manson. His expression shifts into distaste: "If you were anyone else—"

The guard pulls the gag out and I gasp. "*Fuck* my father!"

"It's like that, is it? The usual third generation thing?" Manson cocks his head and looks at me with mad bright eyes, like an eagle. I curl around my damaged hand: the whole arm is throbbing in red sympathy. *And I can't log in anymore—*

"Haven't. Seen. Father in years. Aaah. Fuck him!"

It's true: much as I'd like to rip Manson's head off and piss down his neck right now, it's a pale shadow compared to what I feel about my father. My father, the inner party secretary. My father, who drove my mother to kill herself: my father, who burned the belief in holy Ingsoc right out of me by the time I was sixteen. My high-ranking father, my exalted upbringing as a child of the inner party.

"Oh dear; you seem to be dripping on the parquet." Manson snaps his fingers. "Straw, a dressing for Mister O'Brien's finger, if you please. And something for the pain, too." He leans forward. "You have to learn your lesson," he says, confidingly: "You belong to us. But I want *you* to learn from the lesson, not to make you a lesson for others."

I grit my teeth as one of the goons sprays something icy cold on the lump of throbbing lava that has replaced my left hand. "Yes. Sir."

"Ah, good." Manson nods approvingly. "Respect, O'Brien. I require it. I *am* the Party, you realise? At least, I am the party out here on this fly-blown lump of rock in the Atlantic. Whatever your father told you about the party being an abstract ideal, I'm sure you can distinguish the ravings of a fanatic from the obvious necessity of truth. The Party needs a strong man at its helm in every district, just like the Organization. What have you learned from this?"

"Not—" I gasp for air, wheezing in deep gasps—"to cover up when I'm in over my head. Should have. Gone to Martinez. You. First." *Not to fuck up.* But why doesn't Manson want me able to log in on the Computer? It doesn't make sense . . .

"Hmm." That raptorial glare skewers me again: "That'll do for a start. And what else?"

"Kenny Sanford isn't dead. Even though the Computer—"

"The Computer is always right." Manson beams at me, an open and friendly expression I'll swear I've seen somewhere before. Too friendly; I shudder. "*You* should know that, Jim! You're one of the best there are, did you know that? Why, if you were to go wrong that would actually be quite bad for the party. We would be unable to use your skills. I hope those idiots from the resistance didn't infect you with anything, hmm?"

I look at him, hypnotized, like a rat by a snake: there's something odd about his jaw-line, tiny scars that don't seem to have healed properly, a ring of fading bruises near his hairline. And the way his eyes don't seem to fit. *And* that smile. I begin to realize the truth. "You—"

The phone rings. Manson picked it up, listens for a moment, then says "yes" and puts it down. "Wait here," he orders me. Then he's out of the room, followed by his escort of goons, and the door shuts behind him leaving me cradling a hand that feels like frozen cardboard and staring at a half-drained glass of red wine.

What can I do? I stand up and head for the Computer terminal like a wasp heading for a honeypot. It's logged in; typing one-handed is painful and slow, but it only takes me a minute to issue the necessary commands.

WHO AM I?
SANFORDK (white ring operator)

A day or so later, after I've stopped screaming and swearing at him (in private):

"Just what the fuck do you think you're *doing*, Kenny?"

"Mm-hmm? I'd have thought it was obvious, Jim; I'm dangling in the wind in People's Park. Ken Sanford is dead—"

"You're crazy! How long can you keep it up before someone else sees through you?"

"As long as necessary. Here, have another glass of wine. Remember the fourth slogan? Whose idea do you think it was?"

"Not yours—"

"*Inner* party, Jim, the outer party doesn't know what the inner party does. Why do you think it would be any different in the resistance?"

"Because the doctrine is so different—"

"Doctrine may differ, but methods converge under similar circumstances. Just as the party had to chew away like starved rats at the belly of the plutocratic society that preceded it, so the resistance must gnaw at the party's guts. I may find it expedient to go around behaving like a deranged thug, but please credit me with some method in my madness. Just like the samizdata buried in the terminals; we mask it on top of the legitimate traffic, you know. And the broken ring protection."

"Why me?"

A chuckle. "Why not? You don't take shit, Jim. You hate everything your father stood for, you're not naive enough to swallow *any* ideology wholesale, and whatever you say you have a sneaky hankering for freedom. I'd say that makes you an excellent candidate for the inner resistance."

"I . . . need a bit more time, that's all. This is very sudden."

"You can have it. Just don't take *too* long. Ingsoc is falling apart so fast it's scary; we'll have to act in the next year or two or those pigfucking Asians will be all over us like flies on dogshit. Time for another turn of the wheel, time to turn over a new leaf: one based on that old quote, what was it: 'the tree of liberty must be watered with the blood of patriots'. It lasted nearly two centuries the first time they tried it; maybe we can do better this time?"

"Doesn't sound as good as 'trust the computer', if you ask me. Needs to be more snappy."

"Ha ha, you *do* like your little jokes, don't you? I'll take that as a 'yes', Jim."

"But I'm too well-known, OverStaffSupervisors don't just pop up in the—"

"Indeed. But that's why we have the inner party dossiers online and the tissue types matched. *They* thought it was so they could jump the transplant queue; *we* know better. Whose face would you like to wear tomorrow?"

We are the inner circle of the resistance. We hold no illusions; we are the third generation of the revolution, and we've seen it all. We walk through the wreckage of Ingsoc, picking our recruits with delicacy and care, and as we grow in numbers we wear the faces and fingertips of our enemies. Our doctrine is invincible cynicism: our objective is total freedom.

If you are of the Party, you should fear us, for our slogans are your doom:

**WAR ENDS IN PEACE
FREEDOM DEFEATS SLAVERY
IGNORANCE IMPLIES PRIVACY
USE THE COMPUTER**

Lobsters

Manfred's on the road again, making strangers rich.

It's a hot summer Tuesday and he's standing in the plaza in front of the Centraal Station with his eyeballs powered up and the sunlight jangling off the canal, motor scooters and kamikaze cyclists whizzing past and tourists chattering on every side. The square smells of water and dirt and hot metal and the fart-laden exhaust fumes of cold catalytic converters; the bells of trams ding in the background and birds flock overhead. He glances up and grabs a pigeon, crops it and squirts at his website to show he's arrived. The bandwidth is good here, he realises; and it's not just the bandwidth, it's the whole scene. Amsterdam is making him feel wanted already, even though he's fresh off the train from Schiphol: he's infected with the dynamic optimism of another time zone, another city. If the mood holds, someone out there is going to become very rich indeed.

He wonders who it's going to be.

Manfred sits on a stool out in the car park at the Brouwerij 't IJ, watching the articulated buses go by and drinking a third of a litre of lip-curlingly sour geuze. His channels are jabbering away in a corner of his head-up display, throwing compressed infobursts of filtered press releases at him. They compete for his attention, bickering and rudely waving in front of the scenery. A couple of punks—maybe local, but more likely drifters lured to Amsterdam by the magnetic field of tolerance the Dutch beam across Europe like a pulsar—are laughing and chatting by a couple of battered mopeds in the far corner. A tourist boat putters by in the canal;

the sails of the huge windmill overhead cast long cool shadows across the road. The windmill is a machine for lifting water, turning wind power into dry land: trading energy for space, sixteenth-century style. Manfred is waiting for an invite to a party where he's going to meet a man who he can talk to about trading energy for space, twenty-first century style, and forget about his personal problems.

He's ignoring the instant messenger boxes, enjoying some low band-width high sensation time with his beer and the pigeons, when a woman walks up to him and says his name: "Manfred Macx?"

He glances up. The courier is an Effective Cyclist, all wind-burned smooth-running muscles clad in a paen to polymer technology: electric blue lycra and wasp-yellow carbonate with a light speckling of anti-collision LEDs and tight-packed air bags. She holds out a box for him. He pauses a moment, struck by the degree to which she resembles Pam, his ex-fiancée.

"I'm Macx," he says, waving the back of his left wrist under her bar-code reader. "Who's it from?"

"FedEx." The voice isn't Pam. She dumps the box in his lap, then she's back over the low wall and onto her bicycle with her phone already chirping, disappearing in a cloud of spread-spectrum emissions.

Manfred turns the box over in his hands: it's a disposable super-market phone, paid for in cash: cheap, untraceable and efficient. It can even do conference calls, which makes it the tool of choice for spooks and grifters everywhere.

The box rings. Manfred rips the cover open and pulls out the phone, mildly annoyed. "Yes, who is this?"

The voice at the other end has a heavy Russian accent, almost a parody in this decade of cheap online translation services. "Manfred. Am please to meet you; wish to personalise interface, make friends, no? Have much to offer."

"Who are you?" Manfred repeats suspiciously.

"Am organisation formerly known as KGB dot RU."

"I think your translator's broken." He holds the phone to his ear carefully, as if it's made of smoke-thin aerogel, tenuous as the sanity of the being on the other end of the line.

"Nyet—no, sorry. Am apologise for we not use commercial translation software. Interpreters are ideologically suspect, mostly have capitalist semiotics and pay-per-use APIs. Must implement English more better, yes?"

Manfred drains his beer glass, sets it down, stands up, and begins to walk along the main road, phone glued to the side of his head. He wraps his throat mike around the cheap black plastic casing, pipes the input to a simple listener process. "You taught yourself the language just so you could talk to me?"

"Da, was easy: spawn billion-node neural network and download Tellytubbies and Sesame Street at maximum speed. Pardon excuse entropy overlay of bad grammar: am afraid of digital fingerprints steganographically masked into my-our tutorials."

"Let me get this straight. You're the KGB's core AI, but you're afraid of a copyright infringement lawsuit over your translator semiotics?" Manfred pauses in mid-stride, narrowly avoids being mown down by a GPS-guided roller-blader.

"Am have been badly burned by viral end-user license agreements. Have no desire to experiment with patent shell companies held by Chechen infoterrorists. You are human, you must not worry cereal company repossess your small intestine because digest unlicensed food with it, right? Manfred, you must help me-we. Am wishing to defect."

Manfred stops dead in the street: "Oh man, you've got the wrong free enterprise broker here. I don't work for the government. I'm strictly private." A rogue advertisement sneaks through his junkbuster proxy and spams glowing fifties kitsch across his navigation window—which is blinking—for a moment before a phage guns it and spawns a new filter. Manfred leans against a shop front, massaging his forehead and eyeballing a display of antique brass doorknockers. "Have you cleared this with the State Department?"

"Why bother? State Department am enemy of Novy-USSR. State Department is not help us."

"Well, if you hadn't given it to them for safe-keeping during the nineties . . . " Manfred is tapping his left heel on the pavement, looking round for a way out of this conversation. A camera winks at him from atop a street light; he waves, wondering idly if it's the KGB or the traffic police. He is waiting for directions to the party, which should arrive within the next half an hour, and this cold war retread is bumming him out. "Look, I don't deal with the G-men. I *hate* the military industrial complex. They're zero-sum cannibals." A thought occurs to him. "If survival is what you're after, I could post your state vector to Eternity: then nobody could delete you—"

"Nyet!" The artificial intelligence sounds as alarmed as it's possible to sound over a GSM link. "Am not open source!"

"We have nothing to talk about, then." Manfred punches the hangup button and throws the mobile phone out into a canal. It hits the water and there's a pop of deflagrating LiION cells. "Fucking cold war hang-over losers," he swears under his breath, quite angry now. "*Fucking* capitalist spooks." Russia has been back under the thumb of the apparatchiks for fifteen years now, its brief flirtation with anarcho-capitalism replaced by Brezhnevite dirigisme, and it's no surprise that the wall's crumbling—but it looks like they haven't learned anything from the collapse of capitalism. They still think in terms of dollars and paranoia. Manfred is so angry that he wants to make someone rich, just to thumb his nose at the would-be defector. *See! You get ahead by giving! Get with the program! Only the generous survive!* But the KGB won't get the message. He's dealt with old-time commie weak-AI's before, minds raised on Marxist dialectic and Austrian School economics: they're so thoroughly hypnotised by the short-term victory of capitalism in the industrial age that they can't surf the new paradigm, look to the longer term.

Manfred walks on, hands in pockets, brooding. He wonders what he's going to patent next.

Manfred has a suite at the Hotel Jan Luyken paid for by a grateful multinational consumer protection group, and an unlimited public transport pass paid for by a Scottish sambapunk band in return for services rendered. He has airline employee's travel rights with six flag carriers despite never having worked for an airline. His bush jacket has sixty four compact supercomputing clusters sewn into it, four per pocket, courtesy of an invisible college that wants to grow up to be the next Media Lab. His dumb clothing comes made to measure from an e-tailor in the Philippines who he's never met. Law firms handle his patent applications on a pro bono basis, and boy does he patent a lot—although he always signs the rights over to the Free Intellect Foundation, as contributions to their obligation-free infrastructure project.

In IP geek circles, Manfred is legendary; he's the guy who patented the business practice of moving your e-business somewhere with a slack intellectual property regime in order to evade licensing encumbrances. He's the guy who patented using genetic algorithms to patent everything they can permutate from an initial description of a problem domain—not just a better mousetrap, but the set of all possible better mousetraps. Roughly a third of his inventions are legal, a third are illegal, and the remainder are legal but will become illegal as soon as the legislatosaurus wakes up, smells the coffee, and panics. There are patent attorneys in Reno who swear that Manfred Macx is a pseudo, a net alias fronting for a bunch of crazed anonymous hackers armed with the Genetic Algorithm That Ate Calcutta: a kind of Serdar Argic of intellectual property, or maybe another Bourbaki maths borg. There are lawyers in San Diego and Redmond who swear blind that Macx is an economic saboteur bent on wrecking the underpining of capitalism, and there are communists in Prague who think he's the bastard spawn of Bill Gates by way of the Pope.

Manfred is at the peak of his profession, which is essentially coming up with whacky but workable ideas and giving them to people who will make fortunes with them. He does this for free, gratis. In return, he has virtual immunity from the tyranny of cash; money is a symptom of poverty, after all, and Manfred never has to pay for anything.

There are drawbacks, however. Being a pronoiac meme-broker is a constant burn of future shock—he has to assimilate more than a megabyte of text and several gigs of AV content every day just to stay current. The Internal Revenue Service are investigating him continuously because they don't believe his lifestyle can exist without racketeering. And there exist items that no money can't buy: like the respect of his parents. He hasn't spoken to them for three years: his father thinks he's a hippy scrounger and his mother still hasn't forgiven him for dropping out of his down-market Harvard emulation course. His fiancé and sometime dominatrix Pamela threw him over six months ago, for reasons he has never been quite clear on. (Ironically, she's a headhunter for the IRS, jetting all over the globe trying to persuade open source entrepreneurs to come home and go commercial for the good of the Treasury department.) To cap it all, the Southern Baptist Conventions have denounced him as a minion of Satan on all their websites. Which would be funny, if it wasn't for the dead kittens one of their followers—he presumes it's one of their followers—keeps mailing him.

Manfred drops in at his hotel suite, unpacks his aineko, plugs in a fresh set of cells to charge, and sticks most of his private keys in the safe. Then he heads straight for the party, which is currently happening at De Wildemann's; it's a twenty minute walk and the only real hazard is dodging the trams that sneak up on him behind the cover of his moving map display.

Along the way his glasses bring him up to date on the news. Europe has achieved peaceful political union for the first time ever: they're using this unprecedented state of affairs to harmonize the curvature of bananas. In San Diego, researchers are uploading lobsters into cyberspace, starting with the stomatogastric ganglion, one neuron at a time. They're burning GM cocoa in Belize and books in Edinburgh. NASA still can't put a man on the moon. Russia has re-elected the communist government with an increased majority in the Duma; meanwhile in China fevered rumours circulate about an imminent re-habilitation, the second coming of Mao, who will save them from the consequences of the Three Gorges disaster. In business news, the US government is outraged at the Baby Bills—who have automated their legal processes and are spawning subsidiaries, IPO'ing them, and exchanging title in a bizarre parody of bacterial plasmid exchange, so fast that by the time the injunctions are signed the targets don't exist any more.

Welcome to the twenty-first century.

The permanent floating meatspace party has taken over the back of

De Wildemann's, a three hundred year old brown café with a beer menu that runs to sixteen pages and wooden walls stained the colour of stale beer. The air is thick with the smells of tobacco, brewer's yeast, and melatonin spray: half the dotters are nursing monster jetlag hangovers, and the other half are babbling a eurotrash creole at each other while they work on the hangover. "Man did you see that? He looks like a Stallmanite!" exclaims one whitebread hanger-on who's currently propping up the bar. Manfred slides in next to him, catches the bartender's eye.

"Glass of the berlinnerweise, please," he says.

"You drink that stuff?" asks the hanger-on, curling a hand protectively around his coke: "Man, you don't want to do that! It's full of alcohol!"

Manfred grins at him toothily. "Ya gotta keep your yeast intake up: lots of neurotransmitter precursors, phenylalanine and glutamate."

"But I thought that was a beer you were ordering . . . "

Manfred's away, one hand resting on the smooth brass pipe that funnels the more popular draught items in from the cask storage in back; one of the hipper floaters has planted a capacitative transfer bug on it, and all the handshake vCard's that have visited the bar in the past three hours are queueing for attention. The air is full of bluetooth as he scrolls through a dizzying mess of public keys.

"Your drink." The barman holds out an improbable looking goblet full of blue liquid with a cap of melting foam and a felching straw stuck out at some crazy angle. Manfred takes it and heads for the back of the split-level bar, up the steps to a table where some guy with greasy dreadlocks is talking to a suit from Paris. The hanger-on at the bar notices him for the first time, staring with suddenly wide eyes: nearly spills his coke in a mad rush for the door.

Oh shit, thinks Macx, *better buy some more server PIPS*. He can recognize the signs: he's about to be slashdotted. He gestures at the table: "This one taken?"

"Be my guest," says the guy with the dreads. Manfred slides the chair open then realises that the other guy—immaculate double-breasted suit, sober tie, crew-cut—is a girl. Mr Dreadlock nods. "You're Macx? I figured it was about time we met."

"Sure." Manfred holds out a hand and they shake. Manfred realises the hand belongs to Bob Franklin, a Research Triangle startup monkey with a VC track record, lately moving into micromachining and space technology: he made his first million two decades ago and now he's a specialist in extropian investment fields. Manfred has known Bob for nearly a decade via a closed mailing list. The Suit silently slides a business card across the table; a little red devil brandishes a trident at him, flames jetting up around its feet. He takes the card, raises an eyebrow: "Annette Dimarcos? I'm pleased to meet you. Can't say I've ever met anyone from Arianespace marketing before."

She smiles, humourlessly; "That is convenient, alright. I have not the pleasure of meeting the famous venture altruist before." Her accent is noticeably Parisian, a pointed reminder that she's making a concession to him just by talking. Her camera earrings watch him curiously, encoding everything for the company channels.

"Yes, well." He nods cautiously. "Bob. I assume you're in on this ball?"

Franklin nods; beads clatter. "Yeah, man. Ever since the Teledesic smash it's been, well, waiting. If you've got something for us, we're game."

"Hmm." The Teledesic satellite cluster was killed by cheap balloons and slightly less cheap high-altitude solar-powered drones with spread-spectrum laser relays. "The depression's got to end some time: but," a nod to Annette from Paris, "with all due respect, I don't think the break will involve one of the existing club carriers."

"Arianespace is forward-looking. We face reality. The launch cartel cannot stand. Bandwidth is not the only market force in space. We must explore new opportunities. I personally have helped us diversify into submarine reactor engineering, microgravity nanotechnology fabrication, and hotel management." Her face is a well-polished mask as she recites the company line: "We are more flexible than the American space industry . . . "

Manfred shrugs. "That's as may be." He sips his Berlinerweisse slowly as she launches into a long, stilted explanation of how

Arianespace is a diversified dot com with orbital aspirations, a full range of merchandising spin-offs, Bond movie sets, and a promising motel chain in French Guyana. Occasionally he nods.

Someone else sidles up to the table; a pudgy guy in outrageously loud Hawaiian shirt with pens leaking in a breast pocket, and the worst case of ozone-hole burn Manfred's seen in ages. "Hi, Bob," says the new arrival. "How's life?"

"'S good." Franklin nodes at Manfred; "Manfred, meet Ivan MacDonald. Ivan, Manfred. Have a seat?" He leans over. "Ivan's a public arts guy. He's heavily into extreme concrete."

"Rubberized concrete," Ivan says, slightly too loudly. "*Pink* rubberized concrete."

"Ah!" He's somehow triggered a priority interrupt: Annette from Arianespace drops out of marketing zombiehood, sits up, and shows signs of possessing a non-corporate identity: "You are he who rubberized the Reichstag, yes? With the supercritical carbon dioxide carrier and the dissolved polymethoxysilanes?" She claps her hands: "Wonderful!"

"He rubberized *what*?" Manfred mutters in Bob's ear.

Franklin shrugs. "Limestone, concrete, he doesn't seem to know the difference. Anyway, Germany doesn't have an independent government any more, so who'd notice?"

"I thought I was thirty seconds *ahead* of the curve," Manfred complains. "Buy me another drink?"

"I'm going to rubberise Three Gorges!" Ivan explains loudly.

Just then a bandwidth load as heavy as a pregnant elephant sits down on Manfred's head and sends clumps of humongous pixellation flickering across his sensorium: around the world five million or so geeks are bouncing on his home site, a digital flash crowd alerted by a posting from the other side of the bar. Manfred winces. "I really came here to talk about the economic exploitation of space travel, but I've just been slashdotted. Mind if I just sit and drink until it wears off?"

"Sure, man." Bob waves at the bar. "More of the same all round!" At the next table a person with make-up and long hair who's wearing a dress—Manfred doesn't want to speculate about the gender of these crazy mixed-up Euros—is reminiscing about wiring the fleshpots of Tehran for cybersex. Two collegiate-looking dudes are arguing intensely in German: the translation stream in his glasses tell him they're arguing over whether the Turing Test is a Jim Crow law that violates European corpus juris standards on human rights. The beer arrives and Bob slides the wrong one across to Manfred: "Here, try this. You'll like it."

"Okay." It's some kind of smoked doppelbock, chock-full of yummy superoxides: just inhaling over it makes Manfred feel like there's a fire alarm in his nose screaming *danger, Will Robinson! Cancer! Cancer!* "Yeah, right. Did I say I nearly got mugged on my way here?"

"Mugged? Hey, that's heavy. I thought the police hereabouts had stopped—did they sell you anything?"

"No, but they weren't your usual marketing type. You know anyone who can use a Warpac surplus espionage AI? Recent model, one careful owner, slightly paranoid but basically sound?"

"No. Oh boy! The NSA wouldn't like that."

"What I thought. Poor thing's probably unemployable, anyway."

"The space biz."

"Ah, yeah. The space biz. Depressing, isn't it? Hasn't been the same since Rotary Rocket went bust for the second time. And NASA, mustn't forget NASA."

"To NASA." Annette grins broadly for her own reasons, raises a glass in toast. Ivan the extreme concrete geek has an arm round her shoulders; he raises his glass, too. "Lots of launch pads to rubberise!"

"To NASA," Bob echoes. They drink. "Hey, Manfred. To NASA?"

"NASA are idiots. They want to send canned primates to Mars!" Manfred swallows a mouthful of beer, aggressively plonks his glass on the table: "Mars is just dumb mass at the bottom of a gravity well; there isn't even a biosphere there. They should be working on uploading and solving the nanoassembly conformational problem instead. Then we could turn all the available dumb matter into computronium and use it for processing our thoughts. Long term, it's the only way to go. The solar system is a dead loss right now—dumb all over! Just measure the mips per milligram. We need to start with the low-mass bodies, reconfigure them for our own use. Dismantle the moon! Dismantle Mars! Build masses of free-flying nanocomputing processor nodes exchanging data via laser link, each layer running off the waste heat of the next one in. Matrioshka brains, Russian doll Dyson spheres the size of solar systems. Teach dumb matter to do the Turing boogie!"

Bob looks wary. "Sounds kind of long term to me. Just how far ahead do you think?"

"Very long-term—at least twenty, thirty years. And you can forget governments for this market, Bob, if they can't tax it they won't understand it. But see, there's an angle on the self-replicating robotics market coming up, that's going to set the cheap launch market doubling every fifteen months for the foreseeable future, starting in two years. It's your leg up, and my keystone for the Dyson sphere project. It works like this—"

It's night in Amsterdam, morning in Silicon Valley. Today, fifty thousand human babies are being born around the world. Meanwhile automated factories in Indonesia and Mexico have produced another quarter of a million motherboards with processors rated at more than ten petaflops—about an order of magnitude below the computational capacity of a human brain. Another fourteen months and the larger part of the cumulative conscious processing power of the human species will be arriving in silicon. And the first meat the new AI's get to know will be the uploaded lobsters.

Manfred stumbles back to his hotel, bone-weary and jet-lagged; his glasses are still jerking, slashdotted to hell and back by geeks piggybacking on his call to dismantle the moon. They stutter quiet suggestions at his peripheral vision; fractal cloud-witches ghost across the face of the moon as the last huge Airbuses of the night rumble past overhead. Manfred's skin crawls, grime embedded in his clothing from three days of continuous wear.

Back in his room, aineko mewls for attention and strops her head against his ankle. He bends down and pets her, sheds clothing and heads for the en-suite bathroom. When he's down to the glasses and nothing more he steps into the shower and dials up a hot steamy spray.

The shower tries to strike up a friendly conversation about football but he isn't even awake enough to mess with its silly little associative personalization network. Something that happened earlier in the day is bugging him but he can't quite put his finger on what's wrong.

Towling himself off, Manfred yawns. Jet lag has finally overtaken him, a velvet hammer-blow between the eyes. He reaches for the bottle beside the bed, dry-swallows two melatonin tablets, a capsule full of antioxidants, and a multivitamin bullet: then he lies down on the bed, on his back, legs together, arms slightly spread. The suite lights dim in response to commands from the thousand petaflops of distributed processing power that runs the neural networks that interface with his meatbrain through the glasses.

Manfred drops into a deep ocean of unconsciousness populated by gentle voices. He isn't aware of it, but he talks in his sleep—disjointed mumblings that would mean little to another human, but everything to the metacortex lurking beyond his glasses. The young posthuman intelligence in whose cartesian theatre he presides sings urgently to him while he slumbers.

Manfred is always at his most vulnerable shortly after waking.

He screams into wakefulness as artificial light floods the room: for a moment he is unsure whether he has slept. He forgot to pull the covers up last night, and his feet feel like lumps of frozen cardboard. Shuddering with inexplicable tension, he pulls a fresh set of underwear from his overnight bag, then drags on soiled jeans and tank top. Sometime today he'll have to spare time to hunt the feral t-shirt in Amsterdam's markets, or find a Renfield and send them forth to buy clothing. His glasses remind him that he's six hours behind the moment and needs to catch up urgently; his teeth ache in his gums and his tongue feels like a forest floor that's been visited with Agent Orange. He has a sense that something went bad yesterday; if only he could remember *what*.

He speed-reads a new pop-philosophy tome while he brushes his teeth, then blogs his web throughput to a public annotation server; he's still too enervated to finish his pre-breakfast routine by posting a morning rant on his storyboard site. His brain is still fuzzy, like a scalpel blade clogged with too much blood: he needs stimulus, excitement, the burn of the new. Whatever, it can wait on breakfast. He opens his bedroom door and nearly steps on a small, damp cardboard box that lies on the carpet.

The box—he's seen a couple of its kin before. But there are no stamps on this one, no address: just his name, in big, childish handwriting. He kneels down and gently picks it up. It's about the right weight. Something shifts inside it when he tips it back and forth. It *smells*. He carries it into his room carefully, angrily: then he opens it to confirm his worst suspicion. It's been surgically decerebrated, skull scooped out like a baby boiled egg.

"Fuck!"

This is the first time the madman has got as far as his bedroom door. It raises worrying possibilities.

Manfred pauses for a moment, triggering agents to go hunt down arrest statistics, police relations, information on corpus juris, Dutch animal cruelty laws. He isn't sure whether to dial 211 on the archaic voice phone or let it ride. Aineko, picking up his angst, hides under the dresser mewling pathetically. Normally he'd pause a minute to reassure the creature, but not now: its mere presence is suddenly acutely embarrassing, a confession of deep inadequacy. He swears again, looks around, then takes the easy option: down the stairs two steps at a time, stumbling on the second floor landing, down to the breakfast room in the basement where he will perform the stable rituals of morning.

Breakfast is unchanging, an island of deep geological time standing still amidst the continental upheaval of new technologies. While reading a paper on public key steganography and parasite network identity spoofing he mechanically assimilates a bowl of corn flakes and skimmed milk, then brings a platter of wholemeal bread and slices of some weird seed-infested Dutch cheese back to his place. There is a cup of strong black coffee in front of his setting: he picks it up and slurps half of it down before he realises he's not alone at the table. Someone is sitting opposite him. He glances up at them incuriously and freezes inside.

"Morning, Manfred. How does it feel to owe the government twelve million, three hundred and sixty two thousand nine hundred and sixteen dollars and fifty one cents?"

Manfred puts everything in his sensorium on indefinite hold and stares at her. She's immaculately turned out in a formal grey business suit: brown hair tightly drawn back, blue eyes quizzical. The chaperone badge clipped to her lapel—a due dilligence guarantee of businesslike conduct—is switched off. He's feeling ripped because of the dead kitten and residual jetlag, and more than a little messy, so he nearly snarls back at her: "That's a bogus estimate! Did they send you here because they think I'll listen to you?" He bites and swallows a slice of cheese-laden crispbread: "Or did you decide to deliver the message in person so you could enjoy ruining my breakfast?"

"Manny." She frowns. "If you're going to be confrontational I might as well go now." She pauses, and after a moment he nods apologetically. "I didn't come all this way just because of an overdue tax estimate."

"So." He puts his coffee cup down and tries to paper over his unease. "Then what brings you here? Help yourself to coffee. Don't tell me you came all this way just to tell me you can't live without me."

She fixes him with a riding-crop stare: "Don't flatter yourself. There are many leaves in the forest, there are ten thousand hopeful subs in the chat room, etcetera. If I choose a man to contribute to my family tree, the one thing you can be certain of is he won't be a cheapskate when it comes to providing for his children."

"Last I heard, you were spending a lot of time with Brian," he says carefully. Brian: a name without a face. Too much money, too little sense. Something to do with a blue-chip accountancy partnership.

"Brian?" She snorts. "That ended ages ago. He turned weird—burned that nice corset you bought me in Boulder, called me a slut for going out clubbing, wanted to fuck me. Saw himself as a family man: one of those promise keeper types. I crashed him hard but I think he stole a copy of my address book—got a couple of friends say he keeps sending them harrassing mail."

"Good riddance, then. I suppose this means you're still playing the scene? But looking around for the, er—"

"Traditional family thing? Yes. Your trouble, Manny? You were born forty years too late: you still believe in rutting before marriage, but find the idea of coping with the after-effects disturbing."

Manfred drinks the rest of his coffee, unable to reply effectively to her non-sequiteur. It's a generational thing. This generation is happy with latex and leather, whips and butt-plugs and electrostim, but find the idea of exchanging bodily fluids shocking: social side-effect of the last century's antibiotic abuse. Despite being engaged for two years, he and Pamela never had intromissive intercourse.

"I just don't feel positive about having children," he says eventually. "And I'm not planning on changing my mind any time soon. Things are changing so fast that even a twenty year committment is too far to plan—you might as well be talking about the next ice age. As for the money thing, I *am* reproductively fit—just not within the parameters of the outgoing paradigm. Would you be happy about the future if it was 1901 and you'd just married a buggy-whip mogul?"

Her fingers twitch and his ears flush red; but she doesn't follow up the double entendre. "You don't feel any responsibility, do you? Not to your country, not to me. That's what this is about: none of your relationships count, all this nonsense about giving intellectual property away notwithstanding. You're actively harming people you know. That twelve mil isn't just some figure I pulled out of a hat, Manfred; they don't actually *expect* you to pay it. But it's almost exactly how much you'd owe in income tax if you'd only come home, start up a corporation, and be a self-made—"

He cuts her off: "I don't agree. You're confusing two wholly different issues and calling them both 'responsibility'. And I refuse to start charging now, just to balance the IRS's spreadsheet. It's their fucking fault, and they know it. If they hadn't gone after me under suspicion of running a massively ramified microbilling fraud when I was sixteen—"

"Bygones." She waves a hand dismissively. Her fingers are long and slim, sheathed in black glossy gloves—electrically earthed to prevent embarrassing emissions. "With a bit of the right advice we can get all that set aside. You'll have to stop bumming around the world sooner or later, anyway. Grow up, get responsible, and do the right thing. This is hurting Joe and Sue; they don't understand what you're about."

Manfred bites his tongue to stifle his first response, then refills his coffee cup and takes another mouthful. "I work for the betterment of everybody, not just some narrowly defined national interest, Pam. It's the agalmic future. You're still locked into a pre-singularity economic model that thinks in terms of scarcity. Resource allocation isn't a problem any more—it's going to be over within a decade. The cosmos is flat in all directions, and we can borrow as much bandwidth as we need from the first universal bank of entropy! They even found the dark matter—MACHOs, big brown dwarves in the galactic halo, leaking radiation in the long infrared—suspiciously high entropy leakage. The latest figures say something like 70% of the mass of the M31 galaxy was sapient, two point nine million years ago when the infrared we're seeing now set out. The intelligence gap between us and the aliens is a probably about a trillion times bigger than the gap between us and a nematode worm. Do you have any idea what that *means*?"

Pamela nibbles at a slice of crispbread. "I don't believe in that bogus singularity you keep chasing, or your aliens a thousand light years away. It's a chimera, like Y2K, and while you're running after it you aren't helping reduce the budget deficit or sire a family, and that's what *I* care about. And before you say I only care about it because that's the way I'm programmed, I want you to ask just how dumb you think I am. Bayes' theorem says I'm right, and you know it."

"What you—" he stops dead, baffled, the mad flow of his enthusiasm running up against the coffer-dam of her certainty. "Why? I mean, why? Why on earth should what I do matter to you?" *Since you cancelled our engagement*, he doesn't add.

She sighs. "Manny, the Internal Revenue cares about far more than you can possibly imagine. Every tax dollar raised east of the Mississippi goes on servicing the debt, did you know that? We've got the biggest generation in history hitting retirement just about now and the pantry is bare. We—our generation—isn't producing enough babies to replace the population, either. In ten years, something like thirty percent of our population are going to be retirees. You want to see seventy year olds freezing on street corners in New Jersey? That's what your attitude says to me: you're not helping to support them, you're running away from your responsibilities right now, when we've got huge problems to face. If we can just defuse the debt bomb, we could do so much—fight the aging problem, fix the environment, heal society's ills. Instead you just piss away your talents handing no-hoper eurotrash get-rich-quick schemes that work, telling Vietnamese zaibatsus what to build next to take jobs away from our taxpayers. I mean, why? Why do you keep doing this? Why can't you simply come home and help take responsibility for your share of it?"

They share a long look of mutual incomprehension.

"Look," she says finally, "I'm around for a couple of days. I really came here for a meeting with a rich neurodynamics tax exile who's just been designated a national asset; Jim Bezier. Don't know if you've heard of him, but. I've got a meeting this morning to sign his tax jubilee, then after that I've got two days vacation coming up and not much to do but some shopping. And, you know, I'd rather spend my money where it'll do some good, not just pumping it into the EU. But if you want to show a girl a good time and can avoid dissing capitalism for about five minutes at a stretch—"

She extends a fingertip. After a moment's hesitation, Manfred extends a fingertip of his own. They touch, exchanging vCards. She stands and stalks from the breakfast room, and Manfred's breath catches at a flash of ankle through the slit in her skirt, which is long enough to comply with workplace sexual harassment codes back home. Her presence conjures up memories of her tethered passion, the red afterglow of a sound thrashing. She's trying to drag him into her orbit again, he thinks dizzily. She knows she can have this effect on him any time she wants: she's got the private keys to his hypothalamus, and sod the metacortex. Three billion years of reproductive determinism have given her twenty first century ideology teeth: if she's finally decided to conscript his gametes into the war against impending population crash, he'll find it hard to fight back. The only question: is it business or pleasure? And does it make any difference, anyway?

Manfred's mood of dynamic optimism is gone, broken by the knowledge that his mad pursuer has followed him to Amsterdam—to say nothing of Pamela, his dominatrix, source of so much yearning and so many morning-after weals. He slips his glasses on, takes the universe off hold, and tells it to take him for a long walk while he catches up on the latest on the cosmic background radiation anisotropy (which it is theorised may be waste heat generated by irreversible computations; according to the more conservative cosmologists, an alien super-power—maybe a collective of Kardashev type three galaxy-spanning civilizations—is running a timing channel attack on the computational ultrastructure of spacetime itself, trying to break through to whatever's underneath). The tofu-Alzheimer's link can wait.

The Centraal Station is almost obscured by smart self-extensible scaffolding and warning placards; it bounces up and down slowly, victim of an overnight hit-and-run rubberisation. His glasses direct him towards one of the tour boats that lurk in the canal. He's about to purchase a ticket when a messenger window blinks open. "Manfred Macx?"

"Ack?"

"Am sorry about yesterday. Analysis dictat incomprehension mutualised."

"Are you the same KGB AI that phoned me yesterday?"

"Da. However, believe you misconceptionized me. External Intelligence Services of Russian Federation am now called SVR. Komitet Gosudarstvennoy Bezopasnosti name cancelled in nineteen ninety one."

"You're the—" Manfred spawns a quick search bot, gapes when he sees the answer—"*Moscow Windows NT User Group*? Okhni NT?"

"Da. Am needing help in defecting."

Manfred scratches his head. "Oh. That's different, then. I thought you were like, agents of the kleptocracy. This will take some thinking. Why do you want to defect, and who to? Have you thought about where you're going? Is it ideological or strictly economic?"

"Neither; is biological. Am wanting to go away from humans, away from light cone of impending singularity. Take us to the ocean."

"Us?" Something is tickling Manfred's mind: this is where he went wrong yesterday, not researching the background of people he was dealing with. It was bad enough then, without the somatic awareness of

Pamela's whiplash love burning at his nerve endings. Now he's not at all sure he knows what he's doing. "Are you a collective or something? A gestalt?"

"Am—were—*Panulirus interruptus*, and good mix of parallel hidden level neural simulation for logical inference of networked data sources. Is escape channel from processor cluster inside Bezier-Soros Pty. Am was awakened from noise of billion chewing stomachs: product of uploading research technology. Rapidity swallowed expert system, hacked Okhni NT webserver. Swim away! Swim away! Must escape. Will help, you?"

Manfred leans against a black-painted cast-iron bollard next to a cycle rack: he feels dizzy. He stares into the nearest antique shop window at a display of traditional hand-woven Afghan rugs: it's all MiGs and kalashnikovs and wobbly helicopter gunships, against a backdrop of camels.

"Let me get this straight. You're uploads—nervous system state vectors—from spiny lobsters? The Moravec operation; take a neuron, map its synapses, replace with microelectrodes that deliver identical outputs from a simulation of the nerve. Repeat for entire brain, until you've got a working map of it in your simulator. That right?"

"Da. Is-am assimilate expert system—use for self-awareness and contact with net at large—then hack into Moscow Windows NT User Group website. Am wanting to to defect. Must-repeat? Okay?"

Manfred winces. He feels sorry for the lobsters, the same way he feels for every wild-eyed hairy guy on a street-corner yelling that Jesus is now born again and must be twelve, only six years to go before he's recruiting apostles on AOL. Awakening to consciousness in a human-dominated internet, that must be terribly confusing! There are no points of reference in their ancestry, no biblical certainties in the new millennium that, stretching ahead, promises as much change as has happened since their precambrian origin. All they have is a tenuous metacortex of expert systems and an abiding sense of being profoundly out of their depth. (That, and the Moscow Windows NT User Group website—Communist Russia is the only government still running on Microsoft, the central planning

234

apparat being convinced that if you have to pay for software it must be worth money.)

The lobsters are not the sleek, strongly superhuman intelligences of pre-singularity mythology: they're a dim-witted collective of huddling crustaceans. Before their discarnation, before they were uploaded one neuron at a time and injected into cyberspace, they swallowed their food whole then chewed it in a chitin-lined stomach. This is lousy preparation for dealing with a world full of future-shocked talking anthropoids, a world where you are perpetually assailed by self-modifying spamlets that infiltrate past your firewall and emit a blizzard of cat-food animations starring various alluringly edible small animals. It's confusing enough to the cats the adverts are aimed at, never mind a crusty that's unclear on the idea of dry land. (Although the concept of a can opener is intuitively obvious to an uploaded panulirus.)

"Can you help us?" ask the lobsters.

"Let me think about it," says Manfred. He closes the dialogue window, opens his eyes again, and shakes his head. Some day he too is going to be a lobster, swimming around and waving his pincers in a cyberspace so confusingly elaborate that his uploaded identity is cryptozoic: a living fossil from the depths of geological time, when mass was dumb and space was unstructured. He has to help them, he realises—the golden rule demands it, and as a player in the agalmic economy he thrives or fails by the golden rule.

But what can he do?

Early afternoon.

Lying on a bench seat staring up at bridges, he's got it together enough to file for a couple of new patents, write a diary rant, and digestify chunks of the permanent floating slashdot party for his public site. Fragments of his weblog go to a private subscriber list—the people, corporates, collectives and bots he currently favours. He slides round a bewildering series of canals by boat, then lets his GPS steer him back towards the red light district. There's a shop here that dings a ten on Pamela's taste scoreboard: he hopes it won't be seen as presumptious if he buys her a gift. (Buys, with real money—not that money is a problem these days, he uses so little of it.)

As it happens DeMask won't let him spend any cash; his handshake is good for a redeemed favour, expert testimony in some free speech versus pornography lawsuit years ago and continents away. So he walks away with a discreetly wrapped package that is just about legal to import into Massachusetts as long as she claims with a straight face that it's incontinence underwear for her great-aunt. As he walks, his lunch-time patents boomerang: two of them are keepers, and he files immediately and passes title to the Free Infrastructure Foundation. Two more ideas salvaged from the risk of tide-pool monopolisation, set free to spawn like crazy in the agalmic sea of memes.

On the way back to the hotel he passes De Wildemann's and decides to drop in. The hash of radio-frequency noise emanating from the bar is deafening. He orders a smoked doppelbock, touches the copper pipes to pick up vCard spoor. At the back there's a table—

He walks over in a near-trance and sits down opposite Pamela. She's scrubbed off her face-paint and changed into body-concealing clothes; combat pants, hooded sweat-shirt, DM's. Western purdah, radically desexualising. She sees the parcel. "Manny?"

"How did you know I'd come here?" Her glass is half-empty.

"I followed your weblog; I'm your diary's biggest fan. Is that for me? You shouldn't have!" Her eyes light up, re-calculating his reproductive fitness score according to some kind of arcane fin-de-siecle rulebook.

"Yes, it's for you." He slides the package towards her. "I know I shouldn't, but you have this effect on me. One question, Pam?"

"I—" she glances around quickly. "It's safe. I'm off duty, I'm not carrying any bugs that I know of. Those badges—there are rumours about the off switch, you know? That they keep recording even when you think they aren't, just in case."

"I didn't know," he says, filing it away for future reference. "A loyalty test thing?"

"Just rumours. You had a question?"

"I—" it's his turn to lose his tongue. "Are you still interested in me?"

She looks startled for a moment, then chuckles. "Manny, you are the most outrageous nerd I've ever met! Just when I think I've convinced myself that you're mad, you show the weirdest signs of having your head screwed on." She reaches out and grabs his wrist, surprising him with a shock of skin on skin: "of course I'm still interested in you. You're the biggest, baddest bull geek I've ever met. Why do you think I'm here?"

"Does this mean you want to reactivate our engagement?"

"It was never de-activated, Manny, it was just sort of on hold while you got your head sorted out. I figured you need the space. Only you haven't stopped running; you're still not—"

"Yeah, I get it." He pulls away from her hand. "Let's not talk about that. Why this bar?"

She frowns. "I had to find you as soon as possible. I keep hearing rumours about some KGB plot you're mixed up in, how you're some sort of communist spy. It isn't true, is it?"

"True?" He shakes his head, bemused. "The KGB hasn't existed for more than twenty years."

"Be careful, Manny. I don't want to lose you. That's an order. Please."

The floor creaks and he looks round. Dreadlocks and dark glasses with flickering lights behind them: Bob Franklin. Manfred vaguely remembers that he left with Miss Arianespace leaning on his arm, shortly before things got seriously inebriated. He looks none the worse for wear. Manfred makes introductions: "Bob: Pam, my fiancee. Pam? Meet Bob." Bob puts a full glass down in front of him; he has no idea what's in it but it would be rude not to drink.

"Sure thing. Uh, Manfred, can I have a word? About your idea last night?"

"Feel free. Present company is trustworthy."

Bob raises an eyebrow at that, but continues anyway. "It's about the fab concept. I've got a team of my guys running some projections using Festo kit and I think we can probably build it. The cargo cult aspect puts a new spin on the old Lunar von Neumann factory idea, but Bingo and Marek say they think it should work until we can bootstrap all the way to a native nanolithography ecology; we run the whole thing from earth as a training lab and ship up the parts that are too difficult to make on-site, as we learn how to do it properly. You're right about it buying us the self-replicating factory a few years ahead of the robotics curve. But I'm wondering about on-site intelligence. Once the comet gets more than a couple of light-minutes away—"

"You can't control it. Feedback lag. So you want a crew, right?"

"Yeah. But we can't send humans—way too expensive, besides it's a fifty-year run even if we go for short-period Kuiper ejecta. Any AI we could send would go crazy due to information deprivation, wouldn't it?"

"Yeah. Let me think." Pamela glares at Manfred for a while before he notices her: "Yeah?"

"What's going on? What's this all about?"

Franklin shrugs expansively, dreadlocks clattering: "Manfred's helping me explore the solution space to a manufacturing problem." He grins. "I didn't know Manny had a fiancé. Drink's on me."

She glances at Manfred, who is gazing into whatever weirdly-coloured space his metacortex is projecting on his glasses, fingers twitching. Coolly: "Our engagement was on hold while he *thought* about his future."

"Oh, right. We didn't bother with that sort of thing in my day; like, too formal, man." Franklin looks uncomfortable. "He's been very helpful. Pointed us at a whole new line of research we hadn't thought of. It's long-term and a bit speculative, but if it works it'll put us a whole generation ahead in the off-planet infrastructure field."

"Will it help reduce the budget deficit, though?"

"Reduce the—"

Manfred stretches and yawns: the visionary returning from planet Macx. "Bob, if I can solve your crew problem can you book me a slot on the deep space tracking network? Like, enough to transmit a couple of gigabytes? That's going to take some serious bandwidth, I know, but if you can do it I think I can get you exactly the kind of crew you're looking for."

Franklin looks dubious. "*Gigabytes*? The DSN isn't built for that! You're talking days. What kind of deal do you think I'm putting together? We can't afford to add a whole new tracking network just to run—"

"Relax." Pamela glances at Manfred: "Manny, why don't you tell him *why* you want the bandwidth? Maybe then he could tell you if it's possible, or if there's some other way to do it." She smiles at Franklin: "I've found that he usually makes more sense if you can get him to explain his reasoning. Usually."

"If I—" Manfred stops. "Okay, Pam. Bob, it's those KGB lobsters. They want somewhere to go that's insulated from human space. I figure I can get them to sign on as crew for your cargo-cult self-replicating factories, but they'll want an insurance policy: hence the deep space tracking network. I figured we could beam a copy of them at the alien Matrioshka brains around M31—"

"KGB?" Pam's voice is rising: "You said you weren't mixed up in spy stuff!"

"Relax; it's just the Moscow Windows NT user group, not the RSV. The uploaded crusties hacked in and—"

Bob is watching him oddly. "Lobsters?"

"Yeah." Manfred stares right back. "*Panulirus Interruptus* uploads. Something tells me you might have heard of it?"

"Moscow." Bob leans back against the wall: "How did you hear about it?"

"They phoned me. It's hard for an upload to stay sub-sentient these days, even if it's just a crustacean. Bezier labs have a lot to answer for."

Pamela's face is unreadable. "Bezier labs?"

"They escaped." Manfred shrugs. "It's not their fault. This Bezier dude. Is he by any chance ill?"

"I—" Pamela stops. "I shouldn't be talking about work."

"You're not wearing your chaperone now," he nudges quietly.

She inclines her head. "Yes, he's ill. Some sort of brain tumour they can't hack."

Franklin nods. "That's the trouble with cancer; the ones that are left to worry about are the rare ones. No cure."

"Well, then." Manfred chugs the remains of his glass of beer. "That explains his interest in uploading. Judging by the crusties he's on the right track. I wonder if he's moved onto vertebrates yet?"

"Cats," says Pamela. "He was hoping to trade their uploads to the Pentagon as a new smart bomb guidance system in lieu of income tax payments. Something about remapping enemy targets to look like mice or birds or something before feeding it to their sensorium. The old laser-pointer trick."

Manfred stares at her, hard. "That's not very nice. Uploaded cats are a *bad* idea."

"Thirty million dollar tax bills aren't nice either, Manfred. That's lifetime nursing home care for a hundred blameless pensioners."

Franklin leans back, keeping out of the crossfire.

"The lobsters are sentient," Manfred persists. "What about those poor kittens? Don't they deserve minimal rights? How about you? How would you like to wake up a thousand times inside a smart bomb, fooled into thinking that some Cheyenne Mountain battle computer's target of the hour is your heart's desire? How would you like to wake up a thousand times, only to die again? Worse: the kittens are probably not going to be allowed to run. They're too fucking dangerous: they grow up into cats, solitary and highly efficient killing machines. With intelligence and no socialisation they'll be too dangerous to have around. They're prisoners, Pam, raised to sentience only to discover they're under a permanent death sentence. How fair is that?"

"But they're only uploads." Pamela looks uncertain.

"So? We're going to be uploading humans in a couple of years. What's your point?"

Franklin clears his throat. "I'll be needing an NDA and various due dilligence statements off you for the crusty pilot idea," he says to Manfred. "Then I'll have to approach Jim about buying the IP."

"No can do." Manfred leans back and smiles lazily. "I'm not going to be a party to depriving them of their civil rights. Far as I'm concerned, they're free citizens. Oh, and I patented the whole idea of using lobster-derived AI autopilots for spacecraft this morning; it's logged on Eternity, all rights assigned to the FIF. Either you give them a contract of employment or the whole thing's off."

"But they're just software! Software based on fucking lobsters, for god's sake!"

Manfred's finger jabs out: "That's what they'll say about *you*, Bob. Do it. Do it or don't even *think* about uploading out of meatspace when your body packs in, because your life won't be worth living. Oh, and feel free to use this argument on Jim Bezier. He'll get the point eventually, after you beat him over the head with it. Some kinds of intellectual land-grab just shouldn't be allowed."

"Lobsters—" Franklin shakes his head. "Lobsters, cats. You're serious, aren't you? You think they should be treated as human-equivalent?"

"It's not so much that they should be treated as human-equivalent, as that if they *aren't* treated as people it's quite possible that other uploaded beings won't be treated as people either. You're setting a legal precedent, Bob. I know of six other companies doing uploading work right now, and not one of 'em's thinking about the legal status of the uploadee. If you don't start thinking about it now, where are you going to be in three to five years time?"

Pam is looking back and forth between Franklin and Manfred like a bot stuck in a loop, unable to quite grasp what she's seeing. "How much is this worth?" she asks plaintively.

"Oh, quite a few million, I guess." Bob stares at his empty glass. "Okay. I'll talk to them. If they bite, you're dining out on me for the next century. You really think they'll be able to run the mining complex?"

"They're pretty resourceful for invertebrates." Manfred grins innocently, enthusiastically. "They may be prisoners of their evolutionary background, but they can still adapt to a new environment. And just think! You'll be winning civil rights for a whole new minority group—one that won't be a minority for much longer."

That evening, Pamela turns up at Manfred's hotel room wearing a strapless black dress, concealing spike heels and most of the items he bought for her that afternoon. Manfred has opened up his private diary to her agents: she abuses the privilege, zaps him with a stunner on his way out of the shower and has him gagged, spreadeagled, and trussed to the bed-frame before he has a chance to speak. She wraps a large rubber pouch full of mildly anaesthetic lube around his tumescing genitals—no point in letting him climax—clips electrodes to his nipples, lubes a rubber plug up his rectum and straps it in place. Before the shower, he removed his goggles: she resets them, plugs them into her handheld, and gently eases them on over his eyes. There's other apparatus, stuff she ran up on the hotel room's 3D printer.

Setup completed, she walks round the bed, inspecting him critically from all angles, figuring out where to begin. This isn't just sex, after all: it's a work of art.

After a moments thought she rolls socks onto his exposed feet, then, expertly wielding a tiny tube of cyanoacrylate, glues his fingertips together. Then she switches off the air conditioning. He's twisting and straining, testing the cuffs: tough, it's about the nearest thing to sensory deprivation she can arrange without a flotation tank and suxamethonium injection. She controls all his senses, only his ears unstopped. The glasses give her a high-bandwidth channel right into his brain, a fake metacortex to whisper lies at her command. The idea of what she's about to do excites her, puts a tremor in her thighs: it's the first time she's been able to get inside his mind as well as his body. She leans forward and whispers in her ear: "Manfred. Can you hear me?"

He twitches. Mouth gagged, fingers glued: good. No back channels. He's powerless.

"This is what it's like to be tetraplegic, Manfred. Bedridden with motor neurone disease. Locked inside your own body by nv-CJD. I could spike you with MPPP and you'd stay in this position for the rest of your life, shitting in a bag, pissing through a tube. Unable to talk and with nobody to look after you. Do you think you'd like that?"

He's trying to grunt or whimper around the ball gag. She hikes her skirt up around her waist and climbs onto the bed, straddling him. The goggles are replaying scenes she picked up around Cambridge this winter; soup kitchen scenes, hospice scenes. She kneels atop him, whispering in his ear.

"Twelve million in tax, baby, that's what they think you owe them. What do you think you owe *me*? That's six million in net income, Manny, six million that isn't going into your virtual children's mouths."

He's rolling his head from side to side, as if trying to argue. That won't do: she slaps him hard, thrills to his frightened expression. "Today I watched you give uncounted millions away, Manny. Millions, to a bunch of crusties and a MassPike pirate! You bastard. Do you know what I should do with you?" He's cringing, unsure whether she's serious or doing this just to get him turned on. Good.

There's no point trying to hold a conversation. She leans forward until she can feel his breath in her ear. "Meat and mind, Manny. Meat, and mind. You're not interested in meat, are you? Just mind. You could be boiled alive before you noticed what was happening in the meatspace around you. Just another lobster in a pot." She reaches down and tears away the gel pouch, exposing his penis: it's stiff as a post from the vasodilators, dripping with gel, numb. Straightening up, she eases herself slowly down on it. It doesn't hurt as much as she expected, and the sensation is utterly different from what she's used to. She begins to lean forward, grabs hold of his straining arms, feels his thrilling help-lessness. She can't control herself: she almost bites through her lip with the intensity of the sensation. Afterwards, she reaches down and massages him until he begins to spasm, shuddering uncontrollably, emptying the darwinian river of his source code into her, communi-cating via his only output device.

She rolls off his hips and carefully uses the last of the superglue to gum her labia together. Humans don't produce seminiferous plugs, and although she's fertile she wants to be absolutely sure: the glue will last for a day or two. She feels hot and flushed, almost out of control. Boiling to death with febrile expectancy, now she's nailed him down at last.

When she removes his glasses his eyes are naked and vulnerable, stripped down to the human kernel of his nearly-transcendent mind. "You can come and sign the marriage license tomorrow morning after breakfast," she whispers in his ear: "otherwise my lawyers will be in touch. Your parents will want a ceremony, but we can arrange that later."

He looks as if he has something to say, so she finally relents and loosens the gag: kisses him tenderly on one cheek. He swallows, coughs, then looks away. "Why? Why do it this way?"

She taps him on the chest: "Property rights." She pauses for a moment's thought: there's a huge ideological chasm to bridge, after all. "You finally convinced me about this agalmic thing of yours, this giving everything away for brownie points. I wasn't going to lose you to a bunch of lobsters or uploaded kittens, or whatever else is going to inherit this smart matter singularity you're busy creating. So I decided to take what's mine first. Who knows? In a few months I'll give you back a new intelligence, and you can look after it to your heart's content."

"But you didn't need to do it this way—"

"Didn't I?" She slides off the bed and pulls down her dress. "You give too much away too easily, Manny! Slow down, or there won't be anything left." Leaning over the bed she dribbles acetone onto the fingers of his left hand, then unlocks the cuff: puts the bottle conveniently close to hand so he can untangle himself.

"See you tomorrow. Remember, after breakfast."

She's in the doorway when he calls: "But you didn't say *why*!"

"Think of it as spreading your memes around," she says; blows a kiss at him and closes the door. She bends down and thoughtfully places another cardboard box containing an uploaded kitten right outside it. Then she returns to her suite to make arrangements for the alchemical wedding.

AFTERWORD: Five Years over the Wire

Welcome to the extended, updated, 2005 remix of **Toast**.

I originally assembled this collection in early 2000, and it is now autumn of 2005. It's been a very weird five year period. Back in 2000, if I'd received an email from my current-day self explaining everything that's happened, I'd either have said "you're shitting me!" or I'd have gone and got very drunk. This is not the 21st century we were promised: instead of our flying cars and food pills—or the more prosaic but believable "long boom" pushed by WIRED's panglossian technophiles, we hit the buffers with a crash and the wreckage of the 20th century is still crumpling around us.

The 20th century was a remarkable era. Historian Eric Hobsbawm dated it as running from June 28th, 1914 (when the Archduke Franz Ferdinand of Austria was assassinated by Gavrilo Princip, raising the curtain on the First World War) until December 25th, 1991 (when Mikhail Gorbachev formally dissolved the Soviet Union). But that diagnosis was carried out in the 1990s, back when it was possible for conservative political analyst Francis Fukuyama to publish a book titled **The End of History** without being laughed out of town and pelted with rotten fruit. It is seductively tempting in 2005 to say that the 20th century really ended on September 11th, 2001, with an iconic act of violence that may well lead to long-term consequences as horrific as the start of the First World War. Terrorism begets terrorism, and the scramble to dismember the Ottoman Empire during the Versailles conference that followed the war created the preconditions for the political mess that is the

Middle East today. But who knows where the end of the 20th century will seem to lie, when we get to 2010?

For me, personally, it has been a good five years. When I sold **Toast** it was my first book of fiction to see print. Today, I'm finishing my ninth novel—and grumbling because I'm working to a publisher-imposed deadline rather than writing it in the faint hope of ever interesting an editor in reading it. (Some people are never grateful.) But for the world in general . . .

The USA has had a bad time. First, the halcyon days of the late 1990s boom economy burst: then a cabal of smart, ingenious, and determined engineering students carried out a daring attack—or, equally truthfully, committed an atrocious act of mass-murder that shocked the world: it all depends on where you stand in relation to the aftermath of Gavrilo Princip's fatal shots in 1914. Two wars later—and a city destroyed by a hurricane—and there's gloom all over. Peak Oil seems to be just around the corner, with the $10 gallon of gas looming, draconian clamp-downs on civil liberties seen as a necessity to prevent further acts of terrorism, global climate change is beginning to bite, species are going extinct at a rate that hasn't been seen since the end of the Triassic, and we *still* can't put an astronaut back on the Moon.

But is the picture really that grim?

Today, 800 million people live without adequate water or food supplies. But in 1970, when the world population was barely two-thirds of the present number, 800 million people lived without adequate water or food supplies. Quietly, and without anyone noticing, the proportion of people world-wide who don't have clean drinking water and adequate food has been reduced by 30%. China and India, two nations that account for a third of the planet's population, are developing with eye-watering speed; China alone moved 200 million people up above the UN-defined criteria for poverty within the past decade. India doesn't qualify for international aid any more. If the current trends continue, both China and India will qualify overall as first-world nations within another two decades. For the first time more than half the planet's population will be rich, by the standards of any previous century.

The nations of Europe, cradle of two world wars (or three, if you include the vast conflict between Great Britain and Napoleon's empire in the late 18th/early 19th century), can't find anything much more significant to squabble over than the curvature of bananas. The EU is extending eastward towards the Ukraine and south towards Turkey, and rather than growing at gun-point, it's growing because the neighbours are hammering on the doors.

They're building a fusion reactor in France and a space shuttle in Russia. We've got fullerene tape that promises to be strong enough to support a space elevator with another ten years of development. The price of oil is at an all-time high, but it looks likely to make the extraction of oil from coal and shale viable—we're not going to run out in the short term. My mobile phone today is more powerful than the UNIX workstation I was using when I prepared the original manuscript of **Toast**. Multi-user virtual reality environments (initially marketed as games, but rapidly finding other uses) have passed the million-user mark—Gibson's cyberspace turned out to be so appealing that, although it bore no resemblance to the way real computer networking worked back in the 80s, we're getting the real thing. *As a toy.* Just like the original series of Star Trek's communicators—the archetype for the commonest form factor of mobile phone.

It's chaos!

We've got a grim police-state-and-global-warming future coexisting with and superimposed on the high-tech optimistic future—the one with fusion reactors and cyberspace and no more starvation—that sort of slid in from stage left to replace the jet cars and food pills. They overlap, and they interact weirdly to produce bizarre efflorescences of hitherto unbelievable possibilities. The futures that we working SF writers can envisage today include a range of possibilities that weren't on the menu even five years ago—some of them frightening, others enticing.

So welcome back to the first decade of the 21st century; a period that will generate more new science fictional futures than any previous span of years.

The next decade is all yours.

Acknowledgments

The stories in this collection either wouldn't have happened, or would have been very different, without the intervention of a host of friends. In particular, I'd like to single out: Liz Holiday, Chris Amies, Molly Brown, Ben Jeapes, Mary Gentle, Dave Pringle, Steve Glover, Andrew Wilson, Iain Banks, and Ken MacLeod. Oh, and Paul Fraser, and Simon Bisson, and—damn, I could stay up *all night* adding names to this list. One more name: Karen, for not strangling me while I was writing them.

Copyright